AF235242

Bab:
A Sub-Deb

by

Mary Roberts Rinehart

Double 9
BOOKS

Bab: A Sub-Deb
by Mary Roberts Rinehart

Copyright © 2023

All Rights reserved.

No part of this publication may be reproduced, stored in a retrieval system, or transmitted in any form or by any means, electronic, mechanical, photocopying or Otherwise, without the written permission of the publisher.
The author/editor asserts the moral right to be identified as the author/editor of this work.

ISBN: 978-93-59958-08-8

Published by

DOUBLE 9 BOOKS

2/13-B, Ansari Road
Daryaganj, New Delhi – 110002
info@double9books.com
www.double9books.com
Tel. 011-40042856

This book is under public domain

ABOUT THE AUTHOR

American author Mary Roberts Rinehart, also known as the American Agatha Christie, was born on August 12, 1876, and died on September 22, 1958. The Circular Staircase, Rinehart's debut mystery novel, introduced the "had I but known" narrative approach. Although the exact phrase does not occur in Rinehart's book The Door (1930), she is regarded as the creator of the "the butler did it" story device. As one of the first women to visit the front lines in Belgium during World War I, she also worked to share the tales and experiences of these troops. Mary Roberts Rinehart, who is now known as Rinehart, was born in Pittsburgh, Pennsylvania's Allegheny City. Her father was a frustrated inventor, and the family experienced frequent monetary issues throughout her youth. Mary was just 19 years old when her father committed suicide. She was trained to use her right hand because she was left-handed at a time when that was improper. She attended public schools, received her high school diploma at the age of 16, enrolled in the Pittsburgh Training School for Nurses at the Pittsburgh Homeopathic Hospital, and completed her training there in 1896.

CONTENTS

CHAPTER I
THE SUB-DEB: A THEME WRITTEN AND SUBMITTED IN LITERATURE CLASS BY BARBARA PUTNAM ARCHIBALD, 1917

DEFINITION OF A THEME:

A theme is a piece of writing, either true or made up by the author, and consisting of Introduction, Body and Conclusion. It should contain Unity, Coherence, Emphasis, Perspecuity, Vivacity, and Precision. It may be ornamented with dialogue, description and choice quotations.

SUBJECT OF THEME:

An interesting Incident of My Christmas Holadays.

INTRODUCTION

"A tyrant's power in rigor is exprest." —DRYDEN.

I have decided to relate with precision what occurred during my recent Christmas holiday. Although I was away from this school only four days, returning unexpectedly the day after Christmas, a number of Incidents occurred which I believe I should narrate.

It is only just and fair that the Upper House, at least, should know of the injustice of my exile, and that it is all the result of circumstances over which I had no control.

For I make this appeal, and with good reason. Is it any fault of mine that my sister Leila is 20 months older than I am? Naturally, no.

Is it fair also, I ask, that in the best society, a girl is a Sub-Deb the year before she comes out, and although mature in mind, and even maturer in many ways than her older sister, the latter is treated as a young lady, enjoying many privileges, while the former is treated as a mere child, in spite, as I have observed, of only 20 months difference? I wish to place myself on record that it is NOT fair.

I shall go back, for a short time, to the way things were at home when I was small. I was very strictly raised. With the exception of Tommy Gray, who lives next door and only is about my age, I was never permitted to know any of the Other Sex.

Looking back, I am sure that the present way society is organized is really to blame for everything. I am being frank, and that is the way I feel. I was too strictly raised. I always had a governess tagging along. Until I came here to school I had never walked to the corner of the next street unattended. If it wasn't Mademoiselle, it was mother's maid, and if it wasn't either of them, it was mother herself, telling me to hold my toes out and my shoulder blades in. As I have said, I never knew any of the Other Sex, except the miserable little beasts at dancing school. I used to make faces at them when Mademoiselle was putting on my slippers and pulling out my hair bow. They were totally uninteresting, and I used to put pins in my sash, so that they would get scratched.

Their pumps mostly squeaked, and nobody noticed it, although I have known my parents to dismiss a Butler who creaked at the table.

When I was sent away to school, I expected to learn something of life. But I was disappointed. I do not desire to criticize this institution of learning. It is an excellent one, as is shown by the fact that the best families send their daughters here. But to learn life one must know something of both sides of it, male and female. It was, therefore, a matter of deep regret to me to find that, with the exception of the dancing master, who has three children, and the gardener, there were no members of the sterner sex to be seen.

The athletic coach was a girl! As she has left now to be married, I venture to say that she was not what Lord Chesterfield so euphoniously termed "SUAVITER IN MODO, FORTATER IN RE."

When we go out to walk we are taken to the country, and the three matinees a year we see in the city are mostly Shakespeare, arranged for the young. We are allowed only certain magazines, the Atlantic Monthly and one or two others, and Barbara Armstrong was penalized for having a framed photograph of her brother in running clothes.

At the school dances we are compelled to dance with each other, and the result is that when at home at Holiday parties I always try to lead, which annoys the boys I dance with.

Notwithstanding all this it is an excellent school. We learn a great deal, and our dear principal is a most charming and erudite person. But we see very little of life. And if school is a preparation for life, where are we?

Being here alone since the day after Christmas, I have had time to think everything out. I am naturally a thinking person. And now I am no longer indignant. I realize that I was wrong, and that I am only paying the penalty that I deserve although I consider it most unfair to be given French translation to do. I do not object to going to bed at nine o'clock, although ten is the hour in the Upper House, because I have time then to look back over things, and to reflect, to think.

"There is not hing either good or bad, but thinking makes it so."
SHAKESPEARE.

BODY OF THEME:

I now approach the narrative of what happened during the first four days of my Christmas Holiday.

For a period before the fifteenth of December, I was rather worried. All the girls in the school were getting new clothes for Christmas parties, and their Families were sending on invitations in great numbers, to various festivities that were to occur when they went home.

Nothing, however, had come for me, and I was worried. But on the 16th mother's visiting Secretary sent on four that I was to accept, with tiped acceptances for me to copy and send. She also sent me the good news that I was to have two party dresses, and I was to send on my measurements for them.

One of the parties was a dinner and theater party, to be given by Carter Brooks on New Year's Day. Carter Brooks is the well-known Yale Center, although now no longer such but selling advertizing, ecetera.

It is tragic to think that, after having so long anticipated that party, I am now here in sackcloth and ashes, which is a figure of speech for the Peter Thompson uniform of the school, with plain white for evenings and no jewelry.

It was with anticipatory joy, therefore, that I sent the acceptances and the desired measurements, and sat down to cheerfully while away the time in studies and the various duties of school life, until the Holidays.

However, I was not long to rest in piece, for in a few days I received a letter from Carter Brooks, as follows:

DEAR BARBARA: It was sweet of you to write me so promptly, although I confess to being rather astonished as well as delighted at being called "Dearest." The signature too was charming, "Ever thine." But, dear child, won't you write at once and tell me why the waist, bust and hip measurements? And the request to have them really low in the neck?

Ever thine,
CARTER.

It will be perceived that I had sent him the letter to mother, by mistake.

I was very unhappy about it. It was not an auspicious way to begin the holidays, especially the low neck. Also I disliked very much having told him my waist measure which is large owing to basket ball.

As I have stated before, I have known very few of the Other Sex, but some of the girls had had more experience, and in the days before we went home, we talked a great deal about things. Especially Love. I felt that it was rather over-done, particularly in fiction. Also I felt and observed at divers times that I would never marry. It was my intention to go upon the stage, although modified since by what I am about to relate.

The other girls say that I look like Julia Marlowe.

Some of the girls had boys who wrote to them, and one of them—I refrain from giving her name had—a Code. You read every third word. He called her "Cousin" and he would write like this:

Dear Cousin: I am well. Am just about crazy this week to go home. See notice enclosed you football game.

And so on and on. Only what it really said was "I am crazy to see you."

(In giving this code I am betraying no secrets, as they have quarreled and everything is now over between them.)

As I had nobody, at that time, and as I had visions of a career, I was a man-hater. I acknowledge that this was a pose. But after all, what is life but a pose?

"Stupid things!" I always said. "Nothing in their heads but football and tobacco smoke. Women," I said, "are only their playthings. And when they do grow up and get a little intelligence they use it in making money."

There has been a story in the school — I got it from one of the little girls — that I was disappointed in love in early youth, the object of my attachment having been the tenor in our church choir at home. I daresay I should have denied the soft impeachment, but I did not. It was, although not appearing so at the time, my first downward step on the path that leads to destruction.

"The way of the transgressor is hard" — Bible.

I come now to the momentous day of my return to my dear home for Christmas. Father and my sister Leila, who from now on I will term "Sis," met me at the station. Sis was very elegantly dressed, and she said:

"Hello, Kid," and turned her cheek for me to kiss.

She is, as I have stated, but 20 months older than I, and depends altogether on her clothes for her beauty. In the morning she is plain, although having a good skin. She was trimmed up with a bouquet of violets as large as a dishpan, and she covered them with her hands when I kissed her.

She was waved and powdered, and she had on a perfectly new outfit. And I was shabby. That is the exact word. Shabby. If you have to hang your entire wardrobe in a closet ten inches deep, and put it over you on cold nights, with the steam heat shut off at ten o'clock, it does not make it look any better.

My father has always been my favorite member of the family, and he was very glad to see me. He has a great deal of tact, also, and later on he slipped ten dollars in my purse in the motor. I needed it very much, as after I had paid the porter and bought luncheon, I had only three dollars left and an I. O. U. from one of the girls for seventy-five cents, which this may remind her, if it is read in class, she has forgotten.

"Good heavens, Barbara," Sis said, while I hugged father, "you certainly need to be pressed."

"I daresay I'll be the better for a hot iron," I retorted, "but at least I shan't need it on my hair." My hair is curly while hers is straight.

"Boarding school wit!" she said, and stocked to the motor.

Mother was in the car and glad to see me, but as usual she managed to restrain her enthusiasm. She put her hands over some orchids she was wearing when I kissed her. She and Sis were on their way to something or other.

"Trimmed up like Easter hats, you two!" I said.

"School has not changed you, I fear, Barbara," mother observed. "I hope you are studying hard."

"Exactly as hard as I have to. No more, no less," I regret to confess that I replied. And I saw Sis and mother exchange glances of significance.

We dropped them at the reception and father went to his office and I went on home alone. And all at once I began to be embittered. Sis had everything, and what had I? And when I got home, and saw that Sis had had her room done over, and ivory toilet things on her dressing table, and two perfectly huge boxes of candy on a stand and a ball gown laid out on the bed, I almost wept.

My own room was just as I had left it. It had been the night nursery, and there was still the dent in the mantel where I had thrown a hair brush at Sis, and the ink spot on the carpet at the foot of the bed, and everything.

Mademoiselle had gone, and Hannah, mother's maid, came to help me off with my things. I slammed the door in her face, and sat down on the bed and RAGED.

They still thought I was a little girl. They PATRONIZED me. I would hardly have been surprised if they had sent up a bread and milk supper on a tray. It was then and there that I made up my mind to show them that I was no longer a mere child. That the time was gone when they could shut me up in the nursery and forget me. I was seventeen years and eleven days old, and Juliet, in Shakespeare, was only sixteen when she had her well-known affair with Romeo.

I had no plan then. It was not until the next afternoon that the thing sprung (sprang?) fullblown from the head of Jove.

The evening was rather dreary. The family was going out, but not until nine thirty, and mother and Leila went over my clothes. They sat, Sis in pink chiffon and mother in black and silver, and Hannah took out my things and held them up. I was obliged to silently sit by, while my rags and misery were exposed.

"Why this open humiliation?" I demanded at last. "I am the family Cinderella, I admit it. But it isn't necessary to lay so much emphasis on it, is it?"

"Don't be sarcastic, Barbara," said mother. "You are still only a child, and a very untidy child at that. What do you do with your elbows to rub them through so? It must have taken patience and application."

"Mother" I said, "am I to have the party dresses?"

"Two. Very simple."

"Low in the neck?"

"Certainly not. A small v, perhaps."

"I've got a good neck." She rose impressively.

"You amaze and shock me, Barbara," she said coldly.

"I shouldn't have to wear tulle around my shoulders to hide the bones!" I retorted. "Sis is rather thin."

"You are a very sharp-tongued little girl," mother said, looking up at me. I am two inches taller than she is.

"Unless you learn to curb yourself, there will be no parties for you, and no party dresses."

This was the speech that broke the camel's back. I could endure no more.

"I think," I said, "that I shall get married and end everything."

Need I explain that I had no serious intention of taking the fatal step? But it was not deliberate mendacity. It was despair.

Mother actually went white. She clutched me by the arm and shook me.

"What are you saying?" she demanded.

"I think you heard me, mother" I said, very politely. I was however thinking hard.

"Marry whom? Barbara, answer me."

"I don't know. Anybody."

"She's trying to frighten you, mother" Sis said. "There isn't anybody. Don't let her fool you."

"Oh, isn't there?" I said in a dark and portentous manner.

Mother gave me a long look, and went out. I heard her go into father's dressing-room. But Sis sat on my bed and watched me.

"Who is it, Bab?" she asked. "The dancing teacher? Or your riding master? Or the school plumber?"

"Guess again."

"You're just enough of a little simpleton to get tied up to some wretched creature and disgrace us all."

I wish to state here that until that moment I had no intention of going any further with the miserable business. I am naturally truthful, and deception is hateful to me. But when my sister uttered the above disparaging remark I saw that, to preserve my own dignity, which I value above precious stones, I would be compelled to go on.

"I'm perfectly mad about him," I said. "And he's crazy about me."

"I'd like very much to know," Sis said, as she stood up and stared at me, "how much you are making up and how much is true."

None the less, I saw that she was terrified. The family kitten, to speak in allegory, had become a lion and showed its claws.

When she had gone out I tried to think of some one to hang a love affair to. But there seemed to be nobody. They knew perfectly well that the dancing master had one eye and three children, and that the clergyman at school was elderly, with two wives. One dead.

I searched my past, but it was blameless. It was empty and bare, and as I looked back and saw how little there had been in it but imbibing wisdom and playing basket-ball and tennis, and typhoid fever when I was fourteen and almost having to have my head shaved, a great wave of bitterness agitated me.

"Never again," I observed to myself with firmness. "Never again, if I have to invent a member of the Other Sex."

At that time, however, owing to the appearance of Hannah with a mending basket, I got no further than his name.

It was Harold. I decided to have him dark, with a very small black mustache, and passionate eyes. I felt, too, that he would be jealous. The eyes would be of the smoldering type, showing the green-eyed monster beneath.

I was very much cheered up. At least they could not ignore me any more, and I felt that they would see the point. If I was old enough to have a lover—especially a jealous one with the aforementioned eyes—I was old enough to have the necks of my frocks cut out.

While they were getting their wraps on in the lower hall, I counted my money. I had thirteen dollars. It was enough for a plan I was beginning to have in mind.

"Go to bed early, Barbara," mother said when they were ready to go out.

"You don't mind if I write a letter, do you?"

"To whom?"

"Oh, just a letter," I said, and she stared at me coldly.

"I daresay you will write it, whether I consent or not. Leave it on the hall table, and it will go out with the morning mail."

"I may run out to the box with it."

"I forbid your doing anything of the sort."

"Oh, very well," I responded meekly.

"If there is such haste about it, give it to Hannah to mail."

"Very well," I said.

She made an excuse to see Hannah before she left, and I knew THAT I WAS BEING WATCHED. I was greatly excited, and happier than I had been for weeks. But when I had settled myself in the library, with the paper in front of me, I could not think of anything to say in a letter. So I wrote a poem instead.

"To H— —

"Dear love: you seem so far away,

I would that you were near.

I do so long to hear you say

Again, 'I love you, dear.'

"Here all is cold and drear and strange

With none who with me tarry,

I hope that soon we can arrange

To run away and marry."

The last verse did not scan, exactly, but I wished to use the word "marry" if possible. It would show, I felt, that things were really serious and impending. A love affair is only a love affair, but marriage is marriage, and the end of everything.

It was at that moment, 10 o'clock, that the strange thing occurred which did not seem strange at all at the time, but which developed into so great a mystery later on. Which was to actually threaten my reason and which, flying on winged feet, was to send me back here to school the day after Christmas and put my seed pearl necklace in the safe deposit vault. Which was very unfair, for what had my necklace to do with it? And just now, when I need comfort, it—the necklace—would help to relieve my exile.

Hannah brought me in a cup of hot milk, with a Valentine's malted milk tablet dissolved in it.

As I stirred it around, it occurred to me that Valentine would be a good name for Harold. On the spot I named him Harold Valentine, and I wrote the name on the envelope that had the poem inside, and addressed it to the town where this school gets its mail.

It looked well written out. "Valentine," also, is a word that naturally connects itself with AFFAIRS DE COUR. And I felt that I was safe, for as there was no Harold Valentine, he could not call for the letter at the post office, and would therefore not be able to cause me any trouble, under any circumstances. And, furthermore. I knew that Hannah would not mail the letter anyhow, but would give it to mother. So, even if there was a Harold Valentine, he would never get it.

Comforted by these reflections, I drank my malted milk, ignorant of the fact that destiny, "which never swerves, nor yields to men the helm"— Emerson, was stocking at my heels.

Between sips, as the expression goes, I addressed the envelope to Harold Valentine, and gave it to Hannah. She went out the front door with it, as I had expected, but I watched from a window, and she turned right around and went in the area way. So THAT was all right.

It had worked like a Charm. I could tear my hair now when I think how well it worked. I ought to have been suspicious for that very reason. When things go very well with me at the start, it is a sure sign that they are going to blow up eventually.

Mother and Sis slept late the next morning, and I went out stealthily and did some shopping. First I bought myself a bunch of violets, with a white rose in the center, and I printed on the card:

"My love is like a white, white rose. H." And sent it to myself.

It was deception, I acknowledge, but having put my hand to the plow, I did not intend to steer a crooked course. I would go straight to the end. I am like that in everything I do. But, on deliberating things over, I felt that Violets, alone and unsupported, were not enough. I felt that If I had a photograph, it would make everything more real. After all, what is a love affair without a picture of the Beloved Object?

So I bought a photograph. It was hard to find what I wanted, but I got it at last in a stationer's shop, a young man in a checked suit with a small mustache—the young man, of course, not the suit. Unluckily, he was rather blonde, and had a dimple in his chin. But he looked exactly as though his name ought to be Harold.

I may say here that I chose "Harold," not because it is a favorite name of mine, but because it is romantic in sound. Also because I had never known any one named Harold and it seemed only discrete.

I took it home in my muff and put it under my pillow where Hannah would find it and probably take it to mother. I wanted to buy a ring too, to hang on a ribbon around my neck. But the violets had made a fearful hole in my thirteen dollars.

I borrowed a stub pen at the stationer's and I wrote on the photograph, in large, sprawling letters, "To YOU from ME."

"There," I said to myself, when I put it under the pillow. "You look like a photograph, but you are really a bomb-shell."

As things eventuated, it was. More so, indeed.

Mother sent for me when I came in. She was sitting in front of her mirror, having the vibrator used on her hair, and her manner was changed. I guessed that there had been a family counsel over the poem, and that they had decided to try kindness.

"Sit down, Barbara," she said. "I hope you were not lonely last night?"

"I am never lonely, mother. I always have things to think about."

I said this in a very pathetic tone.

"What sort of things?" mother asked, rather sharply.

"Oh—things," I said vaguely. "Life is such a mess, isn't it?"

"Certainly not. Unless one makes it so."

"But it is so difficult. Things come up and—and it's hard to know what to do. The only way, I suppose, is to be true to one's belief in one's self."

"Take that thing off my head and go out, Hannah," mother snapped. "Now then, Barbara, what in the world has come over you?"

"Over me? Nothing."

"You are being a silly child."

"I am no longer a child, mother. I am seventeen. And at seventeen there are problems. After all, one's life is one's own. One must decide——"

"Now, Barbara, I am not going to have any nonsense. You must put that man out of your head."

"Man? What man?"

"You think you are in love with some driveling young Fool. I'm not blind, or an idiot. And I won't have it."

"I have not said that there is anyone, have I?" I said in a gentle voice. "But if there was, just what would you propose to do, mother?"

"If you were three years younger I'd propose to spank you." Then I think she saw that she was taking the wrong method, for she changed her tactics. "It's the fault of that silly school," she said. (Note: These are my mother's words, not mine.) "They are hotbeds of sickly sentimentality. They——"

And just then the violets came, addressed to me. Mother opened them herself, her mouth set. "My love is like a white, white rose," she said. "Barbara, do you know who sent these?"

"Yes, mother," I said meekly. This was quite true. I did.

I am indeed sorry to record that here my mother lost her temper, and there was no end of a fuss. It ended by mother offering me a string of seed pearls for Christmas, and my party dresses cut V front and back, if I would, as she phrased it, "put him out of my silly head."

"I shall have to write one letter, mother," I said, "to—to break things off. I cannot tear myself out of another's life without a word."

She sniffed.

"Very well," she said. "One letter. I trust you to make it only one."

I come now to the next day. How true it is, that "Man's life is but a jest, a dream, a shadow, bubble, air, a vapor at the best!"

I spent the morning with mother at the dressmakers and she chose two perfectly spiffing things, one of white chiffon over silk, made modified Empire, with little bunches of roses here and there on it, and when she and the dressmaker were haggling over the roses, I took the scissors and cut the neck of the lining two inches lower in front. The effect was positively impressive. The other was blue over orchid, a perfectly passionate combination.

When we got home some of the girls had dropped in, and Carter Brooks and Sis were having tea in the den. I am perfectly sure that Sis threw a cigarette in the fire when I went in. When I think of my sitting here alone, when I have done NOTHING, and Sis playing around and smoking cigarettes, and nothing said, all for a difference of 20 months, it makes me furious.

"Let's go in and play with the children, Leila," he said. "I'm feeling young today."

Which was perfectly silly. He is not Methuselah. Although thinking himself so, or almost.

Well, they went into the drawing room. Elaine Adams was there waiting for me, and Betty Anderson and Jane Raleigh. And I hadn't been in the room five minutes before I knew that they all knew. It turned out later that Hannah was engaged to the Adams' butler, and she had told him, and he had told Elaine's governess, who is still there and does the ordering, and Elaine sends her stockings home for her to darn.

Sis had told Carter, too, I saw that, and among them they had rather a good time. Carter sat down at the piano and struck a few chords, chanting "My Love is like a white, white rose."

"Only you know" he said, turning to me, "that's wrong. It ought to be a 'red, red rose.'"

"Certainly not. The word is 'white.'"

"Oh, is it?" he said, with his head on one side. "Strange that both you and Harold should have got it wrong."

I confess to a feeling of uneasiness at that moment.

Tea came, and Carter insisted on pouring.

"I do so love to pour!" he said. "Really, after a long day's shopping, tea is the only thing that keeps me going until dinner. Cream or lemon, Leila dear?"

"Both," Sis said in an absent manner, with her eyes on me. "Barbara, come into the den a moment. I want to show you mother's Christmas gift."

She stocked in ahead of me, and lifted a book from the table. Under it was the photograph.

"You wretched child!" she said. "Where did you get that?"

"That's not your affair, is it?"

"I'm going to make it my affair. Did he give it to you?"

"Have you read what's written on it?"

"Where did you meet him?"

I hesitated because I am by nature truthful. But at last I said:

"At school."

"Oh," she said slowly. "So you met him at school! What was he doing there? Teaching elocution?"

"Elocution!"

"This is Harold, is it?"

"Certainly." Well, he WAS Harold, if I chose to call him that, wasn't he? Sis gave a little sigh.

"You're quite hopeless, Bab. And, although I'm perfectly sure you want me to take the thing to mother, I'll do nothing of the sort."

SHE FLUNG IT INTO THE FIRE. I was raging. It had cost me a dollar. It was quite brown when I got it out, and a corner was burned off. But I got it.

"I'll thank you to burn your own things," I said with dignity. And I went back to the drawing room.

The girls and Carter Brooks were talking in an undertone when I got there. I knew it was about me. And Jane came over to me and put her arm around me.

"You poor thing!" she said. "Just fight it out. We're all with you."

"I'm so helpless, Jane." I put all the despair I could into my voice. For after all, if they were going to talk about my private affairs behind my back, I felt that they might as well have something to talk about. As Jane's second cousin once removed is in this school and as Jane will probably write her all about it, I hope this theme is read aloud in class, so she will get it all straight. Jane is imaginative and may have a wrong idea of things.

"Don't give in. Let them bully you. They can't really do anything. And they're scared. Leila is positively sick."

"I've promised to write and break it off," I said in a tense tone.

"If he really loves you," said Jane, "the letter won't matter." There was a thrill in her voice. Had I not been uneasy at my deceit, I to would have thrilled.

Some fresh muffins came in just then and I was starving. But I waved them away, and stood staring at the fire.

I am writing all of this as truthfully as I can. I am not defending myself. What I did I was driven to, as any one can see. It takes a real shock to make the average family wake up to the fact that the youngest daughter is not the family baby at seventeen. All I was doing was furnishing the shock. If things turned out badly, as they did, it was because I rather overdid the thing. That is all. My motives were perfectly irreproachable.

Well, they fell on the muffins like pigs, and I could hardly stand it. So I wandered into the den, and it occurred to me to write the letter then. I felt that they all expected me to do something anyhow.

If I had never written the wretched letter things would be better now. As I say, I overdid. But everything had gone so smoothly all day that I was deceived. But the real reason was a new set of furs. I had secured the dresses and the promise of the necklace on a poem and a photograph, and I thought that a good love letter might bring a muff. It all shows that it does not do to be grasping.

HAD I NOT WRITTEN THE LETTER, THERE WOULD HAVE BEEN NO TRAGEDY.

But I wrote it and if I do say it, it was a LETTER. I commenced it "Darling," and I said I was mad to see him, and that I would always love him. But I told him that the family objected to him, and that this was to end everything between us. They had started the phonograph in the library, and were playing "The Rosary." So I ended with a verse from that. It was really a most affecting letter. I almost wept over it myself, because, if there had been a Harold, it would have broken his Heart.

Of course I meant to give it to Hannah to mail, and she would give it to mother. Then, after the family had read it and it had got in its work, including the set of furs, they were welcome to mail it. It would go to the dead letter office, since there was no Harold. It could not come back to me, for I had only signed it "Barbara." I had it all figured out carefully. It looked as if I had everything to gain, including the furs, and nothing to lose. Alas, how little I knew!

"The best laid plans of mice and men gang aft allay." Burns.

Carter Brooks ambled into the room just as I sealed it and stood gazing down at me.

"You're quite a Person these days, Bab," he said. "I suppose all the customary Xmas kisses are being saved this year for what's his name."

"I don't understand you."

"For Harold. You know, Bab, I think I could bear up better if his name wasn't Harold."

"I don't see how it concerns you," I responded.

"Don't you? With me crazy about you for lo, these many years! First as a baby, then as a sub-sub-deb, and now as a sub-deb. Next year, when you are a real debutante——"

"You've concealed your infatuation bravely."

"It's been eating me inside. A green and yellow melancholy—hello! A letter to him!"

"Why, so it is," I said in a scornful tone.

He picked it up, and looked at it. Then he started and stared at me.

"No!" he said. "It isn't possible! It isn't old Valentine!"

Positively, my knees got cold. I never had such a shock.

"It—it certainly is Harold Valentine," I said feebly.

"Old Hal!" he muttered. "Well, who would have thought it! And not a word to me about it, the secretive old duffer!" He held out his hand to me. "Congratulations, Barbara," he said heartily. "Since you absolutely refuse me, you couldn't do better. He's the finest chap I know. If it's Valentine the family is kicking up such a row about, you leave it to me. I'll tell them a few things."

I was stunned. Would anybody have believed it? To pick a name out of the air, so to speak, and off a malted milk tablet, and then to find that it actually belonged to some one—was sickening.

"It may not be the one you know" I said desperately. "It—it's a common name. There must be plenty of Valentines."

"Sure there are, lace paper and cupids—lots of that sort. But there's only one Harold Valentine, and now you've got him pinned to the wall! I'll tell you what I'll do, Barbara. I'm a real friend of yours. Always have been. Always will be. The chances are against the family letting him get this letter. I'll give it to him."

"GIVE it to him?"

"Why, he's here. You know that, don't you? He's in town over the holidays."

"Oh, no!" I said in a gasping Voice.

"Sorry," he said. "Probably meant it as a surprise to you. Yes, he's here, with bells on."

He then put the letter in his pocket before my very eyes, and sat down on the corner of the writing table!

"You don't know how all this has relieved my mind," he said. "The poor chap's been looking down. Not interested in anything. Of course this explains it. He's the sort to take Love hard. At college he took everything hard—like to have died once with German measles."

He picked up a book, and the charred picture was underneath. He pounced on it. "Pounced" is exactly the right word.

"Hello!" he said, "family again, I suppose. Yes, it's Hal, all right. Well, who would have thought it!"

My last hope died. Then and there I had a nervous chill. I was compelled to prop my chin on my hand to keep my teeth from chattering.

"Tell you what I'll do," he said, in a perfectly cheerful tone that made me cold all over. "I'll be the cupid for your Valentine. See? Far be it from me to see love's young dream wiped out by a hardhearted family. I'm going to see this thing through. You count on me, Barbara. I'll arrange that you get a chance to see each other, family or no family. Old Hal has been looking down his nose long enough. When's your first party?"

"Tomorrow night," I gasped out.

"Very well. Tomorrow night it is. It's the Adams', isn't it, at the Club?"

I could only nod. I was beyond speaking. I saw it all clearly. I had been wicked in deceiving my dear family and now I was to pay the penalty. He would know at once that I had made him up, or rather he did not know me and therefore could not possibly be in Love with me. And what then?

"But look here," he said, "if I take him there as Valentine, the family will be on, you know. We'd better call him something else. Got any choice as to a name?"

"Carter" I said frantically. "I think I'd better tell you. I——"

"How about calling him Grosvenor?". he babbled on. "Grosvenor's a good name. Ted Grosvenor—that ought to hit them between the eyes. It's going to be rather a lark, Miss Bab!"

And of course just then mother came in, and the Brooks idiot went in and poured her a cup of tea, with his little finger stuck out at a right angel, and every time he had a chance he winked at me.

I wanted to die.

When they had all gone home it seemed like a bad dream, the whole thing. It could not be true. I went upstairs and manicured my nails, which usually comforts me, and put my hair up like Leila's.

But nothing could calm me. I had made my own fate, and must lie in it. And just then Hannah slipped in with a box in her hands and her eyes frightened.

"Oh, Miss Barbara!" she said. "If your mother sees this!"

I dropped my manicure scissors, I was so alarmed. But I opened the box, and clutched the envelope inside. It said "from H— —." Then Carter was right. There was an H after all!

Hannah was rolling her hands in her apron and her eyes were popping out of her head.

"I just happened to see the boy at the door," she said, with her silly teeth chattering. "Oh, Miss Barbara, if Patrick had answered the bell! What shall we do with them?"

"You take them right down the back stairs," I said. "As if it was an empty box. And put it outside with the waist papers. Quick."

She gathered the thing up, but of course mother had to come in just then and they met in the doorway. She saw it all in one glance, and she snatched the card out of my hand.

"From H— —!" she read. "Take them out, Hannah, and throw them away. No, don't do that. Put them on the Servant's table." Then, when the door had closed, she turned to me. "Just one more ridiculous episode of this kind, Barbara," she said, "and you go back to school—Christmas or no Christmas."

I will say this. If she had shown the faintest softness, I'd have told her the whole thing. But she did not. She looked exactly as gentle as a macadam pavement. I am one who has to be handled with gentleness. A kind word will do anything with me, but harsh treatment only makes me determined. I then become inflexible as iron.

That is what happened then. Mother took the wrong course and threatened, which as I have stated is fatal, as far as I am concerned. I refused to yield an inch, and it ended in my having my dinner in my room, and mother threatening to keep me home from the party the next night. It was not a threat, if she had only known it.

But when the next day went by, with no more flowers, and nothing apparently wrong except that mother was very dignified with me, I began to feel better. Sis was out all day, and in the afternoon Jane called me up.

"How are you?" she said.

"Oh, I'm all right."

"Everything smooth?"

"Well, smooth enough."

"Oh, Bab," she said. "I'm just crazy about it. All the girls are."

"I knew they were crazy about something."

"You poor thing, no wonder you are bitter," she said. "Somebody's coming. I'll have to ring off. But don't you give in, Bab. Not an inch. Marry your heart's desire, no matter who butts in."

Well, you can see how it was. Even then I could have told father and mother, and got out of it somehow. But all the girls knew about it, and there was nothing to do but go on.

All that day every time I thought of the Party my heart missed a beat. But as I would not lie and say that I was ill—I am naturally truthful, as far as possible—I was compelled to go, although my heart was breaking.

I am not going to write much about the party, except a slight description, which properly belongs in every theme.

All Parties for the school set are alike. The boys range from knickerbockers to college men in their freshmen year, and one is likely to dance half the evening with youngsters that one saw last in their perambulators. It is rather startling to have about six feet of black trouser legs and white shirt front come and ask one to dance and then to get one's eyes raised as far as the top of what looks like a particularly thin pair of tree trunks and see a little boy's face.

As this theme is to contain description I shall describe the ball room of the club where the eventful party occurred.

The ball room is white, with red hangings, and looks like a Charlotte Russe with maraschino cherries. Over the fireplace they had put "Merry Christmas," in electric lights, and the chandeliers were made into Christmas trees and hung with colored balls. One of the balls fell off during the cotillion, and went down the back of one of the girl's dresses, and they were compelled to up-end her and shake her out in the dressing room.

The favors were insignificant, as usual. It is not considered good taste to have elaborate things for the school crowd. But when I think of the silver things Sis always brought home, and remember that I took away about six Christmas stockings, a toy balloon, four whistles, a wooden canary in a cage and a box of talcum powder, I feel that things are not fair in this World.

Hannah went with me, and in the motor she said:

"Oh, Miss Barbara, do be careful. The family is that upset."

"Don't be a silly," I said. "And if the family is half as upset as I am, it is throwing a fit at this minute."

We were early, of course. My mother believes in being on time, and besides, she and Sis wanted the motor later. And while Hannah was on her knees taking off my carriage boots, I suddenly decided that I could not go down. Hannah turned quite pale when I told her.

"What will your mother say?" she said. "And you with your new dress and all! It's as much as my life is worth to take you back home now, Miss Barbara."

Well, that was true enough. There would be a riot if I went home, and I knew it.

"I'll see the steward and get you a cup of tea," Hannah said. "Tea sets me up like anything when I'm nervous. Now please be a good girl, Miss Barbara, and don't run off, or do anything foolish."

She wanted me to promise, but I would not, although I could not have run anywhere. My legs were entirely numb.

In a half hour at the utmost I knew all would be known, and very likely I would be a homeless wanderer on the earth. For I felt that never, never could I return to my dear ones, when my terrible actions became known.

Jane came in while I was sipping the tea and she stood off and eyed me with sympathy.

"I don't wonder, Bab!" she said. "The idea of your family acting so outrageously! And look here" She bent over me and whispered it. "Don't trust Carter too much. He is perfectly infatuated with Leila, and he will play into the hands of the enemy. BE CAREFUL."

"Loathsome creature!" was my response. "As for trusting him, I trust no one, these days."

"I don't wonder your faith is gone," she observed. But she was talking with one eye on a mirror.

"Pink makes me pale," she said. "I'll bet the maid has a drawer full of rouge. I'm going to see. How about a touch for you? You look ghastly."

"I don't care how I look," I said, recklessly. "I think I'll sprain my ankle and go home. Anyhow I am not allowed to use rouge."

"Not allowed!" she observed. "What has that got to do with it? I don't understand you, Bab; you are totally changed."

"I am suffering," I said. I was to.

Just then the maid brought me a folded note. Hannah was hanging up my wraps, and did not see it. Jane's eyes fairly bulged.

"I hope you have saved the cotillion for me," it said. And it was signed. H——!

"Good gracious," Jane said breathlessly. "Don't tell me he is here, and that that's from him!"

I had to swallow twice before I could speak. Then I said, solemnly:

"He is here, Jane. He has followed me. I am going to dance the cotillion with him although I shall probably be disinherited and thrown out into the world, as a result."

I have no recollection whatever of going down the staircase and into the ballroom. Although I am considered rather brave, and once saved one of the smaller girls from drowning, as I need not remind the school, when she was skating on thin ice, I was frightened. I remember that, inside the door, Jane said "Courage!" in a low tense voice, and that I stepped on somebody's foot and said "Certainly" instead of apologizing. The shock of that brought me around somewhat, and I managed to find Mrs. Adams and Elaine, and not disgrace myself. Then somebody at my elbow said:

"All right, Barbara. Everything's fixed."

It was Carter.

"He's waiting in the corner over there," he said. "We'd better go through the formality of an introduction. He's positively twittering with excitement."

"Carter" I said desperately. "I want to tell you something first. I've got myself in an awful mess. I——"

"Sure you have," he said. "That's why I'm here, to help you out. Now you be calm, and there's no reason why you two can't have the evening of your young lives. I wish I could fall in love. It must be bully."

"Carter——!"

"Got his note, didn't you?"

"Yes, I——"

"Here we are," said Carter. "Miss Archibald, I would like to present Mr. Grosvenor."

Somebody bowed in front of me, and then straightened up and looked down at me. IT WAS THE MAN OF THE PICTURE, LITTLE MUSTACHE AND ALL. My mouth went perfectly dry.

It is all very well to talk about Romance and Love, and all that sort of thing. But I have concluded that amorous experiences are not always agreeable. And I have discovered something else. The moment anybody is crazy about me I begin to hate him. It is curious, but I am like that. I only care as long as they, or he, is far away. And the moment I touched H's white kid glove, I knew I loathed him.

"Now go to it, you two," Carter said in cautious tone. "Don't be conspicuous. That's all."

And he left us.

"Suppose we dance this. Shall we?" said H. And the next moment we were gliding off. He danced very well. I will say that. But at the time I was too much occupied with hating him to care about dancing, or anything. But I was compelled by my pride to see things through. We are a very proud family and never show our troubles, though our hearts be torn with anguish.

"Think," he said, when we had got away from the band, "think of our being together like this!"

"It's not so surprising, is it? We've got to be together if we are dancing."

"Not that. Do you know, I never knew so long a day as this has been. The thought of meeting you—er—again, and all that."

"You needn't rave for my benefit," I said freezingly. "You know perfectly well that you never saw me before."

"Barbara! With your dear little letter in my breast pocket at this moment!"

"I didn't know men had breast pockets in their evening clothes."

"Oh well, have it your own way. I'm too happy to quarrel," he said. "How well you dance—only, let me lead, won't you? How strange it is to think that we have never danced together before!"

"We must have a talk," I said desperately. "Can't we go somewhere, away from the noise?"

"That would be conspicuous, wouldn't it, under the circumstances? If we are to overcome the family objection to me, we'll have to be cautious, Barbara."

"Don't call me Barbara," I snapped. "I know perfectly well what you think of me, and I——"

"I think you are wonderful," he said. "Words fail me when I try to tell you what I am thinking. You've saved the cotillion for me, haven't you? If not, I'm going to claim it anyhow. IT IS MY RIGHT."

He said it in the most determined manner, as if everything was settled. I felt like a rat in a trap, and Carter, watching from a corner, looked exactly like a cat. If he had taken his hand in its white glove and washed his face with it, I would hardly have been surprised.

The music stopped, and somebody claimed me for the next. Jane came up, too, and clutched my arm.

"You lucky thing!" she said. "He's perfectly handsome. And oh, Bab, he's wild about you. I can see it in his eyes."

"Don't pinch, Jane," I said coldly. "And don't rave. He's an idiot."

She looked at me with her mouth open.

"Well, if you don't want him, pass him on to me," she said, and walked away.

It was too silly, after everything that had happened, to dance the next dance with Willie Graham, who is still in knickerbockers, and a full head shorter than I am. But that's the way with a Party for the school crowd, as I've said before. They ask all ages, from perambulators up, and of course the little boys all want to dance with the older girls. It is deadly stupid.

But H seemed to be having a good time. He danced a lot with Jane, who is a wretched dancer, with no sense of time whatever. Jane is not pretty, but she has nice eyes, and I am not afraid, second cousin once removed or no second cousin once removed, to say she used them.

Altogether, it was a terrible evening. I danced three dances out of four with knickerbockers, and one with old Mr. Adams, who is fat and rotates his partner at the corners by swinging her on his waistcoat. Carter did not dance at all, and every time I tried to speak to him he was taking a crowd of the little girls to the fruit-punch bowl.

I determined to have things out with H during the cotillion, and tell him that I would never marry him, that I would die first. But I was favored a great deal, and when we did have a chance the music was making such a noise that I would have had to shout. Our chairs were next to the band.

But at last we had a minute, and I went out to the verandah, which was closed in with awnings. He had to follow, of course, and I turned and faced him.

"Now" I said, "this has got to stop."

"I don't understand you, Bab."

"You do, perfectly well," I stormed. "I can't stand it. I am going crazy."

"Oh," he said slowly. "I see. I've been dancing too much with the little girl with the eyes! Honestly, Bab, I was only doing it to disarm suspicion. MY EVERY THOUGHT IS OF YOU."

"I mean," I said, as firmly as I could, "that this whole thing has got to stop. I can't stand it."

"Am I to understand," he said solemnly, "that you intend to end everything?"

I felt perfectly wild and helpless.

"After that Letter!" he went on. "After that sweet Letter! You said, you know, that you were mad to see me, and that—it is almost too sacred to repeat, even to YOU—that you would always love me. After that Confession I refuse to agree that all is over. It can NEVER be over."

"I daresay I am losing my mind," I said. "It all sounds perfectly natural. But it doesn't mean anything. There CAN'T be any Harold Valentine; because I made him up. But there is, so there must be. And I am going crazy."

"Look here," he stormed, suddenly quite raving, and throwing out his right hand. It would have been terribly dramatic, only he had a glass of punch in it. "I am not going to be played with. And you are not going to jilt me without a reason. Do you mean to deny everything? Are you going to say, for instance, that I never sent you any violets? Or gave you my Photograph, with an—er—touching inscription on it?" Then, appealingly, "You can't mean to deny that Photograph, Bab!"

And then that lanky wretch of an Eddie Perkins brought me a toy balloon, and I had to dance, with my heart crushed.

Nevertheless, I ate a fair supper. I felt that I needed Strength. It was quite a grown-up supper, with bullion and creamed chicken and baked ham and sandwiches, among other things. But of course they had to show it was a 'kid' party, after all. For instead of coffee we had milk.

Milk! When I was going through a tragedy. For if it is not a tragedy to be engaged to a man one never saw before, what is it?

All through the refreshments I could feel that his eyes were on me. And I hated him. It was all well enough for Jane to say he was handsome. She wasn't going to have to marry him. I detest dimples in chins. I always have. And anybody could see that it was his first mustache, and soft, and that he took it round like a mother pushing a new baby in a perambulator. It was sickening.

I left just after supper. He did not see me when I went upstairs, but he had missed me, for when Hannah and I came down, he was at the door, waiting. Hannah was loaded down with silly favors, and lagged behind, which gave him a chance to speak to me. I eyed him coldly and tried to pass him, but I had no chance.

"I'll see you tomorrow, DEAREST," he whispered.

"Not if I can help it," I said, looking straight ahead. Hannah had dropped a stocking—not her own. One of the Christmas favors—and was fumbling about for it.

"You are tired and unnerved to-night, Bab. When I have seen your father tomorrow, and talked to him——"

"Don't you dare to see my father."

"——and when he has agreed to what I propose," he went on, without paying any attention to what I had said, "you will be calmer. We can plan things."

Hannah came puffing up then, and he helped us into the motor. He was very careful to see that we were covered with the robes, and he tucked Hannah's feet in. She was awfully flattered. Old Fool! And she babbled about him until I wanted to slap her.

"He's a nice young man. Miss Bab," she said. "That is, if he's the One. And he has nice manners. So considerate. Many a party I've taken your sister to, and never before——"

"I wish you'd shut up, Hannah," I said. "He's a pig, and I hate him."

She sulked after that, and helped me out of my things at home without a word. When I was in bed, however, and she was hanging up my clothes, she said:

"I don't know what's got into you, Miss Barbara. You are that cross that there's no living with you."

"Oh, go away," I said.

"And what's more," she added, "I don't know but what your mother ought to know about these goings on. You're only a little girl, with all your high and mightiness, and there's going to be no scandal in this family if I can help it."

I put the bedclothes over my head, and she went out.

But of course I could not sleep. Sis was not home yet, or mother, and I went into Sis's room and got a novel from her table. It was the story of a woman who had married a man in a hurry, and without really loving him, and when she had been married a year, and hated the very way her husband drank his coffee and cut the ends off his cigars, she found some one she really loved with her whole heart. And it was too late. But she wrote him one letter, the other man, you know, and it caused a lot of trouble. So she said—I remember the very words—

"Half the troubles in the world are caused by letters. Emotions are changeable things"—this was after she had found that she really loved her husband after all, but he had had to shoot himself before she found it out, although not fatally—"but the written word does not change. It remains always, embodying a dead truth and giving it apparent life. No woman should ever put her thoughts on paper."

She got the letter back, but she had to steal it. And it turned out that the other man had really only wanted her money all the time.

That story was a real illumination to me. I shall have a great deal of money when I am of age, from my grandmother. I saw it all. It was a trap sure enough. And if I was to get out I would have to have the letter.

IT WAS THE LETTER THAT PUT ME IN HIS POWER.

The next day was Christmas. I got a lot of things, including the necklace, and a mending basket from Sis, with the hope that it would make me tidy, and father had bought me a set of silver fox, which mother did not approve of, it being too expensive for a young girl to wear, according to her. I must say that for an hour or two I was happy enough.

But the afternoon was terrible. We keep open house on Xmas afternoon, and father makes a champagne punch, and somebody pours tea, although nobody drinks it, and there are little cakes from the club, and the house is decorated with poinsettias.

At eleven o'clock the mail came in, and mother sorted it over, while father took a gold piece out to the post-man.

There were about a million cards, and mother glanced at the addresses and passed them round. But suddenly she frowned. There was a small parcel, addressed to me.

"This looks like a gift, Barbara," she said. And proceeded to open it.

My heart skipped two beats, and then hammered. Mother's mouth was set as she tore off the paper and opened the box. There was a card, which she glanced at, and underneath, was a book of poems.

"Love Lyrics," said mother, in a terrible voice. "To Barbara, from H— —"

"Mother— —" I began, in an earnest tone.

"A child of mine receiving such a book from a man!" she went on. "Barbara, I am speechless."

But she was not speechless. If she was speechless for the next half hour, I would hate to hear her really converse. And all that I could do was to bear it. For I had made a Frankenstein—see the book read last term by the Literary Society—not out of grave-yard fragments, but from malted milk tablets, so to speak, and now it was pursuing me to an early grave. For I felt that I simply could not continue to live.

"Now—where does he live?"

"I—don't know, mother."

"You sent him a letter."

"I don't know where he lives, anyhow."

"Leila," mother said, "will you ask Hannah to bring my smelling salts?"

"Aren't you going to give me the book?" I asked. "It—it sounds interesting."

"You are shameless," mother said, and threw the thing into the fire. A good many of my things seemed to be going into the fire at that time. I cannot help wondering what they would have done if it had all happened in the summer, and no fires burning. They would have felt quite helpless, I imagine.

Father came back just then, but he did not see the book, which was then blazing with a very hot red flame. I expected mother to tell him, and I daresay I should not have been surprised to see my furs follow the book. I had got into the way of expecting to see things burning that do not belong in a fireplace. But mother did not tell him.

I have thought over this a great deal, and I believe that now I understand. Mother was unjustly putting the blame for everything on this School, and mother had chosen the School. My father had not been much impressed by the catalog. "Too much dancing room and not enough tennis courts," he had said. This, of course, is my father's opinion. Not mine.

The real reason, then, for mother's silence was that she disliked confessing that she made a mistake in her choice of a School.

I ate very little luncheon and my only comfort was my seed pearls. I was wearing them, for fear the door-bell would ring, and a letter or flowers would arrive from H. In that case I felt quite sure that someone, in a frenzy, would burn the pearls also.

The afternoon was terrible. It rained solid sheets, and Patrick, the butler, gave notice three hours after he had received his Christmas presents, on account of not being let off for early mass.

But my father's punch is famous, and people came, and stood around and buzzed, and told me I had grown and was almost a young lady. And Tommy Gray got out of his cradle and came to call on me, and coughed all the time, with a whoop. He developed the whooping cough later. He had on his first long trousers, and a pair of lavender socks and a tie to match. He said they were not exactly the same shade, but he did not think it would be noticed. Hateful child!

At half past five, when the place was jammed, I happened to look up. Carter Brooks was in the hall, and behind him was H. He had seen me before I saw him, and he had a sort of sickly grin, meant to denote joy. I was talking to our bishop at the time, and he was asking me what sort of services we had in the school chapel.

I meant to say "non-sectarian," but in my surprise and horror I regret to say that I said, "vegetarian." Carter Brooks came over to me like a cat to a saucer of milk, and pulled me off into a corner.

"It's all right," he said. "I phoned mama, and she said to bring him. He's known as Grosvenor here, of course. They'll never suspect a thing. Now, do I get a small 'thank you'?"

"I won't see him."

"Now look here, Bab," he protested, "you two have got to make this thing up You are a pair of idiots, quarreling over nothing. Poor old Hal is all broken up. He's sensitive. You've got to remember how sensitive he is."

"Go, away" I cried, in broken tones. "Go away, and take him with you."

"Not until he had spoken to your Father," he observed, setting his jaw. "He's here for that, and you know it. You can't play fast and loose with a man, you know."

"Don't you dare to let him speak to father!"

He shrugged his shoulders.

"That's between you two, of course," he said. "It's not up to me. Tell him yourself, if you've changed your mind. I don't intend," he went on, impressively, "to have any share in ruining his life."

"Oh piffle," I said. I am aware that this is slang, and does not belong in a theme. But I was driven to saying it.

I got through the crowd by using my elbows. I am afraid I gave the bishop quite a prod, and I caught Mr. Andrews on his rotating waistcoat. But I was desperate.

Alas, I was too late.

The caterer's man, who had taken Patrick's place in a hurry, was at the punch bowl, and father was gone. I was just in time to see him take H. into his library and close the door.

Here words fail me. I knew perfectly well that beyond that door H, whom I had invented and who therefore simply did not exist, was asking for my hand. I made up my mind at once to run away and go on the stage, and I had even got part way up the stairs, when I remembered that, with a dollar for the picture and five dollars for the violets and three dollars for the hat pin I had given Sis, and two dollars and a quarter for mother's handkerchief case, I had exactly a dollar and seventy-five cents in the world.

I WAS TRAPPED.

I went up to my room, and sat and waited. Would father be violent, and throw H. out and then come upstairs, pale with fury and disinherit me? Or would the whole family conspire together, when the people had gone, and send me to a convent? I made up my mind, if it was the convent, to take the veil and be a nun. I would go to nurse lepers, or something, and then, when it was too late, they would be sorry.

The stage or the convent, nun or actress? Which?

I left the door open, but there was only the sound of revelry below. I felt then that it was to be the convent. I pinned a towel around my face, the way the nuns wear whatever they call them, and from the side it was very becoming. I really did look like Julia Marlowe, especially as my face was very sad and tragic.

At something before seven every one had gone, and I heard Sis and mother come upstairs to dress for dinner. I sat and waited, and when I heard father I got cold all over. But he went on by, and I heard him go into mother's room and close the door. Well, I knew I had to go through with it, although my life was blasted. So I dressed and went downstairs.

Father was the first down. HE CAME DOWN WHISTLING.

It is perfectly true. I could not believe my ears.

He approached me with a smiling face.

"Well, Bab," he said, exactly as if nothing had happened, "have you had a nice day?"

He had the eyes of a basilisk, that creature of fable.

"I've had a lovely day, Father," I replied. I could be basilisk-ish also.

There is a mirror over the drawing room mantle, and he turned me around until we both faced it.

"Up to my ears," he said, referring to my height. "And lovers already! Well, I daresay we must make up our minds to lose you."

"I won't be lost," I declared, almost violently. "Of course, if you intend to shove me off your hands, to the first idiot who comes along and pretends a lot of stuff, I— —"

"My dear child!" said father, looking surprised. "Such an outburst! All I was trying to say, before your mother comes down, is that I—well, that I understand and that I shall not make my little girl unhappy by—er—by breaking her heart."

"Just what do you mean by that, father?"

He looked rather uncomfortable, being one who hates to talk sentiment.

"It's like this, Barbara," he said. "If you want to marry this young man— and you have made it very clear that you do—I am going to see that you do it. You are young, of course, but after all your dear mother was not much older than you are when I married her."

"Father!" I cried, from an over-flowing heart.

"I have noticed that you are not happy, Barbara," he said. "And I shall not thwart you, or allow you to be thwarted. In affairs of the heart, you are to have your own way."

"I want to tell you something!" I cried. "I will NOT be cast off! I— —"

"Tut, tut," said Father. "Who is casting you off? I tell you that I like the young man, and give you my blessing, or what is the present-day equivalent for it, and you look like a figure of tragedy!"

But I could endure no more. My own father had turned on me and was rending me, so to speak. With a breaking heart and streaming eyes I flew to my chamber.

There, for hours I paced the floor.

Never, I determined, would I marry H. Better death, by far. He was a scheming fortune-hunter, but to tell the family that was to confess all. And

I would never confess. I would run away before I gave Sis such a chance at me. I would run away, but first I would kill Carter Brooks.

Yes, I was driven to thoughts of murder. It shows how the first false step leads down and down, to crime and even to death. Oh never, never, gentle reader, take that first false step. Who knows to what it may lead!

"One false Step is never retrieved." Gray—On a Favorite Cat.

I reflected also on how the woman in the book had ruined her life with a letter. "The written word does not change," she had said. "It remains always, embodying a dead truth and giving it apparent life."

"Apparent life" was exactly what my letter had given to H. Frankenstein. That was what I called him, in my agony. I felt that if only I had never written the Letter there would have been no trouble. And another awful thought came to me: Was there an H after all? Could there be an H?

Once the French teacher had taken us to the theater in New York, and a woman sitting on a chair and covered with a sheet, had brought a man out of a perfectly empty cabinet, by simply willing to do it. The cabinet was empty, for four respectable looking men went up and examined it, and one even measured it with a Tape-measure.

She had materialized him, out of nothing.

And while I had had no cabinet, there are many things in this world "that we do not dream of in our philosophy." Was H. a real person, or a creature of my disordered brain? In plain and simple language, COULD THERE BE SUCH A PERSON?

I feared not.

And if there was no H, really, and I married him, where would I be?

There was a ball at the Club that night, and the family all went. No one came to say good-night to me, and by half past ten I was alone with my misery. I knew Carter Brooks would be at the ball, and H also, very likely, dancing around as agreeably as if he really existed, and I had not made him up.

I got the book from Sis's room again, and re-read it. The woman in it had been in great trouble, too, with her husband cleaning his revolver and making his will. And at last she had gone to the apartments of the man who had her letters, in a taxicab covered with a heavy veil, and had got them back. He had shot himself when she returned—the husband—but she burned the letters and then called a doctor, and he was saved. Not the doctor, of course. The husband.

The villain's only hold on her had been the letters, so he went to South Africa and was gored by an elephant, thus passing out of her life.

Then and there I knew that I would have to get my letter back from H. Without it he was powerless. The trouble was that I did not know where he was staying. Even if he came out of a cabinet, the cabinet would have to be somewhere, would it not?

I felt that I would have to meet guile with guile. And to steal one's own letter is not really stealing. Of course if he was visiting any one and pretending to be a real person, I had no chance in the world. But if he was stopping at a hotel I thought I could manage. The man in the book had had an apartment, with a Japanese servant, who went away and drew plans of American forts in the kitchen and left the woman alone with the desk containing the letter. But I daresay that was unusually lucky and not the sort of thing to look forward to.

With me, to think is to act. Hannah was out, it being Christmas and her brother-in-law having a wake, being dead, so I was free to do anything I wanted to.

First I called the club and got Carter Brooks on the telephone.

"Carter," I said, "I—I am writing a letter. Where is—where does H. stay?"

"Who?"

"H.—Mr. Grosvenor."

"Why, bless your ardent little heart! Writing, are you? It's sublime, Bab!"

"Where does he live?"

"And is it all alone you are, on Christmas Night!" he burbled. (This is a word from Alice in Wonder Land, and although not in the dictionary, is quite expressive.)

"Yes," I replied, bitterly. "I am old enough to be married off without my consent, but I am not old enough for a real Ball. It makes me sick."

"I can smuggle him here, if you want to talk to him."

"Smuggle!" I said, with scorn. "There is no need to smuggle him. The family is crazy about him. They are flinging me at him."

"Well, that's nice," he said. "Who'd have thought it! Shall I bring him to the 'phone?"

"I don't want to talk to him. I hate him."

"Look here," he observed, "if you keep that up, he'll begin to believe you. Don't take these little quarrels too hard, Barbara. He's so happy to-night in the thought that you——"

"Does he live in a cabinet, or where?"

"In a what? I don't get that word."

"Don't bother. Where shall I send his letter?"

Well, it seemed he had an apartment at the arcade, and I rang off. It was after eleven by that time, and by the time I had got into my school mackintosh and found a heavy veil of mother's and put it on, it was almost half past.

The house was quiet, and as Patrick had gone, there was no one around in the lower hall. I slipped out and closed the door behind me, and looked for a taxicab, but the veil was so heavy that I hailed our own limousine, and Smith had drawn up at the curb before I knew him.

"Where to, lady?" he said. "This is a private car, but I'll take you anywhere in the city for a dollar."

A flush of just indignation rose to my cheek, at the knowledge that Smith was using our car for a taxicab! And just as I was about to speak to him severely, and threaten to tell father, I remembered, and walked away.

"Make it seventy-five cents," he called after me. But I went on. It was terrible to think that Smith could go on renting our car to all sorts of people, covered with germs and everything, and that I could never report it to the family.

I got a real taxi at last, and got out at the arcade, giving the man a quarter, although ten cents would have been plenty as a tip.

I looked at him, and I felt that he could be trusted.

"This," I said, holding up the money, "is the price of silence."

But if he was trustworthy he was not subtle, and he said:

"The what, miss?"

"If any one asks if you have driven me here, YOU HAVE NOT" I explained, in an impressive manner.

He examined the quarter, even striking a match to look at it. Then he replied: "I have not!" and drove away.

Concealing my nervousness as best I could, I entered the doomed building. There was only a hall boy there, asleep in the elevator, and I looked at the thing with the names on it. "Mr. Grosvenor" was on the fourth floor.

I wakened the boy, and he yawned and took me to the fourth floor. My hands were stiff with nervousness by that time, but the boy was half asleep, and evidently he took me for some one who belonged there, for he said "Goodnight" to me, and went on down. There was a square landing with two doors, and "Grosvenor" was on one. I tried it gently. It was unlocked.

"FACILUS DESCENSUS IN AVERNU."

I am not defending myself. What I did was the result of desperation. But I cannot even write of my sensations as I stepped through that fatal portal, without a sinking of the heart. I had, however, had sufficient foresight to prepare an alibi. In case there was someone present in the apartment I intended to tell a falsehood, I regret to confess, and to say that I had got off at the wrong floor.

There was a sort of hall, with a clock and a table, and a shaded electric lamp, and beyond that the door was open into a sitting room.

There was a small light burning there, and the remains of a wood fire in the fireplace. There was no cabinet however.

Everything was perfectly quiet, and I went over to the fire and warmed my hands. My nails were quite blue, but I was strangely calm. I took off mother's veil, and my mackintosh, so I would be free to work, and I then looked around the room. There were a number of photographs of rather smart looking girls, and I curled my lip scornfully. He might have fooled them but he could not deceive me. And it added to my bitterness to think that at that moment the villain was dancing—and flirting probably—while I was driven to actual theft to secure the letter that placed me in his power.

When I had stopped shivering I went to his desk. There were a lot of letters on the top, all addressed to him as Grosvenor. It struck me suddenly as strange that if he was only visiting, under an assumed name, in order to see me, that so many people should be writing to him as Mr. Grosvenor. And it did not look like the room of a man who was visiting, unless he took a freight car with him on his travels.

THERE WAS A MYSTERY. All at once I knew it.

My letter was not on the desk, so I opened the top drawer. It seemed to be full of bills, and so was the one below it. I had just started on the third drawer, when a terrible thing happened.

"Hello!" said some one behind me.

I turned my head slowly, and my heart stopped.

THE PORTERES INTO THE PASSAGE HAD OPENED, AND A GENTLEMAN IN HIS EVENING CLOTHES WAS STANDING THERE.

"Just sit still, please," he said, in a perfectly cold voice. And he turned and locked the door into the hall. I was absolutely unable to speak. I tried once, but my tongue hit the roof of my mouth like the clapper of a bell.

"Now," he said, when he had turned around. "I wish you would tell me some good reason why I should not hand you over to the police."

"Oh, please don't!" I said.

"That's eloquent. But not a reason. I'll sit down and give you a little time. I take it, you did not expect to find me here."

"I'm in the wrong apartment. That's all," I said. "Maybe you'll think that's an excuse and not a reason. I can't help it if you do."

"Well," he said, "that explains some things. It's pretty well known, I fancy, that I have little worth stealing, except my good name."

"I was not stealing," I replied in a sulky manner.

"I beg your pardon," he said. "It IS an ugly word. We will strike it from the record. Would you mind telling me whose apartment you intended to— er—investigate? If this is the wrong one, you know."

"I was looking for a letter."

"Letters, letters!" he said. "When will you women learn not to write letters. Although"—he looked at me closely—"you look rather young for that sort of thing." He sighed. "It's born in you, I daresay," he said.

Well, for all his patronizing ways, he was not very old himself.

"Of course," he said, "if you are telling the truth—and it sounds fishy, I must say—it's hardly a police matter, is it? It's rather one for diplomacy. But can you prove what you say?"

"My word should be sufficient," I replied stiffly. "How do I know that YOU belong here?"

"Well, you don't, as a matter of fact. Suppose you take my word for that, and I agree to believe what you say about the wrong apartment, Even then it's rather unusual. I find a pale and determined looking young lady going through my desk in a business-like manner. She says she has come for a letter. Now the question is, is there a letter? If so, what letter?"

"It is a love letter," I said.

"Don't blush over such a confession," he said. "If it is true, be proud of it. Love is a wonderful thing. Never be ashamed of being in love, my child."

"I am not in love," I cried with bitter fury.

"Ah! Then it is not YOUR letter!"

"I wrote it."

"But to simulate a passion that does not exist—that is sacrilege. It is——"

"Oh, stop talking," I cried, in a hunted tone. "I can't bear it. If you are going to arrest me, get it over."

"I'd rather NOT arrest you, if we can find a way out. You look so young, so new to crime! Even your excuse for being here is so naive, that I—won't you tell me why you wrote a love letter, if you are not in love? And whom you sent it to? That's important, you see, as it bears on the case. I intend," he said, "to be judicial, unimpassioned, and quite fair."

"I wrote a love letter" I explained, feeling rather cheered, "but it was not intended for any one, Do you see? It was just a love letter."

"Oh," he said. "Of course. It is often done. And after that?"

"Well, it had to go somewhere. At least I felt that way about it. So I made up a name from some malted milk tablets——"

"Malted milk tablets!" he said, looking bewildered.

"Just as I was thinking up a name to send it to," I explained, "Hannah— that's mother's maid, you know—brought in some hot milk and some malted milk tablets, and I took the name from them."

"Look here," he said, "I'm unprejudiced and quite calm, but isn't the 'mother's maid' rather piling it on?"

"Hannah is mother's maid, and she brought in the milk and the tablets, I should think," I said, growing sarcastic, "that so far it is clear to the dullest mind."

"Go on," he said, leaning back and closing his eyes. "You named the letter for your mother's maid—I mean for the malted milk. Although you have not yet stated the name you chose; I never heard of any one named Milk, and as to the other, while I have known some rather thoroughly malted people—however, let that go."

"Valentine's tablets," I said. "Of course, you understand," I said, bending forward, "there was no such person. I made him up. The Harold was made up too—Harold Valentine."

"I see. Not clearly, perhaps, but I have a gleam of intelligence."

"But, after all, there was such a person. That's clear, isn't it? And now he considers that we are engaged, and—and he insists on marrying me."

"That," he said, "is really easy to understand. I don't blame him at all. He is clearly a person of discernment."

"Of course," I said bitterly, "you would be on HIS side. Every one is."

"But the point is this," he went on. "If you made him up out of the whole cloth, as it were, and there was no such person, how can there be such a person? I am merely asking to get it all clear in my head. It sounds so reasonable when you say it, but there seems to be something left out."

"I don't know how he can be, but he is," I said, hopelessly. "And he is exactly like his picture."

"Well, that's not unusual, you know."

"It is in this case. Because I bought the picture in a shop, and just pretended it was him. (He?) And it WAS."

He got up and paced the floor.

"It's a very strange case," he said. "Do you mind if I light a cigarette? It helps to clear my brain. What was the name you gave him?"

"Harold Valentine. But he is here under another name, because of my family. They think I am a mere child, you see, and so of course he took a NOM DE PLUME."

"A NOM DE PLUME? Oh I see! What is it?"

"Grosvenor," I said. "The same as yours."

"There's another Grosvenor in the building, That's where the trouble came in, I suppose, Now let me get this straight. You wrote a letter, and somehow or other he got it, and now you want it back. Stripped of the things that baffle my intelligence, that's it, isn't it?"

I rose in excitement.

"Then, if he lives in the building, the letter is probably here. Why can't you go and get it for me?"

"Very neat! And let you slip away while I am gone?"

I saw that he was still uncertain that I was telling him the truth. It was maddening. And only the Letter itself could convince him.

"Oh, please try to get it," I cried, almost weeping. "You can lock me in here, if you are afraid I will run away. And he is out. I know he is. He is at the club ball."

"Naturally," he said "the fact that you are asking me to compound a felony, commit larceny, and be an accessory after the fact does not trouble you. As I told you before, all I have left is my good name, and now ——!"

"Please!" I said.

He stared down at me.

"Certainly," he said. "Asked in that tone, murder would be one of the easiest things I do. But I shall lock you in."

"Very well," I said meekly. And after I had described it—the letter—to him he went out.

I had won, but my triumph was but sackcloth and ashes in my mouth. I had won, but at what a cost! Ah, how I wished that I might live again the past few days! That I might never have started on my path of deception! Or that, since my intentions at the start had been so innocent, I had taken another photograph at the shop, which I had fancied considerably but had heartlessly rejected because of no mustache.

He was gone for a long time, and I sat and palpitated. For what if H. had returned early and found him and called in the police?

But the latter had not occurred, for at ten minutes after one he came back, entering by the window from a fire-escape, and much streaked with dirt.

"Narrow escape, dear child!" he observed, locking the window and drawing the shade. "Just as I got it, your—er—gentleman friend returned and fitted his key in the lock. I am not at all sure," he said, wiping his hands with his handkerchief, "that he will not regard the open window as a suspicious circumstance. He may be of a low turn of mind. However, all's well that ends here in this room. Here it is."

I took it, and my heart gave a great leap of joy. I was saved.

"Now," he said, "we'll order a taxicab and get you home. And while it is coming suppose you tell me the thing over again. It's not as clear to me as it ought to be, even now."

So then I told him—about not being out yet, and Sis having flowers sent her, and her room done over, and never getting to bed until dawn. And that they treated me like a mere child, which was the reason for everything, and about the poem, which he considered quite good. And then about the letter.

"I get the whole thing a bit clearer now," he said. "Of course, it is still cloudy in places. The making up somebody to write to is understandable, under the circumstances. But it is odd to have had the very person materialize, so to speak. It makes me wonder—well, how about burning the letter, now we've got it? It would be better, I think. The way things have been going with you, if we don't destroy it, it is likely to walk off into somebody else's pocket and cause more trouble."

So we burned it, and then the telephone rang and said the taxi was there.

"I'll get my coat and be ready in a jiffy," he said, "and maybe we can smuggle you into the house and no one the wiser. We'll try anyhow."

He went into the other room and I sat by the fire and thought. You remember that when I was planning Harold Valentine, I had imagined him with a small, dark mustache, and deep, passionate eyes? Well, this Mr. Grosvenor had both, or rather, all three. And he had the loveliest smile, with no dimple. He was, I felt, exactly the sort of man I could die for.

It was too tragic that, with all the world to choose from, I had not taken him instead of H.

We walked downstairs, so as not to give the elevator boy a chance to talk, he said. But he was asleep again, and we got to the street and to the taxicab without being seen.

Oh, I was very cheerful. When I think of it—but I might have known, all along. Nothing went right with me that week.

Just before we got to the house he said:

"Goodnight and goodbye, little Barbara. I'll never forget you and this evening. And save me a dance at your coming-out party. I'll be there."

I held out my hand, and he took it and kissed it. It was all perfectly thrilling. And then we drew up in front of the house and he helped me out, and my entire family had just got out of the motor and was lined up on the pavement staring at us!

"All right, are you?" he said, as coolly as if they had not been anywhere in sight. "Well, good night and good luck!" And he got into the taxicab and drove away, leaving me in the hands of the enemy.

The next morning I was sent back to school. They never gave me a chance to explain, for mother went into hysterics, after accusing me of having men dangling around waiting at every corner. They had to have a doctor, and things were awful.

The only person who said anything was Sis. She came to my room that night when I was in bed, and stood looking down at me. She was very angry, but there was a sort of awe in her eyes.

"My hat's off to you, Barbara," she said. "Where in the world do you pick them all up? Things must have changed at school since I was there."

"I'm sick to death of the other sex," I replied languidly. "It's no punishment to send me away. I need a little piece and quiet." And I did.

CONCLUSION

All this holiday week, while the girls are away, I have been writing this theme, for literature class. To-day is New Years and I am putting in the finishing touches. I intend to have it typed in the village and to send a copy to father, who I think will understand, and another copy, but with a few lines cut, to Mr. Grosvenor. The nice one. There were some things he did not quite understand, and this will explain.

I shall also send a copy to Carter Brooks, who came out handsomely with an apology this morning in a letter and a ten pound box of candy.

His letter explains everything. H. is a real person and did not come out of a cabinet. Carter recognized the photograph as being one of a Mr. Grosvenor he went to college with, who had gone on the stage and was playing in a stock company at home. Only they were not playing Christmas week, as business, he says, is rotten then. When he saw me writing the letter he felt that it was all a bluff, especially as he had seen me sending myself the violets at the florists.

So he got Mr. Grosvenor, the blonde one, to pretend he was Harold Valentine. Only things slipped up. I quote from Carter's letter:

"He's a bully chap, Bab, and he went into it for a lark, roses and poems and all. But when he saw that you took it rather hard, he felt it wasn't square. He went to your father to explain and apologized, but your father seemed to think you needed a lesson. He's a pretty good sport, your father. And he said to let it go on for a day or two. A little worry wouldn't hurt you."

However, I do not call it being a good sport to see one's daughter perfectly wretched and do nothing to help. And more than that, to willfully permit one's child to suffer, and enjoy it.

But it was father, after all, who got the jolt, I think, when he saw me get out of the taxicab.

Therefore I will not explain, for a time. A little worry will not hurt him either.

I will not send him his copy for a week.

Perhaps, after all, I will give him something to worry about eventually. For I have received a box of roses, with no card, but a pen and ink drawing of a gentleman in evening clothes crawling onto a fire-escape through an open window. He has dropped his heart, and it is two floors below.

My narrative has now come to a conclusion, and I will close with a few reflections drawn from my own sad and tragic Experience. I trust the girls of this school will ponder and reflect.

Deception is a very sad thing. It starts very easy, and without warning, and everything seems to be going all right, and no rocks ahead. When suddenly the breakers loom up, and your frail vessel sinks, with you on board, and maybe your dear ones, dragged down with you.

Oh, what a tangled Web we weave,
When first we practice to deceive.
Sir Walter Scott.

CHAPTER II
THEME: THE CELEBRITY

We have been requested to write, during this vacation, a true and veracious account of a meeting with any celebrity we happened to meet during the summer. If no celebrity, any interesting character would do, excepting one's own family.

But as one's own family is neither celebrated nor interesting, there is no temptation to write about it.

As I met Mr. Reginald Beecher this summer, I have chosen him as my subject.

Brief history of the Subject: He was born in 1890 at Woodbury, N. J. Attended public high schools, and in 1910 graduated from Princeton University.

Following year produced first Play in New York, called Her Soul. Followed this by the Soul Mate, and this by The Divorce.

Description of Subject. Mr. Beecher is tall and slender, and wears a very small dark Mustache. Although but twenty-six years of age, his hair on close inspection reveals here and there a silver thread. His teeth are good, and his eyes amber, with small flecks of brown in them. He has been vaccinated twice.

It has always been one of my chief ambitions to meet a celebrity. On one or two occasions we have had them at school, but they never sit at the Junior's table. Also, they are seldom connected with either the Drama or The Movies (a slang term but apparently taking a place in our literature).

It was my intention, on being given this subject for my midsummer theme, to seek out Mrs. Bainbridge, a lady author who has a cottage across the bay from ours, and to ask the privilege of sitting at her feet for a few hours, basking in the sunshine of her presence, and learning from her own lips her favorite Flower, her favorite Poem and the favorite child of her brain.

Of all those arts in which the wise excel,

Nature's chief masterpiece is writing well.

Duke of Buckingham

I had meant to write my theme on her, but I learned in time that she was forty years of age. Her work is therefore done. She has passed her active years, and I consider that it is not the past of American Letters which is at stake, but the future. Besides, I was more interested in the drama than in literature.

Possibly it is owing to the fact that the girls think I resemble Julia Marlowe, that from my earliest years my mind has been turned toward the stage. I am very determined and fixed in my ways, and with me to decide to do a thing is to decide to do it. I am not of a romantic nature, however, and as I learned of the dangers of the theater, I drew back. Even a strong nature, such as mine is, on occasions, can be influenced. I therefore decided to change my plans, and to write plays instead of acting in them.

At first I meant to write comedies, but as I realized the gravity of life, and its bitterness and disappointments, I turned naturally to tragedy. Surely, as dear Shakespeare says:

The world is a stage

Where every man must play a part,

And mine a sad one.

This explains my sincere interest in Mr. Beecher. His works were all realistic and sad. I remember that I saw the first one three years ago, when a mere child, and became violently ill from crying and had to be taken home.

The school will recall that last year I wrote a play, patterned on The Divorce, and that only a certain narrowness of view on the part of the faculty prevented it being the class play. If I may be permitted to express an opinion, we of the class of 1917 are not children, and should not be treated as such.

Encouraged by the applause of my class-mates, and feeling that I was of a more serious turn of mind than most of them, who seem to think of pleasure only, I decided to write a play during the summer. I would thus be improving my vacation hours, and, I considered, keeping out of mischief. It was pure idleness which had caused my trouble during the last Christmas holidays. How true it is that the devil finds work for idle hands!

With a play and this theme I believed that the devil would give me up as a total loss, and go elsewhere.

How little we can read the future!

I now proceed to an account of my meeting and acquaintance with Mr. Beecher. It is my intention to conceal nothing. I can only comfort myself with the thought that my motives were innocent, and that I was obeying orders and securing material for a theme. I consider that the attitude of my family is wrong and cruel, and that my sister Leila, being only 20 months older, although out in society, has no need to write me the sort of letters she has been writing. Twenty months is twenty months, and not two years, although she seems to think it is.

I returned home full of happy plans for my vacation. When I look back it seems strange that the gay and innocent young girl of the train can have been! So much that is tragic has since happened. If I had not had a cinder in my eye things would have been different. But why repine? Fate frequently hangs thus on a single hair—an eye-lash, as one may say.

Father met me at the train. I had got the aforementioned cinder in my eye, and a very nice young man had taken it out for me. I still cannot see what harm there was in our chatting together after that, especially as we said nothing to object to. But father looked very disagreeable about it, and the young man went away in a hurry. But it started us off wrong, although I got him—father—to promise not to tell mother.

"I do wish you would be more careful, Bab," he said with a sort of sigh.

"Careful!" I said. "Then it's not doing things, but being found out, that matters!"

"Careful in your conduct, Bab."

"He was a beautiful young man, father," I observed, slipping my arm through his.

"Barbara, Barbara! Your poor mother——"

"Now look here, father" I said. "If it was mother who was interested in him it might be troublesome. But it is only me. And I warn you, here and now, that I expect to be thrilled at the sight of a nice young man right along. It goes up my back and out the roots of my hair."

Well, my father is a real person, so he told me to talk sense, and gave me twenty dollars, and agreed to say nothing about the young man to mother, if I would root for Canada against the Adirondacks for the summer, because of the fishing.

Mother was waiting in the hall for me, but she held me off with both hands.

"Not until you have bathed and changed your clothing, Barbara," she said. "I have never had it."

She meant the whooping cough. The school will recall the epidemic which ravaged us last June, and changed us from a peaceful institution to what sounded like a dog show.

Well, I got the same old room, not much fixed up, but they had put up different curtains anyhow, thank goodness. I had been hinting all spring for new furniture, but my family does not take a hint unless it is chloroformed first, and I found the same old stuff there.

They believe in waiting until a girl makes her debut before giving her anything but the necessities of life.

Sis was off for a week-end, but Hannah was there, and I kissed her. Not that I'm so fond of her, but I had to kiss somebody.

"Well, Miss Barbara!" she said. "How you've grown!"

That made me rather sore, because I am not a child any longer, but they all talk to me as if I were but six years old, and small for my age.

"I've stopped growing, Hannah," I said, with dignity. "At least, almost. But I see I still draw the nursery."

Hannah was opening my suitcase, and she looked up and said: "I tried to get you the blue room, Miss Bab. But Miss Leila said she needed it for house parties."

"Never mind," I said. "I don't care anything about furniture. I have other things to think about, Hannah; I want the school room desk up here."

"Desk!" she said, with her jaw drooping.

"I am writing now," I said. "I need a lot of ink, and paper, and a good lamp. Let them keep the blue room, Hannah, for their selfish purposes. I shall be happy in my work. I need nothing more."

"Writing!" said Hannah. "Is it a book you're writing?"

"A play."

"Listen to the child! A play!"

I sat on the edge of the bed.

"Listen, Hannah," I said. "It is not what is outside of us that matters. It is what is inside. It is what we are, not what we eat, or look like, or wear. I have given up everything, Hannah, to my career."

"You're young yet," said Hannah. "You used to be fond enough of the boys."

Hannah has been with us for years, so she gets rather talky at times, and has to be sat upon.

"I care nothing whatever for the Other Sex," I replied haughtily.

She was opening my suitcase at the time, and I was surveying the chamber which was to be the seen of my Literary Life, at least for some time.

"Now and then," I said to Hannah, "I shall read you parts of it. Only you mustn't run and tell mother."

"Why not?" said she, peering into the Suitcase.

"Because I intend to deal with Life," I said. "I shall deal with real Things, and not the way we think them. I am young, but I have thought a great deal. I shall mince nothing."

"Look here, Miss Barbara," Hannah said, all at once, "what are you doing with this whiskey flask? And these socks? And—you come right here, and tell me where you got the things in this suitcase." I stocked over to the bed, and my blood froze in my veins. IT WAS NOT MINE.

Words cannot fully express how I felt. While fully convinced that there had been a mistake, I knew not when or how. Hannah was staring at me with cold and accusing eyes.

"You're a very young lady, Miss Barbara," she said, with her eyes full of Suspicion, "to be carrying a flask about with you." I was as puzzled as she was, but I remained calm and to all appearances Spartan.

"I am young in years," I remarked. "But I have seen Life, Hannah."

Now I meant nothing by this at the time. But it was getting on my nerves to be put in the infant class all the time. The Christmas before they had done it, and I had had my revenge. Although it had hurt me more than it hurt them, and if I gave them a fright I gave myself a worse one. As I said at that time:

Oh, what a tangled web we weave,

When first we practice to deceive.

Sir Walter Scott.

Hannah gave me a horrified glare, and dipped into the suitcase again. She brought up a tin box of cigarettes, and I thought she was going to have delirium tremens at once.

Well, at first I thought the girls at school had played a trick on me, and a low down mean trick at that. There are always those who think it is funny to do that sort of thing, but they are the first to squeal when anything is done to them. Once I put a small garter snake in a girl's muff, and it went up her sleeve, which is nothing to some of the things she had done to me. And you would have thought the school was on fire.

Anyhow, I said to myself that some Smarty was trying to get me into trouble, and Hannah would run to the family, and they'd never believe me. All at once I saw all my cherished plans for the summer gone, and me in the country somewhere with Mademoiselle, and walking through the pasture with a botany in one hand and a folding cup in the other, in case we found a spring a cow had not stepped in. Mademoiselle was once my Governess, but has retired to private life, except in cases of emergency.

I am naturally very quick in mind. The Archibalds are all like that, and when once we decide on a course we stick to it through thick and thin. But we do not lie. It is ridiculous for Hannah to say I said the cigarettes were mine. All I said was:

"I suppose you are going to tell the family. You'd better run, or you'll burst."

"Oh, Miss Barbara, Miss Barbara!" she said. "And you so young to be so wild!"

This was unjust, and I am one to resent injustice. I had returned home with my mind fixed on serious things, and now I was being told I was wild.

"If I tell your mother she'll have a fit," Hannah said, evidently drawn hither and thither by emotion. "Now see here, Miss Bab, you've just come home, and there was trouble at your last vacation that I'm like to remember to my dying day. You tell me how those things got there, like a good girl, and I'll say nothing about them."

I am naturally sweet in disposition, but to call me a good girl and remind me of last Christmas holidays was too much. My natural firmness came to the front.

"Certainly NOT," I said.

"You needn't stick your lip out at me, Miss Bab, that was only giving you a chance, and forgetting my duty to help you, not to mention probably losing my place when the family finds out."

"Finds out what?"

"What you've been up to, the stage, and writing plays, and now liquor and tobacco!"

Now I may be at fault in the narrative that follows. But I ask the school if this was fair treatment. I had returned to my home full of high ideals, only to see them crushed beneath the heal of domestic tyranny.

Necessity is the argument of tyrants;
it is the creed of slaves.
William Pitt.

How true are these immortal words.

It was with a firm countenance but a sinking heart that I saw Hannah leave the room. I had come home inspired with lofty ambition, and it had ended thus. Heart-broken, I wandered to the bedside, and let my eyes fall on the suitcase, the container of all my woe.

Well, I was surprised, all right. It was not and never had been mine. Instead of my blue serge sailor suit and my 'robe de nuit' and kimono etc., it contained a checked gentleman's suit, a mussed shirt and a cap. At first I was merely astonished. Then a sense of loss overpowered me. I suffered. I was prostrated with grief. Not that I cared a rap for the clothes I'd lost, being most of them to small and patched here and there. But I had lost the plot of my play. My career was gone.

I was undone.

It may be asked what has this recital to do with the account of meeting a celebrity. I reply that it has a great deal to do with it. A bare recital of a meeting may be news, but it is not art.

A theme consists of Introduction, Body and Conclusion.

This is still the Introduction.

When I was at last revived enough to think I knew what had happened. The young man who took the cinder out of my eye had come to sit beside me, which I consider was merely kindness on his part and nothing like flirting, and he had brought his suitcase over, and they had got mixed up. But I knew the family would call it flirting, and not listen to a word I said.

A madness seized me. Now that everything is over, I realize that it was madness. But "there is a divinity that shapes our ends etc." It was to be. It was Karma, or Kismet, or whatever the word is. It was written in the Book of Fate that I was to go ahead, and wreck my life, and generally ruin everything.

I locked the door behind Hannah, and stood with tragic feet, "where the brook and river meet." What was I to do? How hide this evidence of my (presumed) duplicity? I was innocent, but I looked guilty. This, as everyone knows, is worse than guilt.

I unpacked the suitcase as fast as I could, therefore, and being just about distracted, I bundled the things up and put them all together in the toy closet, where all Sis's dolls and mine are, mine being mostly pretty badly gone, as I was always hard on dolls.

How far removed were those innocent years when I played with dolls!

Well, I knew Hannah pretty well, and therefore was not surprised when, having hidden the trousers under a doll buggy, I heard mother's voice at the door.

"Let me in, Barbara," she said.

I closed the closet door, and said: "What is it, mother?"

"Let me in."

So I let her in, and pretended I expected her to kiss me, which she had not yet, on account of the whooping cough. But she seemed to have forgotten that. Also the kiss.

"Barbara," she said, in the meanest voice, "how long have you been smoking?"

Now I must pause to explain this. Had mother approached me in a sweet and maternal manner, I would have been softened, and would have told the whole story. But she did not. She was, as you might say, steaming with rage. And seeing that I was misunderstood, I hardened. I can be as hard as adamant when necessary.

"What do you mean, mother?"

"Don't answer one question with another."

"How can I answer when I don't understand you?"

She simply twitched with fury.

"You—a mere Child!" she raved. "And I can hardly bring myself to mention it—the idea of your owning a flask, and bringing it into this house—it is—it is——"

Well, I was growing cold and more haughty every moment, so I said: "I don't see why the mere mention of a flask upsets you so. It isn't because you aren't used to one, especially when traveling. And since I was a mere baby I have been accustomed to intoxicants."

"Barbara!" she interjected, in the most dreadful tone.

"I mean, in the family," I said. "I have seen wine on our table ever since I can remember. I knew to put salt on a claret stain before I could talk."

Well, you know how it is to see an enemy on the run, and although I regret to refer to my dear mother as an enemy, still at that moment she was such and no less. And she was beating it. It was the reference to my youth that had aroused me, and I was like a wounded lion. Besides, I knew well enough that if they refused to see that I was practically grown up, if not entirely, I would get a lot of Sis's clothes, fixed up with new ribbons. Faded old things! I'd had them for years.

Better to be considered a bad woman than an unformed child.

"However, mother," I finished, "if it is any comfort to you, I did not buy that flask. And I am not a confirmed alcoholic. By no means."

"This settles it," she said, in a melancholy tone. "When I think of the comfort Leila has been to me, and the anxiety you have caused, I wonder where you get your—your DEVILTRY from. I am positively faint."

I was alarmed, for she did look queer, with her face all white around the rouge. So I reached for the flask.

"I'll give you a swig of this," I said. "It will pull you around in no time."

But she held me off fiercely.

"Never!" she said. "Never again. I shall empty the wine cellar. There will be nothing to drink in this house from now on. I do not know what we are coming to."

She walked into the bathroom, and I heard her emptying the flask down the drain pipe. It was a very handsome flask, silver with gold stripes, and all at once I knew the young man would want it back. So I said:

"Mother, please leave the flask here anyhow."

"Certainly not."

"It's not mine, mother."

"Whose is it?"

"It—a friend of mine loaned it to me."

"Who?"

"I can't tell you."

"You can't TELL me! Barbara, I am utterly bewildered. I sent you away a simple child, and you return to me—what?"

Well, we had about an hour's fight over it, and we ended in a compromise. I gave up the flask, and promised not to smoke and so forth, and I was to have some new dresses and a silk sweater, and to be allowed to stay up until ten o'clock, and to have a desk in my room for my work.

"Work!" mother said. "Career! What next? Why can't you be like Leila, and settle down to having a good time?"

"Leila and I are different," I said loftily, for I resented her tone. "Leila is a child of the moment. Life for her is one grand, sweet Song. For me it is a serious matter. 'Life is real, life is earnest, and the grave is not its goal,'" I quoted in impassioned tones.

(Because that is the way I feel. How can the grave be its goal? THERE MUST BE SOMETHING BEYOND. I have thought it all out, and I believe in a world beyond, but not in a hell. Hell, I believe, is the state of mind one gets into in this world as a result of one's wicked acts or one's wicked thoughts, and is in one's self.)

As I have said, the other side of the compromise was that I was not to carry flasks with me, or drink any punch at parties if it had a stick in it, and you can generally find out by the taste. For if it is what Carter Brooks calls "loaded" it stings your tongue. Or if it tastes like cider it's probably champagne. And I was not to smoke any cigarettes.

Mother was holding out on the sweater at that time, saying that Sis had a perfectly good one from Miami, and why not wear that? So I put up a strong protest about the cigarettes, although I have never smoked but once as I think the school knows, and that only half through, owing to getting dizzy. I said that Sis smoked now and then, because she thought it looked smart; but that, if I was to have a career, I felt that the soothing influence of tobacco would help a lot.

So I got the new sweater, and everything looked smooth again, and mother kissed me on the way out, and said she had not meant to be harsh, but that my great uncle Putnam had been a notorious drunkard, and I looked like him, although of a more refined type.

There was a dreadful row that night, however, when father came home. We were all dressed for dinner, and waiting in the drawing room, and Leila was complaining about me, as usual.

"She looks older than I do now, mother," she said. "If she goes to the seashore with us I'll have her always tagging at my heals. I don't see why I can't have my first summer in peace." Oh, yes, we were going to the shore, after all. Sis wanted it, and everybody does what she wants, regardless of what they prefer, even fishing.

"First summer!" I exclaimed. "One would think you were a teething baby!"

"I was speaking to mother, Barbara. Everyone knows that a debutante only has one year nowadays, and if she doesn't go off in that year she's swept away by the flood of new girls the next fall. We might as well be frank. And while Barbara's not a beauty, as soon as the bones in her neck get a little flesh on them she won't be hopeless, and she has a flippant manner that men like."

"I intend to keep Barbara under my eyes this summer," mother said firmly. "After last Christmas's happenings, and our discovery today, I shall keep her with me. She need not, however, interfere with you, Leila. Her hours are mostly different, and I will see that her friends are the younger boys."

I said nothing, but I knew perfectly well she had in mind Eddie Perkins and Willie Graham, and a lot of other little kids that hang around the fruit punch at parties, and throw the peas from the croquettes at each other when the footmen are not near, and pretend they are allowed to smoke, but have sworn off for the summer.

I was naturally indignant at Sis's words, which were not filial, to my mind, but I replied as sweetly as possible:

"I shall not be in your way, Leila. I ask nothing but food and shelter, and that perhaps not for long."

"Why? Do you intend to die?" she demanded.

"I intend to work," I said. "It's more interesting than dieing, and will be a novelty in this house."

Father came in just then, and he said:

"I'll not wait to dress, Clara. Hello, children. I'll just change my collar while you ring for the cocktails."

Mother got up and faced him with majesty.

"We are not going to have, any" she said.

"Any what?" said father from the doorway.

"I have had some fruit juice prepared with a dash of bitters. It is quite nice. And I'll ask you, James, not to explode before the servants. I will explain later."

Father has a very nice disposition but I could see that mother's manner got on his nerves, as it got on mine. Anyhow there was a terrific fuss, with Sis playing the piano so that the servants would not hear, and in the end father had a cocktail. Mother waited until he had had it, and was quieter, and then she told him about me, and my having a flask in my suitcase. Of course I could have explained, but if they persisted in misunderstanding me, why not let them do so, and be miserable?

"It's a very strange thing, Bab," he said, looking at me, "that everything in this house is quiet until you come home, and then we get as lively as kittens in a frying pan. We'll have to marry you off pretty soon, to save our piece of mind."

"James!" said my mother. "Remember last winter, please."

There was no claret or anything with dinner, and father ordered mineral water, and criticized the food, and fussed about Sis's dressmaker's bill. And the second man gave notice immediately after we left the dining room. When mother reported that, as we were having coffee in the drawing room, father said:

"Humph! Well, what can you expect? Those fellows have been getting the best half of a bottle of claret every night since they've been here, and now it's cut off. Damned if I wouldn't like to leave myself."

From that time on I knew that I was watched. It made little or no difference to me. I had my work, and it filled my life. There were times when my soul was so filled with joy that I could hardly bare it. I had one act done in two days. I wrote out the love scenes in full, because I wanted to be sure of what they would say to each other. How I thrilled as each marvelous burst of fantasy flowed from my pen! But the dialogue of less interesting parts I left for the actors to fill in themselves. I consider this the best way, as it gives them a chance to be original, and not to have to say the same thing over and over.

Jane Raleigh came over to see me the day after I came home, and I read her some of the love scenes. She positively wept with excitement.

"Bab," she said, "if any man, no matter who, ever said those things to me, I'd go straight into his arms. I couldn't help it. Whose going to act in it?"

"I think I'll have Robert Edeson, or Richard Mansfield."

"Mansfield's dead," said Jane.

"Honestly?"

"Honest he is. Why don't you get some of these moving picture actors? They never have a chance in the Movies, only acting and not talking."

Well, that sounded logical. And then I read her the place where the cruel first husband comes back and finds her married again and happy, and takes the children out to drown them, only he can't because they can swim, and they pull him in instead. The curtain goes down on nothing but a few bubbles rising to mark his watery grave.

Jane was crying.

"It is too touching for words, Bab!" she said. "It has broken my heart. I can just close my eyes and see the theater dark, and the stage almost dark, and just those bubbles coming up and breaking. Would you have to have a tank?"

"I daresay," I replied dreamily. "Let the other people worry about that. I can only give them the material, and hope that they have intelligence enough to grasp it."

I think Sis must have told Carter Brooks something about the trouble I was in, for he brought me a box of candy one afternoon, and winked at me when mother was not looking.

"Don't open it here," he whispered.

So I was forced to control my impatience, though passionately fond of candy. And when I got to my room later, the box was full of cigarettes. I could have screamed. It just gave me one more thing to hide, as if a man's suit and shirt and so on was not sufficient.

But Carter paid more attention to me than he ever had before, and at a tea dance somebody had at the country club he took me to one side and gave me a good talking to.

"You're being rather a bad child, aren't you?" he said.

"Certainly not."

"Well, not bad, but—er—naughty. Now see here, Bab, I'm fond of you, and you're growing into a mighty pretty girl. But your whole social life is at stake. For heaven's sake, at least until you're married, cut out the cigarettes and booze."

That cut me to the heart, but what could I say?

Well, July came, and we had rented a house at Little Hampton and everywhere one went one fell over an open trunk or a barrel containing silver or linen.

Mother went around with her lips moving as if in prayer, but she was really repeating lists, such as sowing basket, table candles, headache tablets, black silk stockings and tennis rackets.

Sis got some lovely clothes, mostly imported, but they had a woman come in and sew for me. Hannah and she used to interrupt my most precious moments at my desk by running a tape measure around me, or pinning a paper pattern to me. The sewing woman always had her mouth full of pins, and once, owing to my remarking that I wished I had been illegitimate, so I could go away and live my own life, she swallowed one. It caused a grate deal of excitement, with Hannah blaming me and giving her vinegar to swallow to soften the pin. Well, it turned out all right, for she kept on living, but she pretended to have sharp pains all over her here and there, and if the pin had been as lively as a tadpole and wriggled from spot to spot, it could not have hurt in so many places.

Of course they blamed me, and I shut myself up more and more in my sanctuary. There I lived with the creatures of my dreams, and forgot for a while that I was only a Sub-Deb, and that Leila's last year's tennis clothes were being fixed over for me.

But how true what dear Shakespeare says:

dreams,

Which are the children of an idle brain.

Begot of nothing but vain fantasy.

I loved my dreams, but alas, they were not enough. After a tortured hour or two at my desk, living in myself the agonies of my characters, suffering the pangs of the wife with two husbands and both living, struggling in the water with the children, fruit of the first union, dying with number two and blowing my last bubbles heavenward—after all these emotions, I was done out.

Jane came in one day and found me prostrate on my couch, with a light of suffering in my eyes.

"Dearest!" cried Jane, and gliding to my side, fell on her knees.

"Jane!"

"What is it? You are ill?"

I could hardly more than whisper. In a low tone I said:

"He is dead."

"Dearest!"

"Drowned!"

At first she thought I meant a member of my family. But when she understood she looked serious.

"You are too intense, Bab," she said solemnly. "You suffer too much. You are wearing yourself out."

"There is no other way," I replied in broken tones.

Jane went to the Mirror and looked at herself. Then she turned to me.

"Others don't do it."

"I must work out my own Salvation, Jane," I observed firmly. But she had roused me from my apathy, and I went into Sis's room, returning with a box of candy some one had sent her. "I must feel, Jane, or I cannot write."

"Pooh! Loads of writers get fat on it. Why don't you try comedy? It pays well."

"Oh—MONEY!" I said, in a disgusted tone.

"Your FORTE, of course, is love," she said. "Probably that's because you've had so much experience." Owing to certain reasons it is generally supposed that I have experienced the gentle passion. But not so, alas! "Bab," Jane said, suddenly, "I have been your friend for a long time. I have never betrayed you. You can trust me with your life. Why don't you tell me?"

"Tell you what?"

"Something has happened. I see it in your eyes. No girl who is happy and has not a tragic story stays at home shut up at a messy desk when everyone is out at the club playing tennis. Don't talk to me about a career. A girl's career is a man and nothing else. And especially after last winter, Bab. Is—is it the same one?"

Here I made my fatal error. I should have said at once that there was no one, just as there had been no one last winter. But she looked so intense, sitting there, and after all, why should I not have an amorous experience? I am not ugly, and can dance well, although inclined to lead because of dancing with other girls all winter at school. So I lay back on my pillow and stared at the ceiling.

"No. It is not the same man."

"What is he like? Bab, I'm so excited I can't sit still."

"It—it hurts to talk about him," I observed faintly.

Now I intended to let it go at that, and should have, had not Jane kept on asking questions. Because I had had a good lesson the winter before, and did not intend to deceive again. And this I will say—I really told Jane Raleigh nothing. She jumped to her own conclusions. And as for her people saying she cannot chum with me any more, I will only say this: If Jane Raleigh smokes she did not learn it from me.

Well, I had gone as far as I meant to. I was not really in love with anyone, although I liked Carter Brooks, and would possibly have loved him with all the depth of my nature if Sis had not kept an eye on me most of the time. However— —

Jane seemed to be expecting something, and I tried to think of some way to satisfy her and not make any trouble. And then I thought of the suitcase. So I locked the door and made her promise not to tell, and got the whole thing out of the toy closet.

"Wha—what is it?" asked Jane.

I said nothing, but opened it all up. The flask was gone, but the rest was there, and Carter's box too. Jane leaned down and lifted the trousers and poked around somewhat. Then she straitened and said:

"You have run away and got married, Bab."

"Jane!"

She looked at me piercingly.

"Don't lie to me," she said accusingly. "Or else what are you doing with a man's whole outfit, including his dirty collar? Bab, I just can't bare it."

Well, I saw that I had gone to far, and was about to tell Jane the truth when I heard the sewing woman in the hall. I had all I could do to get the things put away, and with Jane looking like death I had to stand there and be fitted for one of Sis's chiffon frocks, with the low neck filled in with net.

"You must remember, Miss Bab," said the human pin cushion, "that you are still a very young girl, and not out yet."

Jane got up off the bed suddenly.

"I—I guess I'll go, Bab," she said. "I don't feel very well."

As she went out she stopped in the doorway and crossed her heart, meaning that she would die before she would tell anything. But I was not comfortable. It is not a pleasant thought that your best friend considers you married and gone beyond recall, when in truth you are not, or even thinking about it, except in idle moments.

The seen now changes. Life is nothing but such changes. No sooner do we alight on one branch, and begin to sip the honey from it, but we are taken up and carried elsewhere, perhaps to the mountains or to the sea-shore, and there left to make new friends and find new methods of enjoyment.

The flight—or journey—was in itself an anxious time. For on my otherwise clear conscience rested the weight of that strange suitcase. Fortunately Hannah was so busy that I was left to pack my belongings myself, and thus for a time my guilty secret was safe. I put my things in on top of the masculine articles, not daring to leave any of them in the closet, owing to house-cleaning, which is always done before our return in the fall.

On the train I had a very unpleasant experience, due to Sis opening my suitcase to look for a magazine, and drawing out a soiled gentleman's collar. She gave me a very piercing glance, but said nothing and at the next opportunity I threw it out of a window, concealed in a newspaper.

We now approach the catastrophe. My book on play writing divides plays into Introduction, Development, Crisis, Denouement and Catastrophe. And so one may divide life. In my case the cinder proved the introduction, as there was none other. I consider that the suitcase was the development, my showing it to Jane Raleigh was the crisis, and the denouement or catastrophe occurred later on.

Let us then proceed to the catastrophe.

Jane Raleigh came to see me off at the train. Her family was coming the next day. And instead of flowers, she put a small bundle into my hands. "Keep it hidden, Bab," she said, "and tear up the card."

I looked when I got a chance, and she had crocheted me a wash cloth, with a pink edge. "For your linen chest," the card said, "and I'm doing a bath towel to match."

I tore up the card, but I put the wash cloth with the other things I was trying to hide, because it is bad luck to throw a gift away. But I hoped, as I seemed to be getting more things to conceal all the time, that she would make me a small bath towel, and not the sort as big as a bed spread.

Father went with us to get us settled, and we had a long talk while mother and Sis made out lists for dinners and so forth.

"Look here, Bab," he said, "something's wrong with you. I seem to have lost my only boy, and have got instead a sort of tear-y young person I don't recognize."

"I'm growing up, father" I said. I did not mean to rebuke him, but ye gods! Was I the only one to see that I was no longer a child?

"Sometimes I think you are not very happy with us."

"Happy?" I pondered. "Well, after all, what is happiness?"

He took a spell of coughing then, and when it was over he put his arms around me and was quite affectionate.

"What a queer little rat it is!" he said.

I only repeat this to show how even my father, with all his affection and good qualities, did not understand and never would understand. My heart was full of a longing to be understood. I wanted to tell him my yearnings for better things, my aspirations to make my life a great and glorious thing. AND HE DID NOT UNDERSTAND.

He gave me five dollars instead. Think of the tragedy of it!

As we went along, and he pulled my ear and finally went asleep with a hand on my shoulder, the bareness of my life came to me. I shook with sobs. And outside somewhere Sis and mother made dinner lists. Then and there I made up my mind to work hard and achieve, to become great and powerful, to write things that would ring the hearts of men—and women, to, of course—and to come back to them some day, famous and beautiful, and when they sued for my love, to be kind and haughty, but cold. I felt that I would always be cold, although gracious.

I decided then to be a writer of plays first, and then later on to act in them. I would thus be able to say what came into my head, as it was my own play. Also to arrange the scenes so as to wear a variety of gowns, including evening things. I spent the rest of the afternoon manicuring my nails in our state room.

Well, we got there at last. It was a large house, but everything was to thin about it. The school will understand this, the same being the condition of the new freshman dormitory. The walls were to thin, and so were the floors. The doors shivered in the wind, and palpitated if you slammed them. Also you could hear every sound everywhere.

I looked around me in despair. Where, oh where, was I to find my cherished solitude? Where?

On account of Hannah hating a new place, and considering the house an insult to the servants, especially only one bathroom for the lot of them, she let me unpack alone, and so far I was safe. But where was I to work? Fate settled that for me however.

There is no armor against fate;
Death lays his icy hand on Kings.
J. Shirley; Dirge.

Previously, however, mother and I had had a talk. She sailed into my room one evening, dressed for dinner, and found me in my ROBE DE NUIT, curled up in the window seat admiring the view of the ocean.

"Well!" she said. "Is this the way you intend going to dinner?"

"I do not care for any dinner," I replied. Then, seeing she did not understand, I said coldly. "How can I care for food, mother, when the sea looks like a dying opal?"

"Dying pussycat!" mother said, in a very nasty way. "I don't know what has come over you, Barbara. You used to be a normal child, and there was some accounting for what you were going to do. But now! Take off that nightgown, and I'll have Tanney hold off dinner for half an hour."

Tanney was the butler who had taken Patrick's place.

"If you insist," I said coldly. "But I shall not eat."

"Why not?"

"You wouldn't understand, mother."

"Oh, I wouldn't? Well, suppose I try," she said, and sat down. "I am not very intelligent, but if you put it clearly I may grasp it. Perhaps you'd better speak slowly, also."

So, sitting there in my room, while the sea throbbed in tireless beats against the shore, while the light faded and the stars issued, one by one, like a rash on the face of the sky, I told mother of my dreams. I intended, I said, to write life as it really is, and not as supposed to be.

"It may in places be, ugly" I said, "but truth is my banner. The truth is never ugly, because it is real. It is, for instance, not ugly if a man is in love with the wife of another, if it is real love, and not the passing fancy of a moment."

Mother opened her mouth, but did not say anything.

"There was a time," I said, "when I longed for things that now have no value whatever to me. I cared for clothes and even for the attentions of the other sex. But that has passed away, mother. I have now no thought but for my career."

I watched her face, and soon the dreadful understanding came to me. She, too, did not understand. My literary aspirations were as nothing to her!

Oh, the bitterness of that moment. My mother, who had cared for me as a child, and obeyed my slightest wish, no longer understood me. And saddest of all, there was no way out. None. Once, in my youth, I had believed that I was not the child of my parents at all, but an adopted one—perhaps of rank and kept out of my inheritance by those who had selfish motives. But now I knew that I had no rank or inheritance, save what I should carve out for myself. There was no way out. None.

Mother rose slowly, staring at me with perfectly fixed and glassy eyes.

"I am absolutely sure," she said, "that you are on the edge of something. It may be typhoid, or it may be an elopement. But one thing is certain. You are not normal."

With this she left me to my thoughts. But she did not neglect me. Sis came up after dinner, and I saw mother's fine hand in that. Although not hungry in the usual sense of the word, I had begun to grow rather empty, and was nibbling out of a box of chocolates when Sis came.

She got very little out of me. To one with softness and tenderness I would have told all, but Sis is not that sort. And at last she showed her claws.

"Don't fool yourself for a minute," she said. "This literary pose has not fooled anybody. Either you're doing it to appear interesting, or you've done something you're scared about. Which is it?"

I refused to reply.

"Because if it's the first, and you're trying to look literary, you are going about it wrong," she said. "Real Literary People don't go round mooning and talking about the opal sea."

I saw mother had been talking, and I drew myself up.

"They look and act like other people," said Leila, going to the bureau and spilling powder all over the place. "Look at Beecher."

"Beecher!" I cried, with a thrill that started inside my elbows. (I have read this to one or two of the girls, and they say there is no such thrill. But not all people act alike under the influence of emotion, and mine is in my arms, as stated.)

"The playwright," Sis said. "He's staying next door. And if he does any languishing it is not by himself."

There may be some who have for a long time had an ideal, but without hoping ever to meet him, and then suddenly learning that he is nearby, with indeed but a wall or two between, can be calm and cool. But I am not like that. Although long suppression has taught me to dissemble at times, where my heart is concerned I am powerless.

For it was at last my heart that was touched. I, who had scorned the other sex and felt that I was born cold and always would be cold, that day I discovered the truth. Reginald Beecher was my ideal. I had never spoken to him, nor indeed seen him, except for his pictures. But the very mention of his name brought a lump to my throat.

Feeling better immediately, I got Sis out of the room and coaxed Hannah to bring me some dinner. While she was sneaking it out of the pantry I was dressing, and soon, as a new being, I was out on the stone bench at the foot of the lawn, gazing with rapt eyes at the sea.

But fate was against me. Eddie Perkins saw me there and came over. He had but recently been put in long trousers, and those not his best ones but only white flannels. He was never sure of his garters, and was always looking to see if his socks were coming down. Well, he came over just as I was sure I saw Reginald Beecher next door on the veranda, and made himself a nuisance right away, trying all sorts of kid tricks, such as snapping a rubber band at me, and pulling out hairpins.

But I felt that I must talk to someone. So I said:

"Eddie, if you had your choice of love or a career, which would it be?"

"Why not both," he said, hitching the rubber band onto one of his front teeth and playing on it. "Neither ought to take up all a fellow's time. Say, listen to this! Talk about a ukelele!"

"A woman can never have both."

He played a while, strumming with one finger until the hand slipped off and stung him on the lip.

"Once," I said, "I dreamed of a career. But I believe love's the most important."

Well, I shall pass lightly over what followed. Why is it that a girl cannot speak of love without every member of the other sex present, no matter how young, thinking it is he? And as for mother maintaining that I kissed that wretched child, and they saw me from the drawing-room, it is not true and never was true. It was but one more misunderstanding which convinced the family that I was carrying on all manner of affairs.

Carter Brooks had arrived that day, and was staying at the Perkins' cottage. I got rid of the Perkins' baby, as his nose was bleeding—but I had not slapped him hard at all, and felt little or no compunction—when I heard Carter coming down the walk. He had called to see Leila, but she had gone to a beach dance and left him alone. He never paid any attention to me when she was around, and I received him coolly.

"Hello!" he said.

"Well?" I replied.

"Is that the way you greet me, Bab?"

"It's the way I would greet most any left-over," I said. "I eat hash at school, but I don't have to pretend to like it."

"I came to see YOU."

"How youthful of you!" I replied, in stinging tones.

He sat down on a bench and stared at me.

"What's got into you lately?" he said. "Just as you're getting to be the prettiest girl around, and I'm strong for you, you—you turn into a regular rattlesnake."

The kindness of his tone upset me considerably, to who so few kind words had come recently. I am compelled to confess that I wept, although I had not expected to, and indeed shed few tears, although bitter ones.

How could I possibly know that the chaste salute of Eddie Perkins and my head on Carter Brooks' shoulder were both plainly visible against the rising moon? But this was the case, especially from the house next door.

But I digress.

Suddenly Carter held me off and shook me somewhat.

"Sit up here and tell me about it," he said. "I'm getting more scared every minute. You are such an impulsive little beast, and you turn the fellows' heads so—look here, is Jane Raleigh lying, or did you run away and get married to someone?"

I am aware that I should have said, then and there, No. But it seemed a shame to spoil things just as they were getting interesting. So I said, through my tears:

"Nobody understands me. Nobody. And I'm so lonely."

"And of course you haven't run away with anyone, have you?"

"Not—exactly."

"Bless you, Bab!" he said. And I might as well say that he kissed me, because he did, although unexpectedly. Somebody just then moved a chair on the porch next door and coughed rather loudly, so Carter drew a long breath and got up.

"There's something about you lately, Bab, that I don't understand," he said. "You—you're mysterious. That's the word. In a couple of years you'll be the real thing."

"Come and see me then," I said in a demure manner. And he went away.

So I sat on my bench and looked at the sea and dreamed. It seemed to me that centuries must have passed since I was a lighthearted girl, running up and down that beach, paddling, and so forth, with no thought of the future farther away than my next meal.

Once I lived to eat. Now I merely ate to live, and hardly that. The fires of genius must be fed, but no more.

Sitting there, I suddenly made a discovery. The boat house was near me, and I realized that upstairs, above the bath-houses, et cetera, there must be a room or two. The very thought intrigued me (a new word for interest, but coming into use, and sounding well).

Solitude—how I craved it for my work. And here it was, or would be when I had got the place fixed up. True, the next door boat-house was close, but a boat-house is a quiet place, generally, and I knew that nowhere, aside from the desert, is there perfect silence.

I investigated at once, but found the place locked and the boatman gone. However, there was a lattice, and I climbed up that and got in. I had a fright there, as it seemed to be full of people, but I soon saw it was only the family bathing suits hung up to dry. Aside from the odor of drying things it was a fine study, and I decided to take a small table there, and the various tools of my profession.

Climbing down, however, I had a surprise. For a man was just below, and I nearly put my foot on his shoulder in the darkness.

"Hello!" he said. "So it's YOU."

I was quite speechless. It was Mr. Beecher himself, in his dinner clothes and bareheaded.

Oh fluttering heart, be still. Oh pen, move steadily. OH TEMPORA O MORES!

"Let me down," I said. I was still hanging to the lattice.

"In a moment," he said. "I have an idea that the instant I do you'll vanish. And I have something to tell you."

I could hardly believe my ears.

"You see," he went on, "I think you must move that bench."

"Bench?"

"You seem to be so very popular," he said. "And of course I'm only a transient and don't matter. But some evening one of the admirers may be on the Patten's porch, while another is with you on the bench. And—the Moon rises beyond it."

I was silent with horror. So that was what he thought of me. Like all the others, he, too, did not understand. He considered me a flirt, when my only thoughts were serious ones, of immortality and so on.

"You'd better come down now," he said. "I was afraid to warn you until I saw you climbing the lattice. Then I knew you were still young enough to take a friendly word of advice."

I got down then and stood before him. He was magnificent. Is there anything more beautiful than a tall man with a gleaming expanse of dress shirt? I think not.

But he was staring at me.

"Look here," he said. "I'm afraid I've made a mistake after all. I thought you were a little girl."

"That needn't worry you. Everybody does," I replied. "I'm seventeen, but I shall be a mere child until I come out."

"Oh!" he said.

"One day I am a child in the nursery," I said. "And the next I'm grown up and ready to be sold to the highest bidder."

"I beg your pardon, I——"

"But I am as grown up now as I will ever be," I said. "And indeed more so. I think a great deal now, because I have plenty of time. But my sister never thinks at all. She is too busy."

"Suppose we sit on the bench. The moon is too high to be a menace, and besides, I am not dangerous. Now, what do you think about?"

"About life, mostly. But of course there is death, which is beautiful but cold. And—one always thinks of love, doesn't one?"

"Does one?" he asked. I could see he was much interested. As for me, I dared not consider whom it was who sat beside me, almost touching. That way lay madness.

"Don't you ever," he said, "reflect on just ordinary things, like clothes and so forth?"

I shrugged my shoulders.

"I don't get enough new clothes to worry about. Mostly I think of my work."

"Work?"

"I am a writer" I said in a low, earnest tone.

"No! How—how amazing. What do you write?"

"I'm on a play now."

"A comedy?"

"No. A tragedy. How can I write a comedy when a play must always end in a catastrophe? The book says all plays end in crisis, denouement and catastrophe."

"I can't believe it," he said. "But, to tell you a secret, I never read any books about plays."

"We are not all gifted from berth, as you are," I observed, not to merely please him, but because I considered it the simple truth.

He pulled out his watch and looked at it in the moonlight.

"All this reminds me," he said, "that I have promised to go to work tonight. But this is so—er—thrilling that I guess the work can wait. Well—now go on."

Oh, the joy of that night! How can I describe it? To be at last in the company of one who understood, who—as he himself had said in "Her Soul"—spoke my own language! Except for the occasional mosquito, there was no sound save the tumescent sea and his voice.

Often since that time I have sat and listened to conversation. How flat it sounds to listen to father conversing about Gold, or Sis about Clothes, or even to the young men who come to call, and always talk about themselves.

We were at last interrupted in a strange manner. Mr. Patten came down their walk and crossed to us, walking very fast. He stopped right in front of us and said:

"Look here, Reg, this is about all I can stand."

"Oh, go away, and sing, or do something," said Mr. Beecher sharply.

"You gave me your word of honor" said the Patten man. "I can only remind you of that. Also of the expense I'm incurring, and all the rest of it. I've shown all sorts of patience, but this is the limit."

He turned on his heel, but came back for a last word or two.

"Now see here," he said, "we have everything fixed the way you said you wanted it. And I'll give you ten minutes. That's all."

He stalked away, and Mr. Beecher looked at me.

"Ten minutes of heaven," he said, "and then perdition with that bunch. Look here," he said, "I—I'm awfully interested in what you are telling me. Let's cut off up the beach and talk."

Oh night of nights! Oh moon of moons!

Our talk was strictly business. He asked me my plot, and although I had been warned not to do so, even to David Belasco, I gave it to him fully. And even now, when all is over, I am not sorry. Let him use it if he will. I can think of plenty of plots.

The real tragedy is that we met father. He had been ordered to give up smoking, and I considered he had done so, mother feeling that I should be encouraged in leaving off cigarettes. So when I saw the cigar I was sure it was not father. It proved to be, however, and although he passed with nothing worse than a glare, I knew I was in more trouble.

At last we reached the bench again, and I said good night. Our relations continued business-like to the last. He said:

"Good night, little authoress, and let's have some more talks."

"I'm afraid I've bored you," I said.

"Bored me!" he said. "I haven't spent such an evening for years!"

The family acted perfectly absurd about it. Seeing that they were going to make a fuss, I refused to say with whom I had been walking. You'd have thought I had committed a crime.

"It has come to this, Barbara," mother said, pacing the floor. "You cannot be trusted out of our sight. Where do you meet all these men? If this is how things are now, what will it be when given your liberty?"

Well, it is to painful to record. I was told not to leave the place for three days, although allowed the boat-house. And of course Sis had to chime in that she'd heard a rumor I had run away and got married, and although of course she knew it wasn't true, owing to no time to do so, still where there was smoke there was fire.

But I felt that their confidence in me was going, and that night, after all were in the land of dreams, I took that wretched suit of clothes and so on to the boathouse, and hid them in the rafters upstairs.

I come now to the strange event of the next day, and its sequel.

The Patten place and ours are close together, and no other house near. Mother had been very cool about the Pattens, owing to nobody knowing them that we knew. Although I must say they had the most interesting people all the time, and Sis was crazy to call and meet some of them.

Jane came that day to visit her aunt, and she ran down to see me first thing.

"Come and have a ride," she said. "I've got the runabout, and after that we'll bathe and have a real time."

But I shook my head.

"I'm a prisoner, Jane," I said.

"Honestly! Is it the play, or something else?"

"Something else, Jane," I said. "I can tell you nothing more. I am simply in trouble, as usual."

"But why make you a prisoner, unless — —" She stopped suddenly and stared at me.

"He has claimed you!" she said. "He is here, somewhere about this place, and now, having had time to think it over, you do not want to go to him. Don't deny it. I see it in your face. Oh, Bab, my heart aches for you."

It sounded so like a play that I kept it up. Alas, with what results!

"What else can I do, Jane?" I said.

"You can refuse, if you do not love him. Oh Bab, I did not say it before, thinking you loved him. But no man who wears clothes like those could ever win my heart. At least, not permanently."

Well, she did most of the talking. She had finished the bath towel, which was a large size, after all, and monogrammed, and she made me promise never to let my husband use it. When she went away she left it with me, and I carried it out and put it on the rafters, with the other things—I seemed to be getting more to hide every day.

Things went all wrong the next day. Sis was in a bad temper, and as much as said I was flirting with Carter Brooks, although she never intends to marry him herself, owing to his not having money and never having asked her.

I spent the morning in fixing up a studio in the boat-house, and felt better by noon. I took two boards on trestles and made a desk, and brought a dictionary and some pens and ink out. I use a dictionary because now and then I am uncertain how to spell a word.

Events now moved swiftly and terribly. I did not do much work, being exhausted by my efforts to fix up the studio, and besides, feeling that nothing much was worth while when one's family did not and never would understand. At eleven o'clock Sis and Carter and Jane and some others went in bathing from our dock. Jane called up to me, but I pretended not to hear. They had a good time judging by the noise, although I should think Jane would cover her arms and neck in the water, being very thin. Legs one can do nothing with, although I should think stripes going around would help. But arms can have sleeves.

However—the people next door went in too, and I thrilled to the core when Mr. Beecher left the bath-house and went down to the beech. What a physique! What shoulders, all brown and muscular! And to think that, strong as they were, they wrote the tender love scenes of his plays. Strong and tender—what descriptive words they are! It was then that I saw he had been vaccinated twice.

To resume. All the Pattens went in, and a new girl with them, in a one piece suit. I do not deny that she was pretty. I only say that she was not modest, and that the way she stood on the Patten's dock and posed for Mr. Beecher's benefit was unnecessary and well, not respectable.

She was nothing to me, nor I to her. But I watched her closely. I confess that I was interested in Mr. Beecher. Why not? He was a public character, and entitled to respect. Nay, even to love. But I maintain and will to my dying day, that such love is different from that ordinarily born to the other sex, and a thing to be proud of.

Well, I was seeing a drama and did not even know it. After the rest had gone, Mr. Patten came to the door into Mr. Beecher's room in the bath-house—they are all in a row, with doors opening on the sand—and he had a box in his hand. He looked around, and no one was looking except me, and he did not see me. He looked very fierce and glum, and shortly after he carried in a chair and a folding card table. I thought this was very strange, but imagine how I felt when he came out carrying Mr. Beecher's clothes! He brought them all, going on his tiptoes and watching every minute. I felt like screaming.

However, I considered that it was a practical joke, and I am no spoil sport. So I sat still and waited. They stayed in the water a long time, and the girl with the figure was always crawling out on the dock and then diving in to show off. Leila and the rest got sick of her actions and came in to lunch. They called up to me, but I said I was not hungry.

"I don't know what's come over Bab," I heard Sis say to Carter Brooks. "She's crazy, I think."

"She's seventeen," he said. "That's all. They get over it mostly, but she has it hard."

I loathed him.

Pretty soon the other crowd came up, and I could see every one knew the joke but Mr. Beecher. They all scuttled into their doorways, and Mr. Patten waited till Mr. Beecher was inside and had thrown out the shirt of his bathing suit. Then he locked the door from the outside.

There was a silence for a minute. Then Mr. Beecher said in a terrible voice.

"So that's the game, is it?"

"Now listen, Reg," Mr. Patten said, in a soothing voice. "I've tried everything but force, and now I'm driven to that. I've got to have that third act. The company's got the first two acts well under way, and I'm getting wires about every hour. I've got to have that script."

"You go to Hell!" said Mr. Beecher. You could hear him plainly through the window, high up in the wall. And although I do not approve of an oath, there are times when it eases the tortured soul.

"Now be reasonable, Reg," Mr. Patten pleaded. "I've put a fortune in this thing, and you're lying down on the job. You could do it in four hours if you'd put your mind to it."

There was no answer to this. And he went on:

"I'll send out food or anything. But nothing to drink. There's champagne on the ice for you when you've finished, however. And you'll find pens and ink and paper on the table."

The answer to this was Mr. Beecher's full weight against the door. But it held, even against the full force of his fine physic.

"Even if you do break it open," Mr. Patten said, "you can't go very far the way you are. Now be a good fellow, and let's get this thing done. It's for your good as well as mine. You'll make a fortune out of it."

Then he went into his own door, and soon came out, looking like a gentleman, unless one knew, as I did, that he was a whited sepulcher.

How long I sat there, paralyzed with emotion, I do not know. Hannah came out and roused me from my trance of grief. She is a kindly soul, although too afraid of mother to be helpful.

"Come in like a good girl, Miss Bab," she said. "There's that fruit salad that cook prides herself on, and I'll ask her to brown a bit of sweetbread for you."

"Hannah," I said in a low voice, "there is a crime being committed in this neighborhood, and you talk to me of food."

"Good gracious, Miss Bab!"

"I cannot tell you any more than that, Hannah," I said gently, "because it is only being done now, and I cannot make up my mind about it. But of course I do not want any food."

As I say, I was perfectly gentle with her, and I do not understand why she burst into tears and went away.

I sat and thought it all over. I could not leave, under the circumstances. But yet, what was I to do? It was hardly a police matter, being between friends, as one may say, and yet I simply could not bare to leave my ideal there in that damp bath-house without either food or, as one may say, raiment.

About the middle of the afternoon it occurred to me to try to find a key for the lock of the bath-house. I therefore left my studio and proceeded to the house. I passed close by the fatal building, but there was no sound from it.

I found a number of trunk-keys in a drawer in the library, and was about to escape with them, when father came in. He gave me a long look, and said:

"Bee still buzzing?"

I had hoped for some understanding from him, but my spirits fell at this speech.

"I am still working, father," I said, in a firm if nervous tone. "I am not doing as good work as I would if things were different, but—I am at least content, if not happy."

He stared at me, and then came over to me.

"Put out your tongue," he said.

Even against this crowning infamy I was silent.

"That's all right," he said. "Now see here, Chicken, get into your riding togs and we'll order the horses. I don't intend to let this play-acting upset your health."

But I refused. "Unless, of course, you insist," I finished. He only shook his head, however, and left the room. I felt that I had lost my last friend.

I did not try the keys myself, but instead stood off a short distance and threw them through the window. I learned later that they struck Mr. Beecher on the head. Not knowing, of course, that I had flung them, and that my reason was pure friendliness and idealism, he threw them out again with a violent exclamation. They fell at my feet, and lay there, useless, rejected, tragic.

At last I summoned courage to speak.

"Can't I do something to help?" I said, in a quaking voice, to the window.

There was no answer, but I could hear a pen scratching on paper.

"I do so want to help you," I said, in a louder tone.

"Go, away" said his voice, rather abstracted than angry.

"May I try the keys?" I asked. Be still, my heart! For the scratching had ceased.

"Who's that?" asked the beloved voice. I say 'beloved' because an ideal is always beloved. The voice was beloved, but sharp.

"It's me."

I heard him mutter something, and I think he came to the door.

"Look here," he said. "Go away. Do you understand? I want to work. And don't come near here again until seven o'clock."

"Very well," I said faintly.

"And then come without fail," he said.

"Yes, Mr. Beecher," I replied. How commanding he was! Strong but tender!

"And if anyone comes around making a noise, before that, you shoot them for me, will you?"

"SHOOT them?"

"Drive them off, or use a bean-shooter. Anything. But don't yell at them. It distracts me."

It was a sacred trust. I, and only I, stood between him and his MAGNUM OPUS. I sat down on the steps of our bath-house, and took up my vigil.

It was about five o'clock when I heard Jane approaching. I knew it was Jane, because she always wears tight shoes, and limps when unobserved. Although having the reputation of the smallest foot of any girl in our set in the city, I prefer comfort and ease, unhampered by heals—French or otherwise. No man will ever marry a girl because she wears a small shoe, and catches her heals in holes in the boardwalk, and has to soak her feet at night before she can sleep. However— —

Jane came on, and found me crouched on the doorstep, in a lowly attitude, and holding my finger to my lips.

She stopped and stared at me.

"Hello," she said. "What do you think you are? A statue?"

"Hush, Jane," I said, in a low tone. "I can only ask you to be quiet and speak in whispers. I cannot give the reason."

"Good heavens!" she whispered. "What has happened, Bab?"

"It is happening now, but I cannot explain."

"WHAT is happening?"

"Jane," I whispered, earnestly, "you have known me a long time and I have always been trustworthy, have I not?"

She nodded. She is never exactly pretty, and now she had opened her mouth and forgot to close it.

"Then ask no questions. Trust me, as I am trusting you." It seemed to me that Mr. Beecher threw his pen at the door, and began to pace the bath-house. Owing of course to his being in his bare feet, I was not certain. Jane heard something, too, for she clutched my arm.

"Bab," she said, in intense tones, "if you don't explain I shall lose my mind. I feel now that I am going to shriek."

She looked at me searchingly.

"Somebody is a prisoner. That's all."

It was the truth, was it not? And was there any reasons for Jane Raleigh to jump to conclusions as she did, and even to repeat later in public that I had told her that my lover had come for me, and that father had locked him up to prevent my running away with him, immuring him in the Patten's bath-house? Certainly not.

Just then I saw the boatman coming who looks after our motor boat, and I tiptoed to him and asked him to go away, and not to come back unless he had quieter boats and would not whistle. He acted very ugly about it, I must say, but he went.

When I came back, Jane was sitting thinking, with her forehead all puckered.

"What I don't understand, Bab," she said, "is, why no noise?"

"Because he is writing," I explained. "Although his clothing has been taken away, he is writing. I don't think I told you, Jane, but that is his business. He is a writer. And if I tell you his name you will faint with surprise."

She looked at me searchingly.

"Locked up—and writing, and his clothing gone! What's he writing, Bab? His will?"

"He is doing his duty to the end, Jane," I said softly. "He is writing the last act of a play. The company is rehearsing the first two acts, and he has to get this one ready, though the heavens fall."

But to my surprise, she got up and said to me, in a firm voice:

"Either you are crazy, Barbara Archibald, or you think I am. You've been stuffing me for about a week, and I don't believe a word of it. And you'll apologize to me or I'll never speak to you again."

She said this loudly, and then went away, And Mr. Beecher said, through the door.

"What the devil's the row about?"

Perhaps my nerves were going, or possibly it was no luncheon and probably no dinner. But I said, just as if he had been an ordinary person:

"Go on and write and get through. I can't stew on these steps all day."

"I thought you were an amiable child."

"I'm not amiable and I'm not a child."

"Don't spoil your pretty face with frowns."

"It's MY face. And you can't see it anyhow," I replied, venting in feminine fashion, my anger at Jane on the nearest object.

"Look here," he said, through the door, "you've been my good angel. I'm doing more work than I've done in two months, although it was a dirty, low-down way to make me do it. You're not going back on me now, are you?"

Well, I was mollified, as who would not be? So I said:

"Well?"

"What did Patten do with my clothes?"

"He took them with him." He was silent, except for a muttered word.

"You might throw those keys back again," he said. "Let me know first, however. You're the most accurate thrower I've ever seen."

So I threw them through the window and I believe hit the ink bottle. But no matter. And he tried them, but none availed.

So he gave up, and went back to work, having saved enough ink to finish with. But a few minutes later he called to me again, and I moved to the doorstep, where I sat listening, while apparently admiring the sea. He explained that having been thus forced, he had almost finished the last act, and it was a corker. And he said if he had his clothes and some money, and a key to get out, he'd go right back to town with it and put it in rehearsal. And at the same time he would give the Pattens something to worry about over night. Because, play or no play, it was a rotten thing to lock a man in a bath-house and take his clothes away.

"But of course I can't get my clothes," he said. "They'll take cussed good care of that. And there's the key too. We're up against it, little sister."

Although excited by his calling me thus, I retained my faculties, and said:

"I have a suit of clothes you can have."

"Thanks awfully," he said. "But from the slight acquaintance we have had, I don't believe they would fit me."

"Gentleman's clothes," I said frigidly.

"You have?"

"In my studio," I said. "I can bring them, if you like. They look quite good, although creased."

"You know" he said, after a moment's silence, "I can't quite believe this is really happening to me! Go and bring the suit of clothes, and—you don't happen to have a cigar, I suppose?"

"I have a large box of cigarettes."

"It is true," I heard him say through the door. "It is all true. I am here, locked in. The play is almost done. And a very young lady on the doorstep is offering me a suit of clothes and tobacco. I pinch myself. I am awake."

Alas! Mingled with my joy at serving my ideal there was also grief. My idle had feet of clay. He was a slave, like the rest of us, to his body. He required clothes and tobacco. I felt that, before long, he might even ask for an apple, or something to stay the pangs of hunger. This I felt I could not bare.

Perhaps I would better pass over quickly the events of the next hour. I got the suit and the cigarettes, and even Jane's bath towel, and threw them in to him. Also I believe he took a shower, as I heard the water running, At about seven o'clock he said he had finished the play. He put on the clothes which he observed almost fitted him, although gayer than he usually wore, and said that if I would give him a hair pin he thought he could pick the lock. But he did not succeed.

Being now dressed, however, he drew a chair to the window and we talked together. It seemed like a dream that I should be there, on such intimate terms with a great playwright, who had just, even if under compulsion, finished a last act, I bared my very soul to him, such as about resembling Julia Marlowe, and no one understanding my craving to achieve a place in the world of art. We were once interrupted by Hannah looking for me for dinner. But I hid in a bath-house, and she went away.

What was food to me compared with such a conversation?

When Hannah had disappeared, he said suddenly:

"It's rather unusual, isn't it, your having a suit of clothes and everything in your—er—studio?"

But I did not explain fully, merely saving that it was a painful story.

At half past seven I saw mother on the veranda looking for me, and I ducked out of sight, I was by this time very hungry, although I did not like to mention the fact, But Mr. Beecher made a suggestion, which was this: that the Pattens were evidently going to let him starve until he got through work, and that he would see them in perdition before he would be the butt for their funny remarks when they freed him. He therefore tried to escape out the window, but stuck fast, and finally gave it up.

At last he said:

"Look here, you're a curious child, but a nervy one. How'd you like to see if you can get the key? If you do we'll go to a hotel and have a real meal, and we can talk about your career."

Although quivering with terror, I consented. How could I do otherwise, with such a prospect? For now I began to see that all other emotions previously felt were as nothing to this one. I confess, without shame, that I felt the stirring of the tender passion in my breast. Ah me, that it should have died ere it had hardly lived!

"Where is the key?" I asked, in a rapt but anxious tone.

He thought a while.

"Generally," he said, "it hangs on a nail at the back entry. But the chances are that Patten took it up to his room this time, for safety, You'd know it if you saw it. It has some buttons off somebody's bathing suit tied to it."

Here it was necessary to hide again, as father came stocking out, calling me in an angry tone. But shortly after-wards I was on my way to the Patten's house, on shaking knees. It was by now twilight, that beautiful period of romance, although the dinner hour also. Through the dusk I sped, toward what? I knew not.

The Pattens and the one-piece lady were at dinner, and having a very good time, in spite of having locked a guest in the bath-house. Being used to servants and prowling around, since at one time when younger I had a habit of taking things from the pantry, I was quickly able to see that the key was not in the entry. I therefore went around to the front door and went in, being prepared, if discovered, to say that someone was in their bath-house and they ought to know it. But I was not heard among their sounds of revelry, and was able to proceed upstairs, which I did.

But not having asked which was Mr. Patten's room, I was at a loss and almost discovered by a maid who was turning down the beds—much too early, also, and not allowed in the best houses until nine-thirty, since otherwise the rooms look undressed and informal.

I had but time to duck into another chamber, and from there to a closet.

I REMAINED IN THAT CLOSET ALL NIGHT.

I will explain. No sooner had the maid gone than a woman came into the room and closed the door. I heard her moving around and I suddenly felt that she was going to bed, and might get her robe de nuit out of the closet. I was petrified. But it seems, while she really WAS undressing at that early hour, the maid had laid her night clothes out, and I was saved.

Very soon a knock came to the door, and somebody came in, like Mrs. Patten's voice and said: "You're not going to bed, surely!"

"I'm going to pretend to have a sick headache," said the other person, and I knew it was the one-piece lady. "He's going to come back in a frenzy, and he'll take it out on me, unless I'm prepared."

"Poor Reggie!" said Mrs. Patten, "To think of him locked in there alone, and no clothes or anything. It's too funny for words."

"You're not married to him."

My heart stopped beating. Was SHE married to him? She was indeed. My dream was over. And the worst part of it was that for a married man I had done without food or exercise and now stood in a hot closet in danger of a terrible fuss.

"No, thank heaven!" said Mrs. Patten. "But it was the only way to make him work. He is a lazy dog. But don't worry. We'll feed him before he sees you. He's always rather tractable after he's fed."

Were ALL my dreams to go? Would they leave nothing to my shattered illusions? Alas, no.

"Jolly him a little, too," said — —can I write it?—Mrs. Beecher. "Tell him he's the greatest thing in the world. That will help some. He's vain, you know, awfully vain. I expect he's written a lot of piffle."

Had they listened they would have heard a low, dry sob, wrung from my tortured heart. But Mrs. Beecher had started a vibrator, and my anguished cry was lost.

"Well," said Mrs. Patten, "Will has gone down to let him out, I expect he'll attack him. He's got a vile temper. I'll sit with you till he comes back, if you don't mind. I'm feeling nervous."

It was indeed painful to recall the next half hour. I must tell the truth however. They discussed us, especially mother, who had not called. They said that we thought we were the whole summer colony, although every one was afraid of mother's tongue, and nobody would marry Leila, except Carter Brooks, and he was poor and no prospects. And that I was an incorrigible, and carried on something ghastly, and was going to be put in a convent. I became justly furious and was about to step out and tell them a few plain facts, when somebody hammered at the door and then came in. It was Mr. Patten.

"He's gone!" he said.

"Well, he won't go far, in bathing trunks," said Mrs. Beecher.

"That's just it. His bathing trunks are there."

"Well, he won't go far without them!"

"He's gone so far I can't locate him."

I heard Mrs. Beecher get up.

"Are you in earnest, Will?" she said. "Do you mean that he has gone without a stitch of clothes, and can't be found?"

Mrs. Patten gave a sort of screech.

"You don't think—oh Will, he's so temperamental. You don't think he's drowned himself?"

"No such luck," said Mrs. Beecher, in a cold tone. I hated her for it. True, he had deceived me. He was not as I had thought him. In our two conversations he had not mentioned his wife, leaving me to believe him free to love "where he listed," as the poet says.

"There are a few clues," said Mr. Patten. "He got out by means of a wire hairpin, for one thing. And he took the manuscript with him, which he'd hardly have done if he meant to drown himself. Or even if, as we fear, he had no pockets. He has smoked a lot of cigarettes out of a candy box, which I did not supply him, and he left behind a bath towel that does not, I think, belong to us."

"I should think he would have worn it," said Mrs. Beecher, in a scornful tone.

"Here's the bath towel," Mr. Patten went on. "You may recognize the initials. I don't."

"B. P. A.," said Mrs. Beecher. "Look here, don't they call that—that flibbertigibbet next door 'Barbara'?"

"The little devil!" said Mr. Patten, in a raging tone. "She let him out, and of course he's done no work on the play or anything. I'd like to choke her."

Nobody spoke then, and my heart beat fast and hard. I leave it to anybody, how they'd like to be shut in a closet and threatened with a violent death from without. Would or would they not ever be the same person afterwords?

"I'll tell you what I'd do," said the Beecher woman. "I'd climb up the back of father, next door, and tell him what his little daughter has done, because I know she's mixed up in it, towel or no towel. Reg is always sappy when they're seventeen. And she's been looking moon-eyed at him for days."

Well, the Pattens went away, and Mrs. Beecher manicured her nails,—I could hear her filing them—and sang around and was not much concerned, although for all she knew he was in the briny deep, a corpse. How true it is that "the paths of glory lead but to the grave."

I got very tired and much hotter, and I sat down on the floor. After what seemed like hours, Mrs. Patten came back, all breathless, and she said:

"The girl's gone too, Clare."

"What girl?"

"Next door. If you want excitement, they've got it. The mother is in hysterics and there's a party searching the beach for her body. The truth is, of course, if that towel means anything."

"That Reg has run away with her, of course," said Mrs. Beecher, in a resigned tone. "I wish he would grow up and learn something. He's becoming a nuisance. And when there are so many interesting people to run away with, to choose that chit!"

Yes, she said that, And in my retreat I could but sit and listen, and of course perspire, which I did freely. Mrs. Patten went away, after talking about the "scandal" for some time. And I sat and thought of the beach being searched for my body, a thought which filled my eyes with tears of pity for what might have been, I still hoped Mrs. Beecher would go to bed, but she did not. Through the key hole I could see her with a book, reading, and not caring at all that Mr. Beecher's body, and mine too, might be washing about in the cruel sea, or have eloped to New York.

I loathed her.

At last I must have slept, for a bell rang, and there I was still in the closet, and she was answering it.

"Arrested?" she said, "Well, I should think he'd better be, if what you say about clothing is true.... Well, then—what's he arrested for?... Oh, kidnapping! Well, if I'm any judge, they ought to arrest the Archibald girl for kidnapping HIM. No, don't bother me with it tonight. I'll try to read myself to sleep."

So this was marriage! Did she flee to her unjustly accused husband's side and comfort him? Not she. She went to bed.

At daylight, being about smothered, I opened the closet door and drew a breath of fresh air. Also I looked at her, and she was asleep, with her hair in patent wavers. Ye gods!

The wife of Reginald Beecher thus to distort her looks at night! I could not bare it.

I averted my eyes, and on my tiptoes made for the window.

My sufferings were over. In a short time I had slid down and was making my way through the dewy morn toward my home. Before the sun was up, or more than starting, I had climbed to my casement by means of a wire trellis, and put on my 'robe de nuit'. But before I settled to sleep I went to the pantry and there satisfied the pangs of hunger having had nothing since breakfast the day before. All the lights seemed to be on, on the lower floor, which I considered wasteful of Tanney, the butler. But being sleepy, gave it no further thought. And so to bed, as the great English dairy-keeper, Pepys, had said in his dairy.

It seemed but a few moments later that I heard a scream, and opening my eyes, saw Leila in the doorway. She screamed again, and mother came and stood beside her. Although very drowsy, I saw that they still wore their dinner clothes.

They stared as if transfixed, and then mother gave a low moan, and said to Sis:

"That unfortunate man has been in jail all night."

And Sis said: "Jane Raleigh is crazy. That's all." Then they looked at me, and mother burst into tears. But Sis said:

"You little imp! Don't tell me you've been in that bed all night. I KNOW BETTER."

I closed my eyes. They were not of the understanding sort, and never would be.

"If that's the way you feel I shall tell you nothing," I said wearily.

"WHERE HAVE YOU BEEN?" mother said, in a slow and dreadful voice.

Well, I saw then that a part of the truth must be disclosed, especially since she has for some time considered sending me to a convent, although without cause, and has not done so for fear of my taking the veil. So I told her this. I said:

"I spent the night shut in a clothes closet, but where is my secret. I cannot tell you."

"Barbara! You MUST tell me."

"It is not my secret alone, mother."

She caught at the foot of the bed.

"Who was shut with you in that closet?" she demanded in a shaking voice. "Barbara, there is another wretched man in all this. It could not have been Mr. Beecher, because he has been in the station house all night."

I sat up, leaning on one elbow, and looked at her earnestly.

"Mother" I said, "you have done enough damage, interfering with careers—not only mine, but another's imperiled now by not having a last act. I can tell you no more, except"—here my voice took on a deep and intense fiber—"that I have done nothing to be ashamed of, although unconventional."

Mother put her hands to her face, and emitted a low, despairing cry.

"Come," Leila said to her, as to a troubled child. "Come, and Hannah can use the vibrator on your spine."

So she went, but before she left she said:

"Barbara, if you will only promise to be a good girl, and give us a chance to live this scandal down, I will give you anything you ask for."

"Mother!" Sis said, in an angry tone.

"What can I do, Leila?" mother said. "The girl is attractive, and probably men will always be following her and making trouble. Think of last winter. I know it is bribery, but it is better than scandal."

"I want nothing, mother," I said, in a low, heart stricken tone, "save to be allowed to live my own life and to have a career."

"My heavens," mother said, "if I hear that word again, I'll go crazy."

So she went away, and Sis came over and looked down at me.

"Well!" she said. "What's happened anyhow? Of course you've been up to some mischief, but I don't suppose anybody will ever know the truth of it. I was hoping you'd make it this time and get married, and stop worrying us."

"Go away, please, and let me sleep," I said. "As to getting married, under no circumstances did I expect to marry him. He has a wife already. Personally, I think she's a total loss. She wears patent wavers at night, and sleeps with her mouth open. But who am I to interfere with the marriage bond? I never have and never will."

But Sis only gave me a wild look and went away.

This, dear readers and schoolmates, is the true story of my meeting with and parting from Reginald Beecher, the playwright. Whatever the papers may say, it is not true, except the fact that he was recognized by Jane Raleigh, who knew the suit he wore, when in the act of pawning his ring to get money to escape from his captors (I. E., The Pattens). It was the necktie which struck her first, and also his guilty expression. As I was missing by that time, Jane put two and two together and made an elopement.

Sometimes I sit and think things over, my fingers wandering "over the ivory keys" of the typewriter they gave me to promise not to elope with anybody—although such a thing is far from my mind—and the world seems a cruel and unjust place, especially to those with ambition.

For Reginald Beecher is no longer my ideal, my night of the pen. I will tell about that in a few words.

Jane Raleigh and I went to a matinee late in September before returning to our institutions of learning. Jane clutched my arm as we looked at our programs and pointed to something.

How my heart beat! For whatever had come between us, I was still loyal to him.

This was a new play by him!

"Ah," my heart seemed to say, "now again you will hear his dear words, although spoken by alien mouths.

"The love scenes— —"

I could not finish. Although married and forever beyond me, I could still hear his manly tones as issuing from the door of the Bath-house. I thrilled with excitement. As the curtain rose I closed my eyes in ecstasy.

"Bab!" Jane said, in a quavering tone.

I looked. What did I see? The bath-house itself, the very one. And as I stared I saw a girl, wearing her hair as I wear mine, cross the stage with a bunch of keys in her hand, and say to the bath-house door.

"Can't I do something to help? I do so want to help you."

MY VERY WORDS.

And a voice from beyond the bath-house door said:

"Who's that?"

HIS WORDS.

I could bare no more. Heedless of Jane's protests and anguish, I got up and went out, into the light of day. My body was bent with misery. Because at last I knew that, like mother and all the rest, he too, did not understand me and never would! To him I was but material, the stuff that plays are made of!

And now we know that he never could know,

And did not understand.

Kipling.

Ignoring Jane's observation that the tickets had cost two dollars each, I gathered up the scattered skeins of my life together, and fled.

CHAPTER III
HER DIARY: BEING THE DAILY JOURNAL OF THE SUB-DEB

JANUARY 1st. I have today received this diary from home, having come back a few days early to make up a French condition.

Weather, clear and cold.

New Year's dinner. Roast chicken (Turkey being very expensive), mashed turnips, sweet potatoes and mince pie.

It is my intention to record in this book the details of my Daily Life, my thoughts which are to sacred for utterance, and my ambitions. Because who is there to whom I can speak them? I am surrounded by those who exist for the mere pleasures of the day, or whose lives are bound up in recitations.

For instance, at dinner today, being mostly faculty and a few girls who live in the far West, the conversation was entirely on buying a phonograph for dancing because the music teacher has the measles and is quarantined in the infirmary. And on Miss Everett's cousin, who has written a play.

When one looks at Miss Everett, one recognizes that no cousin of hers could write a play.

New Year's resolution—to help someone every day. Today helped Mademoiselle to put on her rubbers.

JANUARY 2ND. Today I wrote my French theme, beginning, "Les hommes songent moins a leur ame qua leur corps." Mademoiselle sent for me and objected, saying that it was not a theme for a young girl, and that I must write a new one, on the subject of pears. How is one to develop in this atmosphere?

Some of the girls are coming back. They straggle in, and put the favors they got at cotillions on the dresser, and their holiday gifts, and each one relates some amorous experience while at home. Dear Diary, is there something wrong with me, that love has passed me by? I have had offers of devotion but none that appealed to me, being mostly either too young or not attracting me by physical charm. I am not cold, although frequently accused of it, Beneath my frigid exterior beats a warm heart. I intend to be honest in this diary, and so I admit it. But, except for passing fancies—one being, alas, for a married man—I remain without the divine passion.

What must it be to thrill at the approach of the loved form? To harken to each ring of the telephone bell, in the hope that, if it is not the idolized voice, it is at least a message from it? To waken in the morning and, looking around the familiar room, to muse: "Today I may see him—on the way to the post office, or rushing past in his racing car." And to know that at the same moment HE to is musing: "Today I may see her, as she exercises herself at basket ball, or mounts her horse for a daily canter!"

Although I have no horse. The school does not care for them, considering walking the best exercise.

Have flunked the French again, Mademoiselle not feeling well, and marking off for the smallest thing.

Today's helpful deed—assisted one of the younger girls with her spelling.

JANUARY 4TH. Miss Everett's cousin's play is coming here. The school is to have free tickets, as they are "trying it on the dog." Which means seeing if it is good enough for the large cities.

We have decided, if Everett marks us well in English from now on, to applaud it, but if she is unpleasant, to sit still and show no interest.

JANUARY 5TH, 6TH, 7TH, 8TH. Bad weather, which is depressing to one of my temperament. Also boil on nose.

A few helpful deeds—nothing worth putting down.

JANUARY 9TH. Boil cut.

Again I can face my image in my mirror, and not shrink.

Mademoiselle is sick and no French. MISERICORDE!

Helpful deed—sent Mademoiselle some fudge, but this school does not encourage kindness. Reprimanded for cooking in room. School sympathizes with me. We will go to Miss Everett's cousin's play, but we will damn it with faint praise.

JANUARY 10TH. I have written this date, and now I sit back and regard it. As it is impressed on this white paper, so, Dear Diary, is it written on my soul. To others it may be but the tenth of January. To me it is the day of days. Oh, tenth of January! Oh, Monday. Oh, day of my awakening!

It is now late at night, and around me my schoolmates are sleeping the sleep of the young and heart free. Lights being off, I am writing by the faint luminosity of a candle. Propped up in bed, my mackinaw coat over my 'robe de nuit' for warmth, I sit and dream. And as I dream I still hear in my ears his final words: "My darling. My woman!"

How wonderful to have them said to one night after night, the while being in his embrace, his tender arms around one! I refer to the heroine in the play, to whom he says the above rapturous words.

Coming home from the theater tonight, still dazed with the revelation of what I am capable of, once aroused, I asked Miss Everett if her cousin had said anything about Mr. Egleston being in love with the leading character. She observed:

"No. But he may be. She is very pretty."

"Possibly," I remarked. "But I should like to see her in the morning, when she gets up."

All the girls were perfectly mad about Mr. Egleston, although pretending merely to admire his Art. But I am being honest, as I agreed at the start, and now I know, as I sit here with the soft, although chilly breezes of the night blowing on my hot brow, now I know that this thing that has come to me is Love. Moreover, it is the Love of my Life. He will never know it, but I am his. He is exactly my ideal, strong and tall and passionate. And clever, too. He said some awfully clever things.

I believe that he saw me. He looked in my direction. But what does it matter? I am small, insignificant. He probably thinks me a mere child, although seventeen.

What matters, oh Diary, is that I am at last in Love. It is hopeless. Just now, when I had written that word, I buried my face in my hands. There is no hope. None. I shall never see him again. He passed out of my life on the 11:45 train. But I love him. MON DIEU, how I love him!

JANUARY 11TH. We are going home. WE ARE GOING HOME. WE ARE GOING HOME. WE ARE GOING HOME!

Mademoiselle has the measles.

JANUARY 13TH. The family managed to restrain its ecstasy on seeing me today. The house is full of people, as they are having a dinner-dance tonight. Sis had moved into my room, to let one of the visitors have hers, and she acted in a very unfilial manner when she came home and found me in it.

"Well!" she said. "Expelled at last?"

"Not at all," I replied in a lofty manner. "I am here through no fault of my own. And I'd thank you to have Hannah take your clothes off my bed."

She gave me a bitter glance.

"I never knew it to fail!" she said. "Just as everything is fixed, and we're recovering from you're being here for the holidays, you come back and stir up a lot of trouble. What brought you, anyhow?"

"Measles."

She snatched up her ball gown.

"Very well," she said. "I'll see that you're quarantined, Miss Barbara, all right. And If you think you're going to slip downstairs tonight after dinner and WORM yourself into this party, I'll show you."

She flounced out, and shortly afterward mother took a minute from the florist, and came upstairs.

"I do hope you are not going to be troublesome, Barbara," she said. "You are too young to understand, but I want everything to go well tonight, and Leila ought not to be worried."

"Can't I dance a little?"

"You can sit on the stairs and watch." She looked fidgety. "I—I'll send up a nice dinner, and you can put on your dark blue, with a fresh collar, and—it ought to satisfy you, Barbara, that you are at home and possibly have brought the measles with you, without making a lot of fuss. When you come out——"

"Oh, very well," I murmured, in a resigned tone. "I don't care enough about it to want to dance with a lot of souses anyhow."

"Barbara!" said mother.

"I suppose you have some one on the string for her," I said, with the abandon of my thwarted hopes. "Well, I hope she gets him. Because if not, I daresay I shall be kept in the cradle for years to come."

"You will come out when you reach a proper age," she said, "if your impertinence does not kill me off before my time."

Dear Diary, I am fond of my mother, and I felt repentant and stricken.

So I became more agreeable, although feeling all the time that she does not and never will understand my temperament. I said:

"I don't care about society, and you know it, mother. If you'll keep Leila out of this room, which isn't much but is my castle while here, I'll probably go to bed early."

"Barbara, sometimes I think you have no affection for your sister."

I had agreed to honesty January first, so I replied.

"I have, of course, mother. But I am fonder of her while at school than at home. And I should be a better sister if not condemned to her old things, including hats which do not suit my type."

Mother moved over majestically to the door and shut it. Then she came and stood over me.

"I've come to the conclusion, Barbara," she said, "to appeal to your better nature. Do you wish Leila to be married and happy?"

"I've just said, mother— —"

"Because a very interesting thing is happening," said mother, trying to look playful. "I—a chance any girl would jump at."

So here I sit, Dear Diary, while there are sounds of revelry below, and Sis jumps at her chance, which is the Honorable Page Beresford, who is an Englishman visiting here because he has a weak heart and can't fight. And father is away on business, and I am all alone.

I have been looking for a rash, but no luck.

Ah me, how the strains of the orchestra recall that magic night in the theater when Adrian Egleston looked down into my eyes and although ostensibly to an actress, said to my beating heart: "My Darling! My Woman!"

3 A. M. I wonder if I can control my hands to write.

In mother's room across the hall I can hear furious voices, and I know that Leila is begging to have me sent to Switzerland. Let her beg. Switzerland is not far from England, and in England— —

Here I pause to reflect a moment. How is this thing possible? Can I love members of the other sex? And if such is the case, how can I go on with my life? Better far to end it now, than to perchance marry one, and find the other still in my heart. The terrible thought has come to me that I am fickle.

Fickle or polygamous—which?

Dear Diary, I have not been a good girl. My New Year's Resolutions have gone to airy nothing.

The way they went was this: I had settled down to a quiet evening, spent with his beloved picture which I had clipped from a newspaper. (Adrian's. I had not as yet met the other.) And, as I sat in my chamber, I grew more and more desolate. I love life, although pessimistic at times. And it seemed hard that I should be there, in exile, while my sister, only 20 months older, was jumping at her chance below.

At last I decided to try on one of Sis's frocks and see how I looked in it. I thought, if it looked all right, I might hang over the stairs and see what I then scornfully termed "His Nibs." Never again shall I so call him.

I got an evening gown from Sis's closet, and it fitted me quite well, although tight at the waste for me, owing to basketball. It was also too low, so that when I had got it all hooked about four inches of my lingerie showed. As it had been hard as anything to hook, I was obliged to take the scissors and cut off the said lingerie. The result was good, although very decollete. I have no bones in my neck, or practically so.

And now came my moment of temptation. How easy to put my hair up on my head, and then, by the servant's staircase, make my way to the scene below!

I, however, considered that I looked pale, although mature. I looked at least nineteen. So I went into Sis's room, which was full of evening wraps but empty, and put on a touch of rouge. With that and my eyebrows blackened, I would not have known myself, had I not been certain it was I and no other.

I then made my way down the back stairs.

Ah me, Dear Diary, was that but a few hours ago? Is it but a short time since Mr. Beresford was sitting at my feet, thinking me a debutante, and staring soulfully into my very heart? Is it but a matter of minutes since Leila found us there, and in a manner which revealed the true feeling she has for me, ordered me to go upstairs and take off Maddie Mackenzie's gown?

(Yes, it was not Leila's after all. I had forgotten that Maddie had taken her room. And except for pulling it somewhat at the waist, I am sure I did not hurt the old thing.)

I shall now go to bed and dream. Of which one I know not. My heart is full. Romance has come at last into my dull and dreary life. Below, the revelers have gone. The flowers hang their herbaceous heads. The music has flowed away into the river of the past. I am alone with my Heart.

JANUARY 14TH. How complicated my life grows, Dear Diary! How full and yet how incomplete! How everything begins and nothing ends!

HE is in town.

I discovered it at breakfast. I knew I was in for it, and I got down early, counting on mother breakfasting in bed. I would have felt better if father had been at home, because he understands somewhat the way they keep me down. But he was away about an order for shells (not sea; war), and

I was to bare my chiding alone. I had eaten my fruit and cereal, and was about to begin on sausage, when mother came in, having risen early from her slumbers to take the decorations to the hospital.

"So here you are, wretched child!" she said, giving me one of her coldest looks. "Barbara, I wonder if you ever think whither you are tending."

I ate a sausage.

What, Dear Diary, was there to say?

"To disobey!" she went on. "To force yourself on the attention of Mr. Beresford, in a borrowed dress, with your eyelashes blackened and your face painted — —"

"I should think, mother," I observed, "that if he wants to marry into this family, and is not merely being dragged into it, that he ought to see the worst at the start." She glared, without speaking. "You know," I continued, "it would be a dreadful thing to have the ceremony performed and everything too late to back out, and then have ME sprung on him. It wouldn't be honest, would it?"

"Barbara!" she said in a terrible tone. "First disobedience, and now sarcasm. If your father was only here! I feel so alone and helpless."

Her tone cut me to the heart. After all she was my own mother, or at least maintained so, in spite of numerous questions engendered by our lack of resemblance, moral as well as physical. But I did not offer to embarrass her, as she was at that moment poring out her tea. I hid my misery behind the morning paper, and there I beheld the fated vision. Had I felt any doubt as to the state of my affections it was settled then. My heart leaped in my bosom. My face suffused. My hands trembled so that a piece of sausage slipped from my fork. *His picture looked out at me with that well remembered gaze from the depths of the morning paper!*

Oh, Adrian, Adrian!

Here in the same city as I, looking out over perchance the same newspaper to perchance the same sun, wondering—ah, what was he wondering?

I was not even then, in that first rapture, foolish about him. I knew that to him I was probably but a tender memory. I knew, too, that he was but human and probably very conceited. On the other hand, I pride myself on being a good judge of character, and he carried nobility in every lineament. Even the obliteration of one eye by the printer could only hamper but not destroy his dear face.

"Barbara," mother said sharply. "I am speaking. Are you being sulky?"

"Pardon me, mother," I said in my gentlest tones. "I was but dreaming." And as she made no reply, but rang the bell viciously, I went on, pursuing my line of thought. "Mother, were you ever in love?"

"Love! What sort of love?"

I sat up and stared at her.

"Is there more than one sort?" I demanded.

"There is a very silly, schoolgirl love," she said, eying me, "that people outgrow and blush to look back on."

"Do you?"

"Do I what?"

"Do you blush to look back on it?"

Mother rose and made a sweeping gesture with her right arm.

"I wash my hands of you!" she said. "You are impertinent and indelicate. At your age I was an innocent child, not troubling with things that did not concern me. As for love, I had never heard of it until I came out."

"Life must have burst on you like an explosion," I observed. "I suppose you thought that babies — —"

"Silence!" mother shrieked. And seeing that she persisted in ignoring the real things of life while in my presence, I went out, clutching the precious paper to my heart.

JANUARY 15TH. I am alone in my boudoir (which is really the old schoolroom, and used now for a sewing room).

My very soul is sick, oh Diary. How can I face the truth? How write it out for my eyes to see? But I must. For something must be done! The play is failing.

The way I discovered it was this. Yesterday, being short of money, I sold my amethyst pin to Jane, one of the housemaids, for two dollars, throwing in a lace collar when she seemed doubtful, as I had a special purpose for using funds. Had father been at home I could have touched him, but mother is different.

I then went out to buy a frame for his picture, which I had repaired by drawing in the other eye, although lacking the fire and passionate look of the original. At the shop I was compelled to show it, to buy a frame to fit. The clerk was almost overpowered.

"Do you know him?" she asked, in a low and throbbing tone.

"Not intimately," I replied.

"Don't you love the Play?" she said. "I'm crazy about it. I've been back three times. Parts of it I know off by heart. He's very handsome. That picture don't do him justice."

I gave her a searching glance. Was it possible that, without any acquaintance with him whatever, she had fallen in love with him? It was indeed. She showed it in every line of her silly face.

I drew myself up haughtily. "I should think it would be very expensive, going so often," I said, in a cool tone.

"Not so very. You see, the play is a failure, and they give us girls tickets to dress the house. Fill it up, you know. Half the girls in the store are crazy about Mr. Egleston."

My world shuddered about me. What—fail! That beautiful play, ending "My darling, my woman"? It could not be. Fate would not be cruel. Was there no appreciation of the best in art? Was it indeed true, as Miss Everett has complained, although not in these exact words, that the Theater was only supported now by chorus girls' legs, dancing about in utter abandon?

With an expression of despair on my features, I left the store, carrying the frame under my arm.

One thing is certain. I must see the play again, and judge it with a critical eye. *IF IT IS WORTH SAVING, IT MUST BE SAVED.*

JANUARY 16TH. Is it only a day since I saw you, Dear Diary? Can so much have happened in the single lapse of a few hours? I look in my mirror, and I look much as before, only with perhaps a touch of pallor. Who would not be pale?

I have seen HIM again, and there is no longer any doubt in my heart. Page Beresford is attractive, and if it were not for circumstances as they are I would not answer for the consequences. But things ARE as they are. There is no changing that. And I have read my own heart.

I am not fickle. On the contrary, I am true as steal.

I have put his picture under my mattress, and have given Jane my gold cuff pins to say nothing when she makes my bed. And now, with the house full of people downstairs acting in a flippant and noisy manner, I shall record how it all happened.

My financial condition was not improved this morning, father having not returned. But I knew that I must see the play, as mentioned above, even if it became necessary to borrow from Hannah. At last, seeing no other way, I tried this, but failed.

"What for?" she said, in a suspicious way.

"I need it terribly, Hannah," I said.

"You'd ought to get it from your mother, then, Miss Barbara. The last time I gave you some you paid it back in postage stamps, and I haven't written a letter since. They're all stuck together now, and a total loss."

"Very well," I said, frigidly. "But the next time you break anything——"

"How much do you want?" she asked.

I took a quick look at her, and I saw at once that she had decided to lend it to me and then run and tell mother, beginning, "I think you'd ought to know, Mrs. Archibald——"

"Nothing doing, Hannah," I said, in a most dignified manner. "But I think you are an old clam, and I don't mind saying so."

I was now thrown on my own resources, and very bitter. I seemed to have no friends, at a time when I needed them most, when I was, as one may say, "standing with reluctant feet, where the brook and river meet."

Tonight I am no longer sick of life, as I was then. My throws of anguish have departed. But I was then utterly reckless, and even considered running away and going on the stage myself.

I have long desired a career for myself, anyhow. I have a good mind, and learn easily, and I am not a parasite. The idea of being such has always been repugnant to me, while the idea of a few dollars at a time doled out to one of independent mind is galling. And how is one to remember what one has done with one's allowance, when it is mostly eaten up by small loans, carfare, stamps, church collection, rose water and glycerin, and other mild cosmetics, and the additional food necessary when one is still growing?

— To resume, Dear Diary; having utterly failed with Hannah, and having shortly after met Sis on the stairs, I said to her, in a sisterly tone, intimate rather than fond:

"I daresay you can lend me five dollars for a day or so."

"I daresay I can. But I won't," was her cruel reply.

"Oh, very well," I said briefly. But I could not refrain from making a grimace at her back, and she saw me in a mirror.

"When I think," she said heartlessly, "that that wretched school may be closed for weeks, I could scream."

"Well, scream!" I replied. "You'll scream harder if I've brought the measles home on me. And if you're laid up, you can say good-bye to the dishonorable. You've got him tied, maybe," I remarked, "but not thrown as yet."

(A remark I had learned from one of the girls, Trudie Mills, who comes from Montana.)

I was therefore compelled to dispose of my silver napkin ring from school. Jane was bought up, she said, and I sold it to the cook for fifty cents and half a mince pie although baked with our own materials.

All my fate, therefore, hung on a paltry fifty cents.

I was torn with anxiety. Was it enough? Could I, for fifty cents, steal away from the sordid cares of life, and lose myself in obliviousness, gazing only it his dear face, listening to his dear and softly modulated voice, and wondering if, as his eyes swept the audience, they might perchance light on me and brighten with a momentary gleam in their unfathomable depths? Only this and nothing more, was my expectation.

How different was the reality!

Having ascertained that there was a matinee, I departed at an early hour after luncheon, wearing my blue velvet with my fox furs. White gloves and white topped shoes completed my outfit, and, my own chapeau showing the effect of a rainstorm on the way home from church while away at school, I took a chance on one of Sis's, a perfectly maddening one of rose-colored velvet. As the pink made me look pale, I added a touch of rouge.

I looked fully out, and indeed almost second season. I have a way of assuming a serious and mature manner, so that I am frequently taken for older than I really am. Then, taking a few roses left from the decorations, and thrusting them carelessly into the belt of my coat, I went out the back door, as Sis was getting ready for some girls to play bridge, in the front of the house.

Had I felt any grief at deceiving my family, the bridge party would have knocked them. For, as usual, I had not been asked, although playing a good game myself, and having on more than one occasion won most of the money in the Upper House at school.

I was early at the theater. No one was there, and women were going around taking covers off the seats. My fifty cents gave me a good seat, from which I opined, alas, that the shop girl had been right and business was rotten. But at last, after hours of waiting, the faint tuning of musical instruments was heard.

From that time I lived in a daze. I have never before felt so strange. I have known and respected the other sex, and indeed once or twice been kissed by it. But I had remained cold. My pulses had never fluttered. I was always concerned only with the fear that others had overseen and would perhaps tell. But now—I did not care who would see, if only Adrian would put his arms about me. Divine shamelessness! Brave Rapture! For if one who he could not possibly love, being so close to her in her make-up, if one who was indeed employed to be made love to, could submit in public to his embraces, why should not I, who would have died for him?

These were my thoughts as the play went on. The hours flew on joyous feet. When Adrian came to the footlights and looking apparently square at me, declaimed: "The world owes me a living. I will have it," I almost swooned. His clothes were worn. He looked hungry and gaunt. But how true that

"Rags are royal raiment, when worn for virtue's sake."

(I shall stop here and go down to the pantry. I could eat no dinner, being filled with emotion. But I must keep strong if I am to help Adrian in his trouble. The mince pie was excellent, but after all pastry does not take the place of solid food.)

LATER: I shall now go on with my recital. As the theater was almost empty, at the end of Act One I put on the pink hat and left it on as though absent-minded. There was no one behind me. And, although during act one I had thought that he perhaps felt my presence, he had not once looked directly at me.

But the hat captured his errant gaze, as one may say. And, after capture, it remained on my face, so much so that I flushed and a woman sitting near with a very plain girl in a skunk collar, observed:

"Really, it is outrageous."

Now came a moment which I thrill even to recollect. For Adrian plucked a pink rose from a vase—he was in the millionaire's house, and was starving in the midst of luxury—and held it to his lips.

The rose, not the house, of course. Looking over it, he smiled down at me.

LATER: It is midnight. I cannot sleep. Perchance he too, is lying awake. I am sitting at the window in my robe de nuit. Below, mother and Sis have just come in, and Smith has slammed the door of the car and gone back to the garage. How puny is the life my family leads! Nothing but eating and playing, with no higher thoughts.

A man has just gone by. For a moment I thought I recognized the footstep. But no, it was but the night watchman.

JANUARY 17TH. Father still away. No money, as mother absolutely refuses on account of Maddie Mackenzie's gown, which she had to send away to be repaired.

JANUARY 18TH. Father still away. The Hon. sent Sis a huge bunch of orchids today. She refused me even one. She is always tight with flowers and candy.

JANUARY 19TH. The paper says that Adrian's play is going to close the end of next week. No business. How can I endure to know that he is suffering, and that I cannot help, even to the extent of buying one ticket? Matinee today, and no money. Father still away.

I have tried to do a kind deed today, feeling that perhaps it would soften mother's heart and she would advance my allowance. I offered to manicure her nails for her, but she refused, saying that as Hannah had done it for many years, she guessed she could manage now.

JANUARY 20TH. Today I did a desperate thing, dear Diary.

"The desperate is the wisest course." Butler.

It is Sunday. I went to church, and thought things over. What a wonderful thing it would be if I could save the play! Why should I feel that my sex is a handicap?

The rector preached on "The Opportunities of Women." The Sermon gave me courage to go on. When he said, "Women today step in where men are afraid to tread, and bring success out of failure," I felt that it was meant for me.

Had no money for the plate, and mother attempted to smuggle a half dollar to me. I refused, however, as if I cannot give my own money to the heathen, I will give none. Mother turned pale, and the man with the plate gave me a black look. What can he know of my reasons?

Beresford lunched with us, and as I discouraged him entirely, he was very attentive to Sis. Mother is planing a big wedding, and I found Sis in the store room yesterday looking up mother's wedding veil.

No old stuff for me.

I guess Beresford is trying to forget that he kissed my hand the other night, for he called me "Little Miss Barbara" today, meaning little in the sense of young. I gave him a stern glance.

"I am not any littler than the other night," I observed.

"That was merely an affectionate diminutive," he said, looking uncomfortable.

"If you don't mind," I said coldly, "you might do as you have heretofore—reserve your affectionate advances until we are alone."

"Barbara!" mother said. And began quickly to talk about a Lady Something or other we'd met on a train in Switzerland. Because—they can talk until they are black in the face, dear Diary, but it is true we do not know any of the British Nobility, except the aforementioned and the man who comes once a year with flavoring extracts, who says he is the third son of a baronet.

Every one being out this afternoon, I suddenly had an inspiration, and sent for Carter Brooks. I then put my hair up and put on my blue silk, because while I do not believe in woman using her feminine charm when talking business, I do believe that she should look her best under any and all circumstances.

He was rather surprised not to find Sis in, as I had used her name in telephoning.

"I did it," I explained, "because I knew that you felt no interest in me, and I had to see you."

He looked at me, and said:

"I'm rather flabbergasted, Bab. I—what ought I to say, anyhow?"

He came very close, dear Diary, and suddenly I saw in his eyes the horrible truth. He thought me in love with him, and sending for him while the family was out.

Words cannot paint my agony of soul. I stepped back, but he seized my hand, in a caressing gesture.

"Bab!" he said. "Dear little Bab!"

Had my affections not been otherwise engaged, I should have thrilled at his accents. But, although handsome and of good family, though poor, I could not see it that way.

So I drew my hand away, and retreated behind a sofa.

"We must have an understanding, Carter" I Said. "I have sent for you, but not for the reason you seem to think. I am in desperate trouble."

He looked dumfounded.

"Trouble!" he said. "You! Why, little Bab"

"If you don't mind," I put in, rather pettishly, because of not being little, "I wish you would treat me like almost a debutante, if not entirely. I am not a child in arms."

"You are sweet enough to be, if the arms might be mine."

I have puzzled over this, since, dear Diary. Because there must be some reason why men fall in love with me. I am not ugly, but I am not beautiful, my nose being too short. And as for clothes, I get none except Leila's old things. But Jane Raleigh says there are women like that. She has a cousin who has had four husbands and is beginning on a fifth, although not pretty and very slovenly, but with a mass of red hair.

Are all men to be my lovers?

"Carter," I said earnestly, "I must tell you now that I do not care for you—in that way."

"What made you send for me, then?"

"Good gracious!" I exclaimed, losing my temper somewhat. "I can send for the ice man without his thinking I'm crazy about him, can't I?"

"Thanks."

"The truth is," I said, sitting down and motioning him to a seat in my maturest manner, "I—I want some money. There are many things, but the money comes first."

He just sat and looked at me with his mouth open.

"Well," he said at last, "of course—I suppose you know you've come to a Bank that's gone into the hands of a receiver. But aside from that, Bab, it's a pretty mean trick to send for me and let me think—well, no matter about that. How much do you want?"

"I can pay it back as soon as father comes home," I said, to relieve his mind. It is against my principals to borrow money, especially from one who has little or none. But since I was doing it, I felt I might as well ask for a lot.

"Could you let me have ten dollars?" I said, in a faint tone.

He drew a long breath.

"Well, I guess yes," he observed. "I thought you were going to touch me for a hundred, anyhow. I—I suppose you wouldn't give me a kiss and call it square."

I considered. Because after all, a kiss is not much, and ten dollars is a good deal. But at last my better nature won out.

"Certainly not," I said coldly. "And if there is a string to it I do not want it."

So he apologized, and came and sat beside me, without being a nuisance, and asked me what my other troubles were.

"Carter" I said, in a grave voice, "I know that you believe me young and incapable of affection. But you are wrong. I am of a most loving disposition."

"Now see here, Bab," he said. "Be fair. If I am not to hold your hand, or—or be what you call a nuisance, don't talk like this. I am but human," he said, "and there is something about you lately that—well, go on with your story. Only, as I say, don't try me to far."

"It's like this," I explained. "Girls think they are cold and distant, and indeed, frequently are."

"Frequently!"

"Until they meet the right one. Then they learn that their hearts are, as you say, but human."

"Bab," he said, suddenly turning and facing me, "an awful thought has come to me. You are in love—and not with me!"

"I am in love, and not with you," I said in tragic tones.

I had not thought he would feel it deeply—because of having been interested in Leila since they went out in their perambulators together. But I could see it was a shock to him. He got up and stood looking in the fire, and his shoulders shook with grief.

"So I have lost you," he said in a smothered voice. And then—"Who is the sneaking scoundrel?"

I forgave him this, because of his being upset, and in a rapt attitude I told him the whole story. He listened, as one in a daze.

"But I gather," he said, when at last the recital was over, "that you have never met the—met him."

"Not in the ordinary use of the word," I remarked. "But then it is not an ordinary situation. We have met and we have not. Our eyes have spoken, if not our vocal chords." Seeing his eyes on me I added, "if you do not believe that soul can cry unto soul, Carter, I shall go no further."

"Oh!" he exclaimed. "There is more, is there? I trust it is not painful, because I have stood as much as I can now without breaking down."

"Nothing of which I am ashamed," I said, rising to my full height. "I have come to you for help, Carter. That play must not fail!"

We faced each other over those vital words—faced, and found no solution.

"Is it a good play?" he asked, at last.

"It is a beautiful play. Oh, Carter, when at the end he takes his sweetheart in his arms—the leading lady, and not at all attractive. Jane Raleigh says that the star generally hates his leading lady—there is not a dry eye in the house."

"Must be a jolly little thing. Well, of course I'm no theatrical manager, but if it's any good there's only one way to save it. Advertise. I didn't know the piece was in town, which shows that the publicity has been rotten."

He began to walk the floor. I don't think I have mentioned it, but that is Carter's business. Not walking the floor. Advertising. Father says he is quite good, although only beginning.

"Tell me about it," he said.

So I told him that Adrian was a mill worker, and the villain makes him lose his position, by means of forgery. And Adrian goes to jail, and comes out, and no one will give him work. So he prepares to blow up a millionaire's house, and his sweetheart is in it. He has been to the millionaire for work and been refused and thrown out, saying, just before the butler and three footmen push him through a window, in dramatic tones, "The world owes me a living and I will have it."

"Socialism!" said Carter. "Hard stuff to handle for the two dollar seats. The world owes him a living. Humph! Still, that's a good line to work on. Look here, Bab, give me a little time on this, eh what? I may be able to think of a trick or two. But mind, not a word to any one."

He started out, but he came back.

"Look here," he said. "Where do we come in on this anyhow? Suppose I do think of something—what then? How are we to know that your beloved and his manager will thank us for butting in, or do what we suggest?"

Again I drew myself to my full height.

"I am a person of iron will when my mind is made up," I said. "You think of something, Carter, and I'll see that it is done."

He gazed at me in a rapt manner.

"Dammed if I don't believe you," he said.

It is now late at night. Beresford has gone. The house is still. I take the dear picture out from under my mattress and look at it.

Oh Adrien, my Thespian, my Love.

JANUARY 21ST. I have a bad cold, Dear Diary, and feel rotten. But only my physical condition is such. I am happy beyond words. This morning, while mother and Sis were out I called up the theater and inquired the price of a box. The man asked me to hold the line, and then came back and said it would be ten dollars. I told him to reserve it for Miss Putnam—my middle name.

I am both terrified and happy, dear Diary, as I lie here in bed with a hot water bottle at my feet. I have helped the play by buying a box, and tonight I shall sit in it alone, and he will perceive me there, and consider that I must be at least twenty, or I would not be there at the theater alone. Hannah has just come in and offered to lend me three dollars. I refused haughtily, but at last rang for her and took two. I might as well have a taxi tonight.

1 A. M. The family was there! I might have known it. Never do I have any luck. I am a broken thing, crushed to earth. But "Truth crushed to earth will rise again."—Whittier?

I had my dinner in bed, on account of my cold, and was let severely alone by the family. At seven I rose and with palpitating fingers dressed myself in my best evening frock, which is a pale yellow. I put my hair up, and was just finished, when mother knocked. It was terrible.

I had to duck back into bed and crush everything. But she only looked in and said to try and behave for the next three hours, and went away.

At a quarter to eight I left the house in a clandestine manner by means of the cellar and the area steps, and on the pavement drew a long breath. I was free, and I had twelve dollars.

Act One went well, and no disturbance. Although Adrian started when he saw me. The yellow looked very well.

I had expected to sit back, sheltered by the curtains, and only visible from the stage. I have often read of this method. But there were no curtains. I therefore sat, turning a stoney profile to the audience, and ignoring it, as though it were not present, trusting to luck that no one I knew was there.

He saw me. More than that, he hardly took his eyes from the box wherein I sat. I am sure to that he had mentioned me to the company, for one and all they stared at me until I think they will know me the next time they see me.

I still think I would not have been recognized by the family had I not, in a very quiet scene, commenced to sneeze. I did this several times, and a lot of people looked annoyed, as though I sneezed because I liked to sneeze.

And I looked back at them defiantly, and in so doing, encountered the gaze of my maternal parent.

Oh, Dear Diary, that I could have died at that moment, and thus, when stretched out a pathetic figure, with tuber roses and other flowers, have compelled their pity. But alas, no. I sneezed again!

Mother was wedged in, and I saw that my only hope was flight. I had not had more than between three and four dollars worth of the evening, but I glanced again and Sis was boring holes into me with her eyes. Only Beresford knew nothing, and was trying to hold Sis's hand under her opera cloak. Any fool could tell that.

But, as I was about to rise and stand poised, as one may say, for departure, I caught Adrian's eyes, with a gleam in their deep depths. He was, at the moment, toying with the bowl of roses. He took one out, and while the leading lady was talking, he edged his way toward my box. There, standing very close, apparently by accident, he dropped the rose into my lap.

Oh Diary! Diary!

I picked it up, and holding it close to me, I flew.

I am now in bed and rather chilly. Mother banged at the door some time ago, and at last went away, muttering.

I am afraid she is going to be pettish.

JANUARY 22ND. Father came home this morning, and things are looking up. Mother of course tackled him first thing, and when he came upstairs I expected an awful time. But my father is a real person, so he only sat down on the bed, and said:

"Well, chicken, so you're at it again!"

I had to smile, although my chin shook.

"You'd better turn me out and forget me," I said. "I was born for trouble. My advice to the family is to get out from under. That's all."

"Oh, I don't know," he said. "It's pretty convenient to have a family to drop on when the slump comes." He thumped himself on the chest. "A hundred and eighty pounds," he observed, "just intended for little daughters to fall back on when other things fail."

"Father," I inquired, putting my hand in his, because I had been bearing my burdens alone, and my strength was failing: "do you believe in Love?"

"DO I!"

"But I mean, not the ordinary attachment between two married people. I mean Love—the real thing."

"I see! Why, of course I do."

"Did you ever read Pope, father?"

"Pope? Why I—probably, chicken. Why?"

"Then you know what he says: 'Curse on all laws but those which Love has made.'"

"Look here," he said, suddenly laying a hand on my brow. "I believe you are feverish."

"Not feverish, but in trouble," I explained. And so I told him the story, not saying much of my deep passion for Adrian, but merely that I had formed an attachment for him which would persist during life. Although I had never yet exchanged a word with him.

Father listened and said it was indeed a sad story, and that he knew my deep nature, and that I would be true to the end. But he refused to give me any money, except enough to pay back Hannah and Carter Brooks, saying:

"Your mother does not wish you to go to the theater again, and who are we to go against her wishes? And anyhow, maybe if you met this fellow and talked to him, you would find him a disappointment. Many a pretty girl I have seen in my time, who didn't pan out according to specifications when I finally met her."

At this revelation of my beloved father's true self, I was almost stunned. It is evident that I do not inherit my being true as steel from him. Nor from my mother, who is like steel in hardness but not in being true to anything but social position.

As I record this awful day, dear Dairy, there comes again into my mind the thought that I DO NOT BELONG HERE. I am not like them. I do not even resemble them in features. And, if I belonged to them, would they not treat me with more consideration and less discipline? Who, in the family, has my nose?

It is all well enough for Hannah to observe that I was a pretty baby with fat cheeks. May not Hannah herself, for some hidden reason, have brought me here, taking away the real I to perhaps languish unseen and "waste my sweetness on the desert air"? But that way lies madness. Life must be made the best of as it is, and not as it might be or indeed ought to be.

Father promised before he left that I was not to be scolded, as I felt far from well, and was drinking water about every minute.

"I just want to lie here and think about things," I said, when he was going. "I seem to have so many thoughts. And father— —"

"Yes, chicken."

"If I need any help to carry out a plan I have, will you give it to me, or will I have to go to total strangers?"

"Good gracious, Bab!" he exclaimed. "Come to me, of course."

"And you'll do what you're told?"

He looked out into the hall to see if mother was near. Then, dear Dairy, he turned to me and said:

"I always have, Bab. I guess I'll run true to form."

JANUARY 23RD. Much better today. Out and around. Family (mother and Sis) very dignified and nothing much to say. Evidently have promised father to restrain themselves. Father rushed and not coming home to dinner.

Beresford on edge of proposing. Sis very jumpy.

LATER: Jane Raleigh is home for her cousin's wedding! Is coming over. We shall take a walk, as I have much to tell her.

6 P. M. What an afternoon! How shall I write it? This is a Milestone in my Life.

I have met him at last. Nay, more. I have been in his dressing room, conversing as though accustomed to such things all my life. I have concealed under the mattress a real photograph of him, beneath which he has written, "Yours always, Adrian Egleston."

I am writing in bed, as the room is chilly—or I am—and by putting out my hand I can touch his pictured likeness.

Jane came around for me this afternoon, and mother consented to a walk. I did not have a chance to take Sis's pink hat, as she keeps her door locked now when not in her room. Which is ridiculous, because I am not her type, and her things do not suit me very well anyhow. And I have never borrowed anything but gloves and handkerchiefs, except Maddie's dress and the hat.

She had, however, not locked her bathroom, and finding a bunch of violets in the washbowl I put them on. It does not hurt violets to wear them, and anyhow I knew Carter Brooks had sent them and she ought to wear only Beresford's flowers if she means to marry him.

Jane at once remarked that I looked changed.

"Naturally," I said, in a blase' manner.

"If I didn't know you, Bab," she observed, "I would say that you are rouged."

I became very stiff and distant at that. For Jane, although my best friend, had no right to be suspicious of me.

"How do I look changed?" I demanded.

"I don't know. You—Bab, I believe you are up to some mischief!"

"Mischief?"

"You don't need to pretend to me," she went on, looking into my very soul. "I have eyes. You're not decked out this way for ME."

I had meant to tell her nothing, but spying just then a man ahead who walked like Adrian, I was startled. I clutched her arm and closed my eyes.

"Bab!" she said.

The man turned, and I saw it was not he. I breathed again. But Jane was watching me, and I spoke out of an overflowing heart.

"For a moment I thought—Jane, I have met THE ONE at last."

"Barbara!" she said, and stopped dead. "Is it any one I know?"

"He is an actor."

"Ye gods!" said Jane, in a tense voice. "What a tragedy!"

"Tragedy indeed," I was compelled to admit. "Jane, my heart is breaking. I am not allowed to see him. It is all off, forever."

"Darling!" said Jane. "You are trembling all over. Hold on to me. Do they disapprove?"

"I am never to see him again. Never."

The bitterness of it all overcame me. My eyes suffused with tears.

But I told her, in broken accents, of my determination to stick to him, no matter what. "I might never be Mrs. Adrian Egleston, but——"

"Adrian Egleston!" she cried, in amazement. "Why Barbara, you lucky thing!"

So, finding her fuller of sympathy than usual, I violated my vow of silence and told her all.

And, to prove the truth of what I said, I showed her the sachet over my heart containing his rose.

"It's perfectly wonderful," Jane said, in an awed tone. "You beat anything I've ever known for adventures! You are the type men like, for one thing. But there is one thing I could not stand, in your place—having to know that he is making love to the heroine every evening and twice on Wednesdays and—Bab, this is Wednesday!"

I glanced at my wrist watch. It was but two o'clock. Instantly, dear Dairy, I became conscious of a dual going on within me, between love and duty. Should I do as instructed and see him no more, thus crushing my inclination under the iron heel of resolution? Or should I cast my parents to the winds, and go?

Which?

At last I decided to leave it to Jane. I observed: "I'm forbidden to try to see him. But I daresay, if you bought some theater tickets and did not say what the play was, and we went and it happened to be his, it would not be my fault, would it?"

I cannot recall her reply, or much more, except that I waited in a pharmacy, and Jane went out, and came back and took me by the arm.

"We're going to the matinee, Bab," she said. "I'll not tell you which one, because it's to be a surprise." She squeezed my arm. "First row," she whispered.

I shall draw a veil over my feelings. Jane bought some chocolates to take along, but I could eat none. I was thirsty, but not hungry. And my cold was pretty bad, to.

So we went in, and the curtain went up. When Adrian saw me, in the front row, he smiled although in the midst of a serious speech about the world owing him a living. And Jane was terribly excited.

"Isn't he the handsomest thing!" she said. "And oh, Bab, I can see that he adores you. He is acting for you. All the rest of the people mean nothing to him. He sees but you."

Well, I had not told her that we had not yet met, and she said I could do nothing less than send him a note.

"You ought to tell him that you are true, in spite of everything," she said.

If I had not deceived Jane things would be better. But she was set on my sending the note. So at last I wrote one on my visiting card, holding it so she could not read it. Jane is my best friend and I am devoted to her, but she has no scruples about reading what is not meant for her. I said:

"Dear Mr. Egleston: I think the play is perfectly wonderful. And you are perfectly splendid in it. It is perfectly terrible that it is going to stop.

"(Signed) The girl of the rose."

I know that this seems bold. But I did not feel bold, dear Dairy. It was such a letter as any one might read, and contained nothing compromising. Still, I daresay I should not have written it. But "out of the fulness of the heart the mouth speaketh."

I was shaking so much that I could not give it to the usher. But Jane did. However, I had sealed it up in an envelope.

Now comes the real surprise, dear Dairy. For the usher came down and said Mr. Egleston hoped I would go back and see him after the act was over. I think a pallor must have come over me, and Jane said:

"Bab! Do you dare?"

I said yes, I dared, but that I would like a glass of water. I seemed to be thirsty all the time. So she got it, and I recovered my savoir fair, and stopped shaking.

I suppose Jane expected to go along, but I refrained from asking her. She then said:

"Try to remember everything he says, Bab. I am just crazy about it."

Ah, dear Dairy, how can I write how I felt when being led to him. The entire scene is engraved on my soul. I, with my very heart in my eyes, in spite of my efforts to seem cool and collected. He, in front of his mirror, drawing in the lines of starvation around his mouth for the next scene, while on his poor feet a valet put the raged shoes of Act II!

He rose when I entered, and took me by the hand.

"Well!" he said. "At last!"

He did not seem to mind the valet, whom he treated like a chair or table. And he held my hand and looked deep into my eyes.

Ah, dear Dairy, Men may come and Men may go in my life, but never again will I know such ecstasy as at that moment.

"Sit down," he said. "Little Lady of the rose—but it's violets today, isn't it? And so you like the play?"

I was by that time somewhat calmer, but glad to sit down, owing to my knees feeling queer.

"I think it is magnificent," I said.

"I wish there were more like you," he observed. "Just a moment, I have to make a change here. No need to go out. There's a screen for that very purpose."

He went behind the screen, and the man handed him a raged shirt over the top of it, while I sat in a chair and dreamed. What I reflected, would the School say if it but knew! I felt no remorse. I was there, and beyond the screen, changing into the garments of penury, was the only member of the other sex I had ever felt I could truly care for.

Dear Dairy, I am tired and my head aches. I cannot write it all. He was perfectly respectful, and only his eyes showed his true feelings. The woman who is the adventuress in the play came to the door, but he motioned her away with a wave of the hand. And at last it was over, and he was asking me to come again soon, and if I would care to have one of his pictures.

I am very sleepy tonight, but I cannot close this record of a w-o-n-d-e-r-f-u-l d-a-y——

JANUARY 24TH. Cold worse.

Not hearing from Carter Brooks I telephoned him just now. He is sore about Beresford and said he would not come to the house. So I have asked him to meet me in the park, and said that there were only two more days, this being Thursday.

LATER: I have seen Carter, and he has a fine plan. If only father will do it.

He says the theme is that the world owes Adrian a living, and that the way to do is to put that strongly before the people.

"Suppose," he said, "that this fellow would go to some big factory, and demand work. Not ask for it. Demand it. He could pretend to be starving and say: 'The world owes me a living, and I intend to have it.'"

"But suppose they were sorry for him and gave it to him?" I observed.

"Tut, child," he said. "That would have to be all fixed up first. It ought to be arranged that he not only be refused, but what's more, that he'll be thrown out. He'll have to cut up a lot, d'you see, so they'll throw him out. And we'll have Reporters there, so the story can get around. You get it, don't you? Your friend, in order to prove that the idea of the play is right, goes out for a job, and proves that he cannot demand labor and get it." He stopped and spoke with excitement: "Is he a real sport? Would he stand being arrested? Because that would cinch it."

But here I drew a line. I would not subject him to such humiliation. I would not have him arrested. And at last Carter gave in.

"But you get the idea," he said. "There'll be the deuce of a row, and it's good for a half column on the first page of the evening papers. Result, a jam that night at the performance, and a new lease of life for the Play. Egleston comes on, bruised and battered, and perhaps with a limp. The Labor Unions take up the matter—it's a knock out. I'd charge a thousand dollars for that idea if I were selling it."

"Bruised!" I exclaimed. "Really bruised or painted on?"

He glared at me impatiently.

"Now see here, Bab," he said. "I'm doing this for you. You've got to play up. And if your young man won't stand a bang in the eye, for instance, to earn his bread and butter, he's not worth saving."

"Who are you going to get to—to throw him out?" I asked, in a faltering tone.

He stopped and stared at me.

"I like that!" he said. "It's not my play that's failing, is it? Go and tell him the scheme, and then let his manager work it out. And tell him who I am, and that I have a lot of ideas, but this is the only one I'm giving away."

We had arrived at the house by that time and I invited him to come in. But he only glanced bitterly at the windows and observed that they had taken in the mat with 'Welcome' on it, as far as he was concerned. And went away.

Although we have never had a mat with 'Welcome' on it.

Dear Diary, I wonder if father would do it? He is gentle and kindhearted, and it would be painful to him. But to who else can I turn in my extremity?

I have but one hope. My father is like me. He can be coaxed and if kindly treated will do anything. But if approached in the wrong way, or asked to do something against his principals, he becomes a roaring lion.

He would never be bully-ed into giving a man work, even so touching a personality as Adrian's.

LATER: I meant to ask father tonight, but he has just heard of Beresford and is in a terrible temper. He says Sis can't marry him, because he is sure there are plenty of things he could be doing in England, if not actually fighting.

"He could probably run a bus, and release some one who can fight," he shouted. "Or he could at least do an honest day's work with his hands. Don't let me see him, that's all."

"Do I understand that you forbid him the house?" Leila asked, in a cold fury.

"Just keep him out of my sight," father snapped. "I suppose I can't keep him from swilling tea while I am away doing my part to help the Allies."

"Oh, rot!" said Sis, in a scornful manner. "While you help your bank account, you mean. I don't object to that, father, but for heaven's sake don't put it on altruistic grounds."

She went upstairs then and banged her door, and mother merely set her lips and said nothing. But when Beresford called, later, Tanney had to tell him the family was out.

Were it not for our affections, and the necessity for getting married, so there would be an increase in the population, how happy we could all be!

LATER: I have seen father.

It was a painful evening, with Sis shut away in her room, and father cutting the ends off cigars in a viscious manner. Mother was NON EST, and had I not had my memories, it would have been a sickning time.

I sat very still and waited until father softened, which he usually does, like ice cream, all at once and all over. I sat perfectly still in a large chair, and except for an occasional sneeze, was quiet.

Only once did my parent address me in an hour, when he said:

"What the devil's making you sneeze so?"

"My nose, I think, sir," I said meekly.

"Humph!" he said. "It's rather a small nose to be making such a racket."

I was cut to the heart, Dear Diary. One of my dearest dreams has always been a delicate nose, slightly arched and long enough to be truly aristocratic. Not really acqualine but on the verge. I HATE my little nose—hate it—hate it—HATE IT.

"Father" I said, rising and on the point of tears. "How can you! To taunt me with what is not my own fault, but partly hereditary and partly carelessness. For if you had pinched it in infancy it would have been a good nose, and not a pug. And——"

"Good gracious!" he exclaimed. "Why, Bab, I never meant to insult your nose. As a matter of fact, it's a good nose. It's exactly the sort of nose you ought to have. Why, what in the world would YOU do with a Roman nose?"

I have not been feeling very well, dear Diary, and so I suddenly began to weep.

"Why, chicken!" said my father. And made me sit down on his knee. "Don't tell me that my bit of sunshine is behind a cloud!"

"Behind a nose," I said, feebly.

So he said he liked my nose, even although somewhat swollen, and he kissed it, and told me I was a little fool, and at last I saw he was about ready to be tackled. So I observed:

"Father, will you do me a favor?"

"Sure," he said. "How much do you need? Business is pretty good now, and I've about landed the new order for shells for the English War Department. I—suppose we make it fifty! Although, we'd better keep it a secret between the two of us."

I drew myself up, although tempted. But what was fifty dollars to doing something for Adrian? A mere bagatelle.

"Father," I said, "do you know Miss Everett, my English teacher?"

He remembered the name.

"Would you be willing to do her a great favor?" I demanded intensely.

"What sort of a favor?"

"Her cousin has written a play. She is very fond of her cousin, and anxious to have him succeed. And it is a lovely play."

He held me off and stared at me.

"So THAT is what you were doing in that box alone!" he exclaimed. "You incomprehensible child! Why didn't you tell your mother?"

"Mother does not always understand," I said, in a low voice. "I thought, by buying a box, I would do my part to help Miss Everett's cousin's play succeed. And as a result I was dragged home, and shamefully treated in the most mortifying manner. But I am accustomed to brutality."

"Oh, come now," he said. "I wouldn't go as far as that, chicken. Well, I won't finance the play, but short of that I'll do what I can."

However he was not so agreeable when I told him Carter Brooks' plan. He delivered a firm no.

"Although," he said, "somebody ought to do it, and show the fallacy of the play. In the first place, the world doesn't owe the fellow a living, unless he will hustle around and make it. In the second place an employer has a right to turn away a man he doesn't want. No one can force a business to employ Labor."

"Well," I said, "as long as Labor talks and makes a lot of noise, and Capitol is too dignified to say anything, most people are going to side with Labor."

He gazed at me.

"Right!" he said. "You've put your finger on it, in true feminine fashion."

"Then why won't you throw out this man when he comes to you for work? He intends to force you to employ him."

"Oh, he does, does he?" said father, in a fierce voice. "Well, let him come. I can stand up for my principals, too. I'll throw him out, all right."

Dear Diary, the battle is over and I have won. I am very happy. How true it is that strategy will do more than violence!

We have arranged it all. Adrian is to go to the mill, dressed like a decayed gentleman, and father will refuse to give him work. I have said nothing about violence, leaving that to arrange itself.

I must see Adrian and his manager. Carter has promised to tell some reporters that there may be a story at the mill on Saturday morning. I am to excited to sleep.

Feel horrid. Forbidden to go out this morning.

JANUARY 25TH. Beresford was here to lunch and he and mother and Sis had a long talk. He says he has kept it a secret because he did not want his business known. But he is here to place a shell order for the English War Department.

"Well," Leila said, "I can hardly wait to tell father and see him curl up."

"No, no," said Beresford, hastily. "Really you must allow me. I must inform him myself. I am sure you can see why. This is a thing for men to settle. Besides, it is a delicate matter. Mr. Archibald is trying to get the order, and our New York office, if I am willing, is ready to place it with him."

"Well!" said Leila, in a thunderstruck tone. "If you British don't beat anything for keeping your own Counsel!"

I could see that he had her hand under the table. It was sickening.

Jane came to see me after lunch. The wedding was that night, and I had to sit through silver vegetable dishes, and after-dinner coffee sets and plates and a grand piano and a set of gold vases and a cabushion sapphire and the bridesmaid's clothes and the wedding supper and heaven knows what. But at last she said:

"You dear thing—how weary and wan you look!"

I closed my eyes.

"But you don't intend to give him up, do you?"

"Look at me!" I said, in imperious tones. "Do I look like one who would give him up, because of family objections?"

"How brave you are!" she observed. "Bab, I am green with envy. When I think of the way he looked at you, and the tones of his voice when he made love to that—that creature, I am positively SHAKEN."

We sat in somber silence. Then she said:

"I daresay he detests the heroine, doesn't he?"

"He tolerates her," I said, with a shrug.

More silence. I rang for Hannah to bring some ice water. We were in my boudoir.

"I saw him yesterday," said Jane, when Hannah had gone.

"Jane!"

"In the park. He was with the woman that plays the Adventuress. Ugly old thing."

I drew a long breath of relief. For I knew that the adventuress was at least thirty and perhaps more. Besides being both wicked and cruel, and not at all feminine.

Hannah brought the ice-water and then came in the most maddening way and put her hand on my forehead.

"I've done nothing but bring you ice-water for two days," she said. "Your head's hot. I think you need a mustard foot bath and to go to bed."

"Hannah," Jane said, in her loftiest fashion, "Miss Barbara is worried, not ill. And please close the door when you go out."

Which was her way of telling Hannah to go. Hannah glared at her.

"If you take my advice, Miss Jane," she said. "You'll keep away from Miss Barbara."

And she went out, slamming the door.

"Well!" gasped Jane. "Such impertinence. Old servant or not, she ought to have her mouth slapped."

Well, I told Jane the plan and she was perfectly crazy about it. I had a headache, but she helped me into my street things, and got Sis's rose hat for me while Sis was at the telephone. Then we went out.

First we telephoned Carter Brooks, and he said tomorrow morning would do, and he'd give a couple of reporters the word to hang around father's office at the mill. He said to have Adrian there at ten o'clock.

"Are you sure your father will do it?" he asked. "We don't want a fliver, you know."

"He's making a principal of it," I said. "When he makes a principal of a thing, he does it."

"Good for father!" Carter said. "Tell him not to be to gentle. And tell your actor-friend to make a lot of fuss. The more the better. I'll see the policeman at the mill, and he'll probably take him up. But we'll get him out for the matinee. And watch the evening papers."

It was then that a terrible thought struck me. What if Adrian considered it beneath his profession to advertize, even if indirectly? What if he preferred the failure of Miss Everett's cousin's play to a bruise on the eye? What, in short, if he refused?

Dear Dairy, I was stupified. I knew not which way to turn. For men are not like women, who are dependable and anxious to get along, and will sacrifice anything for success. No, men are likely to turn on the ones they love best, if the smallest things do not suit them, such as cold soup, or sleeves too long from the shirt-maker, or plans made which they have not been consulted about beforehand.

"Darling!" said Jane, as I turned away, "you look STRICKEN!"

"My head aches," I said, with a weary gesture toward my forehead. It did ache, for that matter. It is aching now, dear Dairy.

However, I had begun my task and must go through with it. Abandoning Jane at a corner, in spite of her calling me cruel and even sneaking, I went to Adrian's hotel, which I had learned of during my seance in his room while he was changing his garments behind a screen, as it was marked on a dressing case.

It was then five o'clock.

How nervous I felt as I sent up my name to his chamber. Oh, Dear Diary, to think that it was but five hours ago that I sat and waited, while people who guessed not the inner trepidation of my heart past and repast, and glanced at me and at Leila's pink hat above.

At last he came. My heart beat thunderously, as he approached, striding along in that familiar walk, swinging his strong and tender arms. And I! I beheld him coming and could think of not a word to say.

"Well!" he said, pausing in front of me. "I knew I was going to be lucky today. Friday is my best day."

"I was born on Friday," I said. I could think of nothing else.

"Didn't I say it was my lucky day? But you mustn't sit here. What do you say to a cup of tea in the restaurant?"

How grown up and like a debutante I felt, Dear Diary, going to have tea as if I had it every day at school, with a handsome actor across! Although somewhat uneasy also, owing to the possibility of the family coming in. But it did not and I had a truly happy hour, not at all spoiled by looking out the window and seeing Jane going by, with her eyes popping out, and walking very slowly so I would invite her to come in.

WHICH I DID NOT.

Dear Diary, HE WILL DO IT. At first he did not understand, and looked astounded. But when I told him of Carter being in the advertizing business, and father owning a large mill, and that there would be reporters and so on, he became thoughtful.

"It's really incredibly clever," he said. "And if it's pulled off right it ought to be a stampede. But I'd like to see Mr. Brooks. We can't have it fail, you know." He leaned over the table. "It's straight goods, is it, Miss er—Barbara? There's nothing phoney about it?"

"Phoney!" I said, drawing back. "Certainly not."

He kept on leaning over the table.

"I wonder," he said, "what makes you so interested in the play?"

Oh, Diary, Diary!

And just then I looked up, and the adventuress was staring in the door at me with the meanest look on her face.

I draw a veil over the remainder of our happy hour. Suffice it to say that he considers me exactly the type he finds most attractive, and that he does not consider my nose too short. We had a long dispute about this. He thinks I am wrong and says I am not an aquiline type. He says I am romantic and of a loving disposition. Also somewhat reckless, and he gave me good advice about doing what my family consider for my good, at least until I come out.

But our talk was all too short, for a fat man with three rings on came in, and sat down with us, and ordered a whiskey and soda. My blood turned cold, for fear some one I knew would come in and see me sitting there in a drinking party.

And my blood was right to turn cold. For, just as he had told the manager about the arrangement I had made, and the manager said "Bully" and raised his glass to drink to me I looked across and there was mother's aunt, old Susan Paget, sitting near, with the most awful face I ever saw!

I collapsed in my chair.

Dear Diary, I only remember saying, "Well, remember, ten o'clock. And dress up like a gentleman in hard luck," and his saying: "Well, I hope I'm a gentleman, and the hard luck's no joke," and then I went away.

And now, Dear Diary, I am in bed, and every time the telephone rings I have a chill. And in between times I drink ice-water and sneeze. How terrible a thing is love.

LATER: I can hardly write. Switzerland is a settled thing. Father is not home tonight and I cannot appeal to him. Susan Paget said I was drinking too, and mother is having the vibrator used on her spine. If I felt better I would run away.

JANUARY 26TH. How can I write what has happened? It is so terrible.

Beresford went at ten o'clock to ask for Leila, and did not send in his card for fear father would refuse to see him. And father thought, from his saying that he had come to ask for something, and so on, that it was Adrian, and threw him out. He ordered him out first, and Beresford refused to go, and they had words, and then there was a fight. The reporters got it, and it is in all the papers. Hannah has just brought one in. It is headed "Manufacturer assaults Peer." Leila is in bed, and the doctor is with her.

LATER: Adrian has disappeared. The manager has just called up, and with shaking knees I went to the telephone. Adrian went to the mill a little after ten, and has not been seen since.

It is in vain I protest that he has not eloped with me. It is almost time now for the matinee and no Adrian. What shall I do?

SATURDAY, 11 P.M. Dear Diary, I have the measles. I am all broken out, and look horrible. But what is a sickness of the body compared to the agony of my mind? Oh, Dear Diary, to think of what has happened since last I saw your stainless pages!

What is a sickness to a broken heart? And to a heart broken while trying to help another who did not deserve to be helped. But if he deceived me, he has paid for it, and did until he was rescued at ten o'clock tonight.

I have been given a sleeping medicine, and until it takes affect I shall write out the tragedy of this day, omitting nothing. The trained nurse is asleep on a cot, and her cap is hanging on the foot of the bed.

I have tried it on, Dear Diary, and it is very becoming. If they insist on Switzerland I think I shall run away and be a trained nurse. It is easy work, although sleeping on a cot is not always comfortable. But at least a trained nurse leads her own life and is not bullied by her family. And more, she does good constantly.

I feel tonight that I should like to do good, and help the sick, and perhaps go to the front. I know a lot of college men in the American Ambulance.

I shall never go on the stage, Dear Diary. I know now its deceitfulness and vicissitudes. My heart has bled until it can bleed no more, as a result of a theatrical Adonis. I am through with the theater forever.

I shall begin at the beginning. I left off where Adrian had disappeared.

Although feeling very strange, and looking a queer red color in my mirror, I rose and dressed myself. I felt that something had slipped, and I must find Adrian. (It is strange with what coldness I write that once beloved name.)

While dressing I perceived that my chest and arms were covered with small red dots, but I had no time to think of myself. I slipped downstairs and outside the drawing room I heard mother conversing in a loud and angry tone with a visitor. I glanced in, and ye gods!

It was the adventuress.

Drawing somewhat back, I listened. Oh, Diary, what a revelation!

"But I MUST see her," she was saying. "Time is flying. In a half hour the performance begins, and—he cannot be found."

"I can't understand," mother said, in a stiff manner. "What can my daughter Barbara know about him?"

The adventuress sniffed. "Humph!" she said. "She knows, alright. And I'd like to see her in a hurry, if she is in the house."

"Certainly she is in the house," said mother.

"ARE YOU SURE OF THAT? Because I have every reason to believe she has run away with him. She has been hanging around him all week, and only yesterday afternoon I found them together. She had some sort of a scheme, he said afterwards, and he wrinkled a coat under his mattress last night. He said it was to look as if he had slept in it. I know nothing further of your daughter's scheme. But I know he went out to meet her. He has not been seen since. His manager has hunted for to hours."

"Just a moment," said mother, in a frigid tone. "Am I to understand that this—this Mr. Egleston is——"

"He is my Husband."

Ah, Dear Diary, that I might then and there have passed away. But I did not. I stood there, with my heart crushed, until I felt strong enough to escape. Then I fled, like a guilty soul. It was ghastly.

On the doorstep I met Jane. She gazed at me strangely when she saw my face, and then clutched me by the arm.

"Bab!" she cried. "What on the earth is the matter with your complexion?"

But I was desperate.

"Let me go!" I said. "Only lend me two dollars for a taxi and let me go. Something horrible has happened."

She gave me ninety cents, which was all she had, and I rushed down the street, followed by her piercing gaze.

Although realizing that my life, at least the part of it pertaining to sentiment, was over, I knew that, single or married, I must find him. I could not bare to think that I, in my desire to help, had ruined Miss Everett's cousin's play. Luckily I got a taxi at the corner, and I ordered it to drive to the mill. I sank back, bathed in hot perspiration, and on consulting my bracelet watch found I had but twenty five minutes until the curtain went up.

I must find him, but where and how! I confess for a moment that I doubted my own father, who can be very fierce on occasion. What if, maddened by his mistake about Beresford, he had, on being approached by Adrian, been driven to violence? What if, in my endeavor to help one who was unworthy, I had led my poor paternal parent into crime?

Hell is paved with good intentions. SAMUEL JOHNSTON.

On driving madly into the mill yard, I suddenly remembered that it was Saturday and a half holiday. The mill was going, but the offices were closed. Father, then, was immured in the safety of his club, and could not be reached except by pay telephone. And the taxi was now ninety cents.

I got out, and paid the man. I felt very dizzy and queer, and was very thirsty, so I went to the hydrant in the yard and got a drink of water. I did not as yet suspect measles, but laid it all to my agony of mind.

Having thus refreshed myself, I looked about, and saw the yard policeman, a new one who did not know me, as I am away at school most of the time, and the family is not expected to visit the mill, because of dirt and possible accidents.

I approached him, however, and he stood still and stared at me.

"Officer" I said, in my most dignified tones. "I am looking for a—for a gentleman who came here this morning to look for work."

"There was about two hundred lined up here this morning, Miss," he said. "Which one would it be, now?"

How my heart sank!

"About what time would he be coming?" he said. "Things have been kind of mixed-up around here today, owing to a little trouble this morning. But perhaps I'll remember him."

But, although Adrian is of an unusual type, I felt that I could not describe him, besides having a terrible headache. So I asked if he would lend me carfare, which he did with a strange look.

"You're not feeling sick, Miss, are you?" he said. But I could not stay to converse, as it was then time for the curtain to go up, and still no Adrian.

I had but one refuge in mind, Carter Brooks, and to him I fled on the wings of misery in the street car. I burst into his advertizing office like a fury.

"Where is he?" I demanded. "Where have you and your plotting hidden him?"

"Who? Beresford?" he asked in a placid manner. "He is at his hotel, I believe, putting beefsteak on a bad eye. Believe me, Bab——"

"Beresford!" I cried, in scorn and wretchedness. "What is he to me? Or his eye either? I refer to Mr. Egleston. It is time for the curtain to go up now, and unless he has by this time returned, there can be no performance."

"Look here," Carter said suddenly, "you look awfully queer, Bab. Your face——"

I stamped my foot.

"What does my face matter?" I demanded. "I no longer care for him, but I have ruined Miss Everett's cousin's play unless he turns up. Am I to be sent to Switzerland with that on my soul?"

"Switzerland!" he said slowly. "Why, Bab, they're not going to do that, are they? I—I don't want you so far away."

Dear Dairy, I am unsuspicious by nature, believing all mankind to be my friends until proven otherwise. But there was a gloating look in Carter Brooks' eyes as they turned on me.

"Carter!" I said, "you know where he is and you will not tell me. You WISH to ruin him."

I was about to put my hand on his arm, but he drew away.

"Look here," he said. "I'll tell you something, but please keep back. Because you look like smallpox to me. I was at the mill this morning. I do not know anything about your actor-friend. He's probably only been run over or something. But I saw Beresford going in, and I—well, I suggested that he'd better walk in on your father or he wouldn't get in. It worked, Bab. HOW IT DID WORK! He went in and said he had come to ask your father for something, and your father blew up by saying that he knew about it, but that the world only owed a living to the man who would hustle for it, and that he would not be forced to take any one he did not want.

"And in two minutes Beresford hit him, and got a response. It was a million dollars worth."

So he babbled on. But what were his words to me?

Dear Diary, I gave no thought to the smallpox he had mentioned, although fatal to the complexion. Or to the fight at the mill. I heard only Adrian's possible tragic fate. Suddenly I collapsed, and asked for a drink of water, feeling horrible, very wobbly and unable to keep my knees from bending.

And the next thing I remember is father taking me home, and Adrian's fate still a deep mystery, and remaining such, while I had a warm sponge to bring out the rest of the rash, followed by a sleep—it being measles and not smallpox.

Oh, Dear Diary, what a story I learned when having wakened and feeling better, my father came tonight and talked to me from the doorway, not being allowed in.

Adrian had gone to the mill, and father, having thrown Beresford out and asserted his principals, had not thrown him out, BUT HAD GIVEN HIM A JOB IN THE MILL. And the Policeman had given him no chance to escape, which he attempted. He was dragged to the shell plant and there locked in, because of spies. The plant is under military guard.

And there he had been compelled to drag a wheelbarrow back and forth containing charcoal for a small furnace, for hours!

Even when Carter found him he could not be released, as father was in hiding from reporters, and would not go to the telephone or see callers.

He labored until 10 p.m., while the theater remained dark, and people got their money back.

I have ruined him. I have also ruined Miss Everett's cousin.

The nurse is still asleep. I think I will enter a hospital. My career is ended, my life is blasted.

I reach under the mattress and draw out the picture of him who today I have ruined, compelling him to do manual labor for hours, although unaccustomed to it. He is a great actor, and I believe has a future. But my love for him is dead. Dear Diary, he deceived me, and that is one thing I cannot forgive.

So now I sit here among my pillows, while the nurse sleeps, and I reflect about many things. But one speech rings in my ears over and over.

Carter Brooks, on learning about Switzerland, said it in a strange manner, looking at me with inscrutable eyes.

"Switzerland! Why, Bab—I don't want you to go so far away."

WHAT DID HE MEAN BY IT?

Dear Dairy, you will have to be burned, I daresay. Perhaps it is as well. I have p o r e d out my H-e-a-r-t——

CHAPTER IV
BAB'S BURGLAR

I

"MONEY is the root of all Evil."

I do not know who said the above famous words, but they are true. I know it but to well. For had I never gone on an Allowence, and been in debt and always worried about the way silk stockings wear out, et cetera, I would be having a much better time. For who can realy enjoy a dress when it is not paid for or only partialy so?

I have decided to write out this story, which is true in every particuler, except here and there the exact words of conversation, and then sell it to a Magazine. I intend to do this for to reasons. First, because I am in Debt, especialy for to tires, and second, because parents will then read it, and learn that it is not possable to make a good appearence, including furs, theater tickets and underwear, for a Thousand Dollars a year, even if one wears plain uncouth things beneath. I think this, too. My mother does not know how much clothes and other things, such as manacuring, cost these days. She merely charges things and my father gets the bills. Nor do I consider it fair to expect me to atend Social Functions and present a good appearence on a small Allowence, when I would often prefer a simple game of tennis or to lie in a hammick, or to converce with some one I am interested in, of the Other Sex.

It was mother who said a Thousand dollars a year and no extras. But I must confess that to me, after ten dollars a month at school, it seemed a large sum. I had but just returned for the summer holadays, and the Familey was having a counsel about me. They always have a counsel when I come home, and mother makes a list, begining with the Dentist.

"I should make it a Thousand," she said to father. "The child is in shameful condition. She is never still, and she fidgits right through her clothes."

"Very well," said father, and got his Check Book. "That is $83.33-1/3 cents a month. Make it thirty four cents. But no bills, Barbara."

"And no extras," my mother observed, in a stern tone.

"Candy, tennis balls and matinee tickets?" I asked.

"All included," said father. "And Church collection also, and ice cream and taxicabs and Xmas gifts."

Although pretending to consider it small, I realy felt that it was a large amount, and I was filled with joy when father ordered a Check Book for me with my name on each Check. Ah, me! How happy I was!

I was two months younger then and possably childish in some ways. For I remember that in my exhiliration I called up Jane Raleigh the moment she got home. She came over, and I showed her the book.

"Bab!" she said. "A thousand dollars! Why, it is wealth."

"It's not princly," I observed. "But it will do, Jane."

We then went out and took a walk, and I treated her to a Facial Masage, having one myself at the same time, having never been able to aford it before.

"It's Heavenley, Bab," Jane observed to me, through a hot towle. "If I were you I should have one daily. Because after all, what are features if the skin is poor?"

We also had manacures, and as the young person was very nice, I gave her a dollar. As I remarked to Jane, it had taken all the lines out of my face, due to the Spring Term and examinations. And as I put on my hat, I could see that it had done somthing else. For the first time my face showed Character. I looked mature, if not, indeed, even more.

I paid by a Check, although they did not care about taking it, prefering cash. But on calling up the Bank accepted it, and also another check for cold cream, and a fancy comb.

I had, as I have stated, just returned from my Institution of Learning, and now, as Jane and I proceded to a tea place I had often viewed with hungry eyes but no money to spend, it being expencive, I suddenly said:

"Jane, do you ever think how ungrateful we are to those who cherish us through the school year and who, although stern at times, are realy our Best Friends?"

"Cherish us!" said Jane. "I haven't noticed any cherishing. They tolarate me, and hardly that."

"I fear you are pessamistic," I said, reproving her but mildly, for Jane's school is well known to be harsh and uncompromizing. "However, my own feelings to my Instructers are diferent and quite friendly, especialy at a distance. I shall send them flowers."

It was rather awful, however, after I had got inside the shop, to find that violets, which I had set my heart on as being the school flour, were five dollars a hundred. Also there were more teachers than I had considered, some of them making but small impression on account of mildness.

There were eight.

"Jane!" I said, in desparation. "Eight without the housekeeper! And she must be remembered because if not she will be most unpleasant next fall, and swipe my chaffing dish. Forty five dollars is a lot of Money."

"You only have to do it once," said Jane, who could aford to be calm, as it was costing her nothing.

However, I sent the violets and paid with a check. I felt better by subtracting the amount from one thousand. I had still $945.00, less the facials and so on, which had been ten.

This is not a finantial story, although turning on Money. I do not wish to be considered as thinking only of Wealth. Indeed, I have always considered that where my heart was in question I would always decide for Love and penury rather than a Castle and greed. In this I differ from my sister Leila, who says that under no circumstanses would she ever inspect a refrigerater to see if the cook was wasting anything.

I was not worried about the violets, as I consider Money spent as but water over a damn, and no use worrying about. But I was no longer hungry, and I observed this to Jane.

"Oh, come on," she said, in an impatient maner. "I'll pay for it."

I can read Jane's inmost thoughts, and I read them then. She considered that I had cold feet financially, although with almost $945.00 in the bank. Therefore I said at once:

"Don't be silly. It is my party. And we'll take some candy home."

However, I need not have worried, for we met Tommy Gray in the tea shop, and he paid for everything.

I pause here to reflect. How strange to look back, and think of all that has since hapened, and that I then considered that Tommy Gray was interested in Jane and never gave me a thought. Also that I considered that the look he gave me now and then was but a friendly glanse! Is it not strange that Romanse comes thus into our lives, through the medium of a tea-cup, or an eclair, unheralded and unsung, yet leaving us never the same again?

Even when Tommy bought us candy and carried mine under his arm while leaving Jane to get her own from the counter, I suspected nothing. But when he said to me, "Gee, Bab, you're geting to be a regular Person," and made no such remark to Jane, I felt that it was rather pointed.

Also, on walking up the Avenue, he certainly walked nearer me than Jane. I beleive she felt it, to, for she made a sharp speach or to about his Youth, and what he meant to do when he got big. And he replied by saying that she was big enough allready, which hurt because Jane is plump and will eat starches anyhow.

Tommy Gray had improved a great deal since Xmas. He had at that time apeared to long for his head. I said this to Jane, *soto voce*, while he was looking at some neckties in a window.

"Well, his head is big enough now," she said in a snapish maner. "It isn't very long, Bab, since you considered him a mere Child."

"He is twenty," I asserted, being one to stand up for my friends under any and all circumstanses.

Jane snifed.

"Twenty!" she exclaimed. "He's not eighteen yet. His very noze is imature."

Our discourse was interupted by the object of it, who requested an opinion on the ties. He ignored Jane entirely.

We went in, and I purchaced a handsome tie for father, considering it but right thus to show my apreciation of his giving me the Allowence.

It was seventy five cents, and I made out a check for the amount and took the tie with me. We left Jane soon after, as she insisted on adressing Tommy as dear child, or "*mon enfant*" and strolled on together, oblivious to the World, by the World forgot. Our conversation was largely about ourselves, Tommy maintaining that I gave an impression of fridgidity, and that all the College men considered me so.

"Better fridgidity," I retorted, "than softness. But I am sincere. I stick to my friends through thick and thin."

Here he observed that my Chin was romantic, but that my Ears were stingy, being small and close to my head. This irratated me, although glad they are small. So I bought him a gardenia to wear from a flour-seller, but as the flour-seller refused a check, he had to pay for it.

In exchange he gave me his Frat pin to wear.

"You know what that means, don't you, Bab?" he said, in a low and thriling tone. "It means, if you wear it, that you are my—well, you're my girl."

Although thriled, I still retained my practacality.

"Not exclusively, Tom," I said, in a firm tone. "We are both young, and know little of Life. Some time, but not as yet."

He looked at me with a searching glanse.

"I'll bet you have a couple of dozen Frat pins lying around, Bab," he said savigely. "You're that sort. All the fellows are sure to be crasy about you. And I don't intend to be an Also-ran."

"Perhaps," I observed, in my most dignafied maner. "But no one has ever tried to bully me before. I may be young, but the Other Sex have always treated me with respect."

I then walked up the steps and into my home, leaving him on the pavment. It was cruel, but I felt that it was best to start right.

But I was troubled and *distrait* during dinner, which consisted of mutton and custard, which have no appeal for me owing to having them to often at school. For I had, although not telling an untruth, allowed Tom to think that I had a dozen or so Frat pins, although I had none at all.

Still, I reflected, why not? Is it not the only way a woman can do when in conflict with the Other Sex, to meet Wile with Gile? In other words, to use her intellagence against brute force? I fear so.

Men do not expect truth from us, so why disapoint them?

During the salid mother inquired what I had done during the afternoon.

"I made a few purchases," I said.

"I hope you bought some stockings and underclothes," she observed. "Hannah cannot mend your chemises any more, and as for your——"

"Mother!" I said, turning scarlet, for George—who was the Butler, as Tanney had been found kissing Jane—was at that moment bringing in the cheeze.

"I am not going to interfere with your Allowence," she went on. "But I recall very distinctly that during Leila's first year she came home with three evening wraps and one nightgown, having to borrow from one of her schoolmates, while that was being washed. I feel that you should at least be warned."

How could I then state that instead of bying nightgowns, et cetera, I had been sending violets? I could not. If Life to my Familey was a matter of petticoats, and to me was a matter of fragrant flours, why cause them to suffer by pointing out the diference?

I did not feel superior. Only diferent.

That evening, while mother and Leila were out at a Festivaty, I gave father his neck-tie. He was overcome with joy and for a moment could not speak. Then he said:

"Good gracious, Bab! What a—what a *diferent* necktie."

I explained my reasons for buying it for him, and also Tom Gray's objecting to it as to juvenile.

"Young impudense!" said father, refering to Tom. "I darsay I am quite an old fellow to him. Tie it for me, Bab."

"Though old of body, you are young in mentalaty," I said. But he only laughed, and then asked about the pin, which I wore over my heart.

"Where did you get that?" he asked in quite a feirce voice.

I told him, but not quite all. It was the first time I had concealed an *amour* from my parents, having indeed had but few, and I felt wicked and clandestine. But, alas, it is the way of the heart to conceal its deepest feelings, save for blushes, which are beyond bodily control.

My father, however, mearly sighed and observed:

"So it has come at last!"

"What has come at last?" I asked, but feeling that he meant Love. For although forty-two and not what he once was, he still remembers his Youth.

But he refused to anser, and inquired politely if I felt to much grown-up, with the Allowence and so on, to be held on knees and occasionaly tickeled, as in other days.

Which I did not.

That night I stood at the window of my Chamber and gazed with a heaving heart at the Gray residense, which is next door. Often before I had gazed at its walls, and considered them but brick and morter, and needing paint. Now my emotions were diferent. I realized that a House is but a shell, covering and protecting its precious contents from weather and curious eyes, et cetera.

As I stood there, I percieved a light in an upper window, where the nursery had once been in which Tom—in those days when a child, Tommy—and I had played as children, he frequently pulling my hair and never thinking of what was to be. As I gazed, I saw a figure come to the window and gaze fixedly at me. *It was he.*

Hannah was in my room, making a list of six of everything which I needed, so I dared not call out. But we exchanged gestures of afection and trust across the void, and with a beating heart I retired to bed.

Before I slept, however, I put to myself this question, but found no anser to it. How can it be that two people of Diferent Sexes can know each other well, such as calling by first names and dancing together at dancing school, and going to the same dentist, and so on, and have no interest in each other except to have a partner at parties or make up a set at tennis? And then nothing happens, but there is a diference, and they are always hoping to meet on the street or elsewhere, and although quareling sometimes when together, are not happy when apart! How strange is Life!

Hannah staid in my room that evening, fussing about my not hanging up my garments when undressing. As she has lived with us for a long time, and used to take me for walks when Mademoiselle had the toothache, which was often, because she hated to walk, she knows most of the Familey affairs, and is sometimes a nusance.

So, while I said my prayers, she looked in my Check Book. I was furious, and snached it from her, but she had allready seen to much.

"Humph!" she said. "Well, all I've got to say is this, Miss Bab. You'll last just twenty days at the rate you are going, and will have to go stark naked all year."

At this indelacate speach I ordered her out of the room, but she only tucked the covers in and asked me if I had brushed my teeth.

"You know," she said, "that you'll be coming to me for money when you run out, Miss Bab, as you've always done, and expecting me to patch and mend and make over your old things, when I've got my hands full anyhow. And you with a Fortune fritered away."

"I wish to think, Hannah," I said in a plaintive tone. "Please go away."

But she came and stood over me.

"Now you're going to be a good girl this Summer and not give any trouble, aren't you?" she asked. "Because we're upset enough as it is, and your poor mother most distracted, without you're cutting loose as usual and driving everybody crazy."

I sat up in bed, forgetful that the window was now open for the night, and that I was visable from the Gray's in my *robe de nuit*.

"Whose distracted about what?" I asked.

But Hannah would say no more, and left me a pray to doubt and fear.

Alas, Hannah was right. There was something wrong in the house. Coming home as I had done, full of the joy of no rising bell or French grammar, or meat pie on Mondays from Sunday's roast, I had noticed nothing.

I fear I am one who lives for the Day only, and as such I beleive that when people smile they are happy, forgetfull that to often a smile conceals an aching and tempestuous Void within.

Now I was to learn that the demon Strife had entered my domacile, there to make his—or her—home. I do not agree with that poet, A. J. Ryan, date forgoten, who observed:

> *Better a day of strife*
> *Than a Century of sleep.*

Although naturaly no one wishes to sleep for a Century, or even approxamately.

There was Strife in the house. The first way I noticed it, aside from Hannah's anonamous remark, was by observing that Leila was mopeing. She acted very strangely, giving me a pair of pink hoze without more than a hint on my part, and not sending me out of the room when Carter Brooks came in to tea the next day.

I had staid at home, fearing that if I went out I should purchace some *crepe de chene* combinations I had been craving in a window, and besides thinking it possable that Tom would drop in to renew our relations of yesterday, not remembering that there was a Ball Game.

Mother having gone out to the Country Club, I put my hair on top of my head, thus looking as adult as possable. Taking a new detective story of Jane's under my arm, I descended the staircase to the library.

Sis was there, curled up in a chair, knitting for the soldiers. Having forgoten the Ball Game, as I have stated, I asked her, in case I had a caller, to go away, which, considering she has the house to herself all winter, I considered not to much.

"A caller!" she said. "Since when have you been allowed to have callers?"

I looked at her steadily.

"I am young," I observed, "and still in the school room, Leila. I admit it, so don't argue. But as I have not taken the veil, and as this is not a Penitentary, I darsay I can see my friends now and anon, especialy when they live next door."

"Oh!" she said. "It's the Gray infant, is it!"

This remark being purely spiteful, I ignored it and sat down to my book, which concerned the stealing of some famous Emerelds, the heroine being a girl detective who could shoot the cork out of a bottle at a great distance, and whose name was Barbara!

It was for that reason Jane had loaned me the book.

I had reached the place where the Duchess wore the Emerelds to a ball, above white satin and lillies, the girl detective being dressed as a man and driving her there, because the Duchess had been warned and hautily refused to wear the paste copies she had—when Sis said, peavishly:

"Why don't you knit or do somthing useful, Bab?"

I do not mind being picked on by my parents or teachers, knowing it is for my own good. But I draw the line at Leila. So I replied:

"Knit! If that's the scarf you were on at Christmas, and it looks like it, because there's the crooked place you wouldn't fix, let me tell you that since then I have made three socks, heals and all, and they are probably now on the feet of the Allies."

"Three!" she said. "Why *three*?"

"I had no more wool, and there are plenty of one-legged men anyhow."

I would fane have returned to my book, dreaming between lines, as it were, of the Romanse which had come into my life the day before. It is, I have learned, much more interesting to read a book when one has, or is, experiencing the Tender Passion at the time. For during the love seens one can then fancy that the impasioned speaches are being made to oneself, by the object of one's afection. In short, one becomes, even if but a time, the Heroine.

But I was to have no privacy.

"Bab," Sis said, in a more mild and fraternal tone, "I want you to do somthing for me."

"Why don't you go and get it yourself?" I said. "Or ring for George?"

"I don't want you to get anything. I want you to go to father and mother for somthing."

"I'd stand a fine chance to get it!" I said. "Unless it's Calomel or advice."

Although not suspicous by nature, I now looked at her and saw why I had recieved the pink hoze. It was not kindness. It was bribery!

"It's this," she explained. "The house we had last year at the seashore is empty, and we can have it. But mother won't go. She—well, she won't go. They're going to open the country house and stay there."

A few days previously this would have been sad news for me, owing to not being allowed to go to the Country Club except in the mornings, and no chance to meet any new people, and no bathing save in the usual tub. But now I thriled at the information, because the Grays have a place near the Club also.

For a moment I closed my eyes and saw myself, all in white and decked with flours, wandering through the meadows and on the links with a certain Person whose name I need not write, having allready related my feelings toward him.

I am older now by some weeks, older and sader and wiser. For Tradgedy has crept into my life, so that somtimes I wonder if it is worth while to live on and suffer, especialy without an Allowence, and being again obliged to suplicate for the smallest things.

But I am being brave. And, as Carter Brooks wrote me in a recent letter, acompanying a box of candy:

"After all, Bab, you did your durndest. And if they do not understand, I do, and I'm proud of you. As for being 'blited,' as per your note to me, remember that I am, also. Why not be blited together?"

This latter, of course, is not serious, as he is eight years older than I, and even fills in at middle-aged Dinners, being handsome and dressing well, although poor.

Sis's remarks were interupted by the clamor of the door bell. I placed a shaking hand over the Frat pin, beneath which my heart was beating only for *him*. And waited.

What was my dispair to find it but Carter Brooks!

Now there had been a time when to have Carter Brooks sit beside me, as now, and treat me as fully out in Society, would have thriled me to the core. But that day had gone. I realized that he was not only to old, but to flirtatous. He was one who would not look on a woman's Love as precious, but as a plaything.

"Barbara," he said to me. "I do not beleive that Sister is glad to see me."

"I don't have to look at you," Sis said, "I can knit."

"Tell me, Barbara," he said to me beseachingly, "am I as hard to look at as all that?"

"I rather like looking at you," I rejoined with cander. "Across the room."

He said we were not as agreable as we might be, so he picked up a magazine and looked at the Automobile advertizments.

"I can't aford a car," he said. "Don't listen to me, either of you. I'm only talking to myself. But I like to read the ads. Hello, here's a snappy one for five hundred and fifty. Let me see. If I gave up a couple of Clubs, and smokeing, and flours to Debutantes—except Barbara, because I intend to buy every pozy in town when she comes out—I might——"

"Carter," I said, "will you let me see that ad?"

Now the reason I had asked for it was this: in the book the Girl Detective had a small but powerful car, and she could do anything with it, even going up the Court House steps once in it and interupting a trial at the criticle moment.

But I did not, at that time, expect to more than wish for such a vehical. How pleasant, my heart said, to have a car holding to, and since there was to be no bathing, et cetera, and I was not allowed a horse in the country, except my old pony and the basket faeton, to ramble through the lanes with a choice Spirit, and talk about ourselves mostly, with a sprinkling of other subjects!

Five hundred and fifty from nine hundred and forty-five leaves three hundred and forty-five. But I need few garments at school, wearing mostly unaforms of blue serge with one party frock for Friday nights and receptions to Lecturers and Members of the Board. And besides, to own a machine would mean less carfare and no shoes to speak of, because of not walking.

Jane Raleigh came in about then and I took her upstairs and closed the door.

"Jane," I said, "I want your advise. And be honest, because it's a serious matter."

"If it's Tommy Gray," she said, in a contemptable manner, "don't."

How could I know, as revealed later, that Jane had gone on a Diet since yesterday, owing to a certain remark, and had had nothing but an apple all day? I could not. I therfore stared at her steadily and observed:

"I shall never ask for advise in matters of the Heart. There I draw the line."

However, she had seen some caromels on my table, and suddenly burst into emotion. I was worried, not knowing the trouble and fearing that Jane was in love with Tom. It was a terrable thought, for which should I do? Hold on to him and let her suffer, or remember our long years of intimacy and give him up to her?

Should I or should I not remove his Frat pin?

However, I was not called upon to renunciate anything. In the midst of my dispair Jane asked for a Sandwitch and thus releived my mind. I got her some cake and a bottle of cream from the pantrey and she became more normle. She swore she had never cared for Tom, he being not her style, as she had never loved any one who had not black eyes.

"Nothing else matters, Bab," she said, holding out the Sandwitch in a dramatic way. "I see but his eyes. If they are black, they go through me like a knife."

"Blue eyes are true eyes," I observed.

"There is somthing feirce about black eyes," she said, finishing the cream. "I feel this way. One cannot tell what black eyes are thinking. They are a mystery, and as such they atract me. Almost all murderers have black eyes."

"Jane!" I exclaimed.

"They mean passion," she muzed. "They are *strong* eyes. Did you ever see a black-eyed man with glasses? Never. Bab, are you engaged to Tom?"

"Practicaly."

I saw that she wished details, but I am not that sort. I am not the kind to repeat what has been said to me in the emotion of Love. I am one to bury sentament deep in my heart, and have therfore the reputation of being cold and indiferent. But better that than having the Male Sex afraid to tell me how I effect them for fear of it being repeated to other girls, as some do.

"Of course it cannot be soon, if at all," I said. "He has three more years of College, and as you know, here they regard me as a child."

"You have your own income."

That reminded me of the reason for my having sought the privasy of my Chamber. I said:

"Jane, I am thinking of buying an automobile. Not a Limousine, but somthing styleish and fast. I must have Speed, if nothing else."

She stopped eating a caromel and gave me a stunned look.

"What for?"

"For emergencies."

"Then they disaprove of him?" she said, in a low, tence voice.

"They know but little, although what they suspect—Jane," I said, my bitterness bursting out, "what am I now? Nothing. A prisoner, or the equivalent of such, forbiden everything because I am to young! My Soul hampered by being taken to the country where there is nothing to do, given a pony cart, although but 20 months younger than Leila, and not going to come out until she is married, or permanently engaged."

"It *is* hard," said Jane. "Heart-breaking, Bab."

We sat, in deep and speachless gloom. At last Jane said:

"Has she anyone in sight?"

"How do I know? They keep me away at School all year. I am but a stranger here, although I try hard to be otherwise."

"Because we might help along, if there is anyone. To get her married is your only hope, Bab. They're afraid of you. That's all. You're the tipe to atract Men, except your noze, and you could help that by pulling it. My couzin did that, only she did it to much, and made it pointed."

I looked in my mirror and sighed. I have always desired an aristocratic noze, but a noze cannot be altered like teeth, unless broken and then generaly not improved.

"I have tried a shell hair pin at night, but it falls off when I go to sleep," I said, in a despondant manner.

We sat for some time, eating caromels and thinking about Leila, because there was nothing to do with my noze, but Leila was diferent.

"Although," Jane said, "you will never be able to live your own Life until she is gone, Bab."

"There is Carter Brooks," I suggested. "But he is poor. And anyhow she is not in Love with him."

"Leila is not one to care about Love," said Jane. "That makes it eazier."

"But whom?" I said. "Whom, Jane?"

We thought and thought, but of course it was hard, for we knew none of those who filled my sister's life, or sent her flours and so on.

At last I said:

"There must be a way, Jane. *There must be.* And if not, I shall make one. For I am desparate. The mere thought of going back to school, when I am as old as at present and engaged also, is madening."

But Jane held out a warning hand.

"Go slow, dearie," she said, in a solemn tone. "Do nothing rash. Remember this, that she is your sister, and should be hapily married if at all. Also she needs one with a strong hand to control her. And such are not easy to find. You must not ruin her Life."

Considering the fatal truth of that, is it any wonder that, on contemplateing the events that folowed, I am ready to cry, with the great poet Hood: 1835-1874: whose numerous works we studied during the spring term:

> *Alas, I have walked through life*
> *To heedless where I trod;*
> *Nay, helping to trampel my fellow worm,*
> *And fill the burial sod.*

II

If I were to write down all the surging thoughts that filled my brain this would have to be a Novel instead of a Short Story. And I am not one who beleives in beginning the life of Letters with a long work. I think one should start with breif Romanse. For is not Romanse itself but breif, the thing of an hour, at least to the Other Sex?

Women and girls, having no interest outside their hearts, such as baseball and hockey and earning saleries, are more likely to hug Romanse to their breasts, until it is finaly drowned in their tears.

I pass over the next few days, therfore, mearly stating that my *affaire de couer* went ōn rapidly, and that Leila was sulkey *and had no Male visitors*. On the day after the Ball Game Tom took me for a walk, and in a corner of the park, he took my hand and held it for quite a while. He said he had never been a hand-holder, but he guessed it was time to begin. Also he remarked that my noze need not worry me, as it exactly suited my face and nature.

"How does it suit my nature?" I asked.

"It's—well, it's cute."

"I do not care about being cute, Tom," I said ernestly. "It is a word I despize."

"Cute means kissible, Bab!" he said, in an ardent manner.

"I don't beleive in kissing."

"Well," he observed, "there is kissing and kissing."

But a nurse with a baby in a perambulater came along just then and nothing happened worth recording. As soon as she had passed, however, I mentioned that kissing was all right if one was engaged, but not otherwise. And he said:

"But we are, aren't we?"

Although understood before, it had now come in full force. I, who had been but Barbara Archibald before, was now engaged. Could it be I who heard my voice saying, in a low tone, the "yes" of Destiny? It was!

We then went to the corner drug-store and had some soda, although forbiden by my Familey because of city water being used. How strange to me to recall that I had once thought the Clerk nice-looking, and had even purchaced things there, such as soap and chocolate, in order to speak a few words to him!

I was engaged, dear Reader, but not yet kissed. Tom came into our vestabule with me, and would doubtless have done so when no one was passing, but that George opened the door suddenly.

However, what difference, when we had all the rest of our Lives to kiss in? Or so I then considered.

Carter Brooks came to dinner that night because his people were out of town, and I think he noticed that I looked mature and dignafied, for he stared at me a lot. And father said:

"Bab, you're not eating. Is it possable that that boarding school hollow of yours is filling up?"

One's Familey is apt to translate one's finest Emotions into terms of food and drink. Yet could I say that it was my Heart and not my Stomache that was full? I could not.

During dinner I looked at Leila and wondered how she could be married off. For until so I would continue to be but a Child, and not allowed to be engaged or anything. I thought if she would eat some starches it would help, she being pretty but thin. I therfore urged her to eat potatos and so on, because of evening dress and showing her coller bones, but she was quite nasty.

"Eat your dinner," she said in an unfraternal maner, "and stop watching me. They're *my* bones."

"I have no intention of being criticle," I said. "And they are your bones, although not a matter to brag about. But I was only thinking, if you were fater and had a permanant wave put in your hair, because one of the girls did and it hardly broke off at all— —"

She then got up and flung down her napkin.

"Mother!" she said. "Am I to stand this sort of thing indefinately? Because if I am I shall go to France and scrub floors in a Hospitle."

Well, I reflected, that would be almost as good as having her get married. Besides being a good chance to marry over there, the unaform being becoming to most, especialy of Leila's tipe.

That night, in the drawing room, while Sis sulked and father was out and mother was ofering the cook more money to go to the country, I said to Carter Brooks:

"Why don't you stop hanging round, and make her marry you?"

"I'd like to know what's running about in that mad head of yours, Bab," he said. "Of course if you say so I'll try, but don't count to much on it. I don't beleive she'll have me. But why this unseemly haste?"

So I told him, and he understood perfectly, although I did not say that I had already plited my troth.

"Of course," he said. "If that fails there is another method of aranging things, although you may not care to have the Funeral Baked Meats set fourth to grace the Marriage Table. If she refuses me, we might become engaged. You and I."

To proposals in one day. Ye gods!

I was obliged therfore to tell him I was already engaged, and he looked very queer, especialy when I told him to whom it was.

"Pup!" he said, in a manner which I excused because of his natural feelings at being preceded. "And of course this is the real thing?"

"I am not one to change easily, Carter," I said. "When I give I give freely. A thing like this, with me, is to Eternaty, and even beyond."

He is usualy most polite, but he got up then and said:

"Well, I'm dammed."

He went away soon after, and left Sis and me to sit alone, not speaking, because when she is angry she will not speak to me for days at a time. But I found a Magazine picture of a Duchess in a nurse's dress and wearing a fringe, which is English for bangs, and put it on her dressing table.

I felt that this was subtile and would sink in.

The next day Jane came around early.

"There's a sail on down town, Bab," she said. "Don't you want to begin laying away underclothes for your *Trouseau*? You can't begin to soon, because it takes such a lot."

I have no wish to reflect on Jane in this story. She meant well. But she knew I had decided to buy an automobile, saying nothing to the Familey until to late, when I had learned to drive it and it could not be returned. Also she knew my Income, which was not princly although suficient.

But she urged me to take my Check Book and go to the sail.

Now, if I have a weakness, it is for fine under things, with ribbon of a pale pink and everything maching. Although I spent but fifty-eight dollars and sixty-five cents on the *Trouseau* that day, I felt uneasy, especialy as, just afterwards, I saw in a window a costume for a woman *chauffeur*, belted lether coat and leggings, skirt and lether cap.

I gave a check for it also, and on going home hid my Check Book, as Hannah was always snooping around and watching how much I spent. But luckaly we were packing for the country, and she did not find it.

During that evening I reflected about marrying Leila off, as the Familey was having a dinner and I was sent a tray to my Chamber, consisting of scrambeled eggs, baked potatos and junket, which considering that I was engaged and even then colecting my *Trouseau*, was to juvenile for words.

I decided this: that Leila was my sister and therfore bound to me by ties of Blood and Relationship. She must not be married to anyone, therfore, whom she did not love or at least respect. I would not doom her to be unhappy.

Now I have a qualaty which is well known at school and frequently used to obtain holadays and so on. It may be Magnatism, it may be Will. I have a very strong Will, having as a child had a way of lying on the floor and kicking my feet if thwarted. In school, by fixing my eyes ridgidly on the teacher, I have been able to make her do as I wish, such as not calling on me when unprepared, et cetera.

Full well I know the danger of such a Power, unless used for good.

I now made up my mind to use this Will, or Magnatism, on Leila, she being unsuspicious at the time and thinking that the thought of Marriage was her own, and no one else's.

Being still awake when the Familey came upstairs, I went into her room and experamented while she was taking down her hair.

"Well?" she said at last. "You needn't stare like that. I can't do my hair this way without a Swich."

"I was merely thinking," I said in a lofty tone.

"Then go and think in bed."

"Does it or does it not concern you as to what I was thinking?" I demanded.

"It doesn't greatly concern me," she replied, wraping her hair around a kid curler, "but I darsay I know what it was. It's written all over you in letters a foot high. You'd like me to get married and out of the way."

I was exultent yet terrafied at this result of my Experament. Already! I said to my wildly beating heart. And if thus in five minutes what in the entire summer?

On returning to my Chamber I spent a pleasant hour planing my maid-of-honor gown, which I considered might be blue to mach my eyes, with large pink hat and carrying pink flours.

The next morning father and I breakfasted alone, and I said to him:

"In case of festivaty in the Familey, such as a Wedding, is my Allowence to cover clothes and so on for it?"

He put down his paper and searched me with a peircing glanse. Although pleasant after ten A.M. he is not realy paternal in the early morning, and when Mademoiselle was still with us was quite hateful to her at times, asking her to be good enough not to jabber French at him untill evening when he felt stronger.

"Whose Wedding?" he said.

"Well," I said. "You've got to Daughters and we might as well look ahead."

"I intend to have to Daughters," he said, "for some time to come. And while we're on the subject, Bab, I've got somthing to say to you. Don't let that romantic head of yours get filled up with Sweethearts, because you are still a little girl, with all your airs. If I find any boys mooning around here, I'll—I'll shoot them."

Ye gods! How intracate my life was becoming! I engaged and my masculine parent convercing in this homacidal manner! I withdrew to my room and there, when Jane Raleigh came later, told her the terrable news.

"Only one thing is to be done, Jane," I said, my voice shaking. "Tom must be warned."

"Call him up," said Jane, "and tell him to keep away."

But this I dare not do.

"Who knows, Jane," I observed, in a forlorn manner, "but that the telephone is watched? They must suspect. But how? *How?*"

Jane was indeed a *fidus Achates*. She went out to the drug store and telephoned to Tom, being careful not to mention my name, because of the clerk at the soda fountain listening, saying merely to keep away from a Certain Person for a time as it was dangerous. She then merely mentioned the word "revolver" as meaning nothing to the clerk but a great deal to Tom. She also aranged a meeting in the Park at 3 P.M. as being the hour when father signed his mail before going to his Club to play bridge untill dinner.

Our meeting was a sad one. How could it be otherwise, when to loving Hearts are forbiden to beat as one, or even to meet? And when one or the other is constantly saying:

"Turn your back. There is some one I know coming!"

Or:

"There's the Peters's nurse, and she's the worst talker you ever heard of." And so on.

At one time Tom would have been allowed to take out their Roadster, but unfortunately he had been forbiden to do so, owing to having upset it while taking his Grandmother Gray for an airing, and was not to drive again until she could walk without cruches.

"Won't your people let you take out a car?" he asked. "Every girl ought to know how to drive, in case of war or the *chauffeur* leaving——"

"—— or taking a Grandmother for an airing!" I said coldly. Because I did not care to be criticized when engaged only a few hours.

However, after we had parted with mutual Protestations, I felt the desire that every engaged person of the Femanine Sex always feels, to apear perfect to the one she is engaged to. I therfore considered whether to ask Smith to teach me to drive one of our cars or to purchace one of my own, and be responsable to no one if muddy, or arrested for speeding, or any other Vicissatude.

On the next day Jane and I looked at automobiles, starting with ones I could not aford so as to clear the air, as Jane said. At last we found one

I could aford. Also its lining matched my costume, being tan. It was but six hundred dollars, having been more but turned in by a lady after three hundred miles because she was of the kind that never learns to drive but loses its head during an emergensy and forgets how to stop, even though a Human Life be in its path.

The Salesman said that he could tell at a glanse that I was not that sort, being calm in danger and not likly to chase a chicken into a fense corner and murder it, as some do when excited.

Jane and I consulted, for buying a car is a serious matter and not to be done lightly, especialy when one has not consulted one's Familey and knows not where to keep the car when purchased. It is not like a dog, which I have once or twice kept in a clandestine manner in the Garage, because of flees in the house.

"The trouble is," Jane said, "that if you don't take it some one will, and you will have to get one that costs more."

True indeed, I reflected, with my Check Book in my hand.

Ah, would that some power had whispered in my ear "No. By purchacing the above car you are endangering that which lies near to your Heart and Mind. Be warned in time."

But no sign came. No warning hand was outstretched to put my Check Book back in my pocket book. I wrote the Check and sealed my doom.

How weak is human nature! It is terrable to remember the rapture of that moment, and compare it with my condition now, with no Allowence, with my faith gone and my heart in fragments. And with, alas, another year of school.

As we were going to the country in but a few days, I aranged to leave my new Possesion, merely learning to drive it meanwhile, and having my first lesson the next day.

"Dearest," Jane said as we left. "I am thriled to the depths. The way you do things is wonderfull. You have no fear, none whatever. With your father's Revenge hanging over you, and to secrets, you are calm. Perfectly calm."

"I fear I am reckless, Jane," I said, wistfully. "I am not brave. I am reckless, and also desparate."

"You poor darling!" she said, in a broken voice. "When I think of all you are suffering, and then see your smile, my Heart aches for you."

We then went in and had some ice cream soda, which I paid for, Jane having nothing but a dollar, which she needed for a manacure. I also bought a key ring for Tom, feeling that he should have somthing of mine, a token, in exchange for the Frat pin.

I shall pass over lightly the following week, during which the Familey was packing for the country and all the servants were in a bad humer. In the mornings I took lessons driving the car, which I called the Arab, from the well-known song, which we have on the phonograph;

From the Dessert I come to thee,
On my Arab shod with fire.

The instructer had not heard the song, but he said it was a good name, because very likly no one else would think of having it.

"It sounds like a love song," he observed.

"It is," I replied, and gave him a steady glanse. Because, if one realy loves, it is silly to deny it.

"Long ways to a Dessert, isn't it?" he inquired.

"A Dessert may be a place, or it may be a thirsty and emty place in the Soul," I replied. "In my case it is Soul, not terratory."

But I saw that he did not understand.

How few there are who realy understand! How many of us, as I, stand thirsty in the market place, holding out a cup for a kind word or for some one who sees below the surface, and recieve nothing but indiference!

On Tuesday the Grays went to their country house, and Tom came over to say good-bye. Jane had told him he could come, as the Familey would be out.

The thought of the coming seperation, although but for four days, caused me deep greif. Although engaged for only a short time, already I felt how it feels to know that in the vicinaty is some one dearer than Life itself. I felt I must speak to some one, so I observed to Hannah that I was most unhappy, but not to ask me why. I was dressing at the time, and she was hooking me up.

"Unhappy!" she said, "with a thousand dollars a year, and naturaly curly hair! You ought to be ashamed, Miss Bab."

"What is money, or even hair?" I asked, "when one's Heart aches?"

"I guess it's your stomache and not your Heart," she said. "With all the candy you eat. If you'd take a dose of magnezia to-night, Miss Bab, with some orange juice to take the taste away, you'd feel better right off."

I fled from my chamber.

I have frequently wondered how it would feel to be going down a staircase, dressed in one's best frock, low neck and no sleaves, to some loved one lurking below, preferably in evening clothes, although not necesarily so. To move statuesqly and yet tenderly, apearing indiferent but inwardly seathing, while below pasionate eyes looked up as I floated down.

However, Tom had not put on evening dress, his clothes being all packed. He was taking one of father's cigars as I entered the library, and he looked very tall and adolesent, although thin. He turned and seeing me, observed:

"Great Scott, Bab! Why the raiment?"

"For you," I said in a low tone.

"Well, it makes a hit with me all right," he said.

And came toward me.

When Jane Raleigh was first kissed by a member of the Other Sex, while in a hammick, she said she hated to be kissed until he did it, and then she liked it. I at the time had considered Jane as flirtatous and as probably not hating it at all. But now I knew she was right, for as I saw Tom coming toward me after laying father's cigar on the piano, I felt that *I could not bear it*.

And this I must say, here and now. I do not like kissing. Even then, in that first embrase of to, I was worried because I could smell the varnish burning on the Piano. I therfore permited but one salute on the cheek and no more before removing the cigar, which had burned a large spot.

"Look here," he said, in a stern manner, "are we engaged or aren't we? Because I'd like to know."

"If you are to demonstrative, no!" I replied, firmly.

"If you call that a kiss, I don't."

"It sounded like one," I said. "I suppose you know more than I do what is a kiss and what is not. But I'll tell you this—there is no use keeping our amatory affairs to ourselves and then kissing so the Butler thinks the fire whistle is blowing."

We then sat down, and I gave him the key ring, which he said was a dandy. I then told him about getting Sis married and out of the way. He thought it was a good idea.

"You'll never have a chance as long as she's around," he observed, smoking father's cigar at intervals. "They're afraid of you, and that's flat. It's your Eyes. That's what got me, anyhow." He blue a smoke ring and sat back with his legs crossed. "Funny, isn't it?" he said. "Here we are, snug as weavils in a cotton thing-un-a-gig, and only a week ago there was nothing between us but to brick walls. Hot in here, don't you think?"

"Only a week!" I said. "Tom, I've somthing to tell you. That is the nice part of being engaged—to tell things that one would otherwise bury in one's own Bosom. I shall have no secrets from you from henceforward."

So I told him about the car and how we could drive together in it, and no one would know it was mine, although I would tell the Familey later on, when to late to return it. He said little, but looked at me and kept on smoking, and was not as excited as I had expected, although interested.

But in the midst of my Narative he rose quickly and observed:

"Bab, I'm poizoned!"

I then perceived that he was pale and hagard. I rose to my feet, and thinking it might be the cigar, I asked him if he would care for a peice of chocolate cake to take the taste away. But to my greif he refused very snappishly and without a Farewell slamed out of the house, leaving his hat and so forth in the hall.

A bitter night ensued. For I shall admit that terrable thoughts filled my mind, although how perpetrated I knew not. Would those who loved me stoop to such depths as to poizon my afianced? And if so, whom?

The very thought was sickning.

I told Jane the next morning, but she pretended to beleive that the cigar had been to strong for him, and that I should remember that, although very good-hearted, he was a mere child. But, if poizon, she suggested Hannah.

That day, although unerved from anxiety, I took the Arab out alone, having only Jane with me. Except that once I got into reverce instead of low geer, and broke a lamp on a Gentleman behind, I had little or no trouble, although having one or to narrow escapes, owing to putting my foot on the gas throttle instead of the brake.

It was when being backed off the payment by to Policemen and a man from a milk wagon, after one of the aforsaid mistakes, that I first saw he who was to bring such wrechedness to me.

Jane had got out to see how much milk we had spilt—we had struck the milk wagon—and I was getting out my check book, because the man was very nasty and insisted on having my name, when I first saw him. He had stopped and was looking at the gutter, which was full of milk. Then he looked at me.

"How much damages does he want?" he said in a respectful tone.

"Twenty dollars," I replied, not considering it flirting to merely reply in this manner.

The Stranger then walked over to the milkman and said:

"A very little spilt milk goes a long way. Five dollars is plenty for that and you know it."

"How about me getting a stitch in my chin, and having to pay for that?"

I beleive I have not said that the milk man was cut in the chin by a piece of a bottle.

"Ten, then," said my friend in need.

When it was all over, and I had given two dollars to the old woman who had been in the milk wagon and was knocked out although only bruized, I went on, thinking no more about the Stranger, and almost running into my father, who did not see me.

That afternoon I realized that I must face the state of afairs, and I added up the Checks I had made out. Ye gods! Of all my Money there now remaind for the ensuing year but two hundred and twenty nine dollars and forty five cents.

I now realized that I had been extravagant, having spent so much in six days. Although I did not regard the Arab as such, because of saving car fare and half soleing shoes. Nor the *Trouseau*, as one must have clothing. But facial masage and manacures and candy et cetera I felt had been wastefull.

At dinner that night mother said:

"Bab, you must get yourself some thin frocks. You have absolutely nothing. And Hannah says you have bought nothing. After all a thousand dollars is a thousand dollars. You can have what you ought to have. Don't be to saving."

"I have not the interest in clothes I once had, mother," I replied. "If Leila will give me her old things I will use them."

"Bab!" mother said, with a peircing glanse, "go upstairs and bring down your Check Book."

I turned pale with fright, but father said:

"No, my dear. Suppose we let this thing work itself out. It is Barbara's money, and she must learn."

That night, when I was in bed and trying to divide $229.45 by 12 months, father came in and sat down on the bed.

"There doesn't happen to be anything you want to say to me, I suppose, Bab?" he inquired in a gentle tone.

Although not a weeping person, shedding but few tears even when punished in early years, his kind tone touched my Heart, and made me lachrymoze. Such must always be the feelings of those who decieve.

But, although bent, I was not yet broken. I therfore wept on in silence while father patted my back.

"Because," he said, "while I am willing to wait until you are ready, when things begin to get to thick I want you to know that I'm around, the same as usual."

He kissed the back of my neck, which was all that was visable, and went to the door. From there he said, in a low tone:

"And by the way, Bab, I think, since you bought me the Tie, it would be rather nice to get your mother somthing also. How about it? Violets, you know, or—or somthing."

Ye gods! Violets at five dollars a hundred. But I agreed. I then sat up in bed and said:

"Father, what would you say if you knew some one was decieving you?"

"Well," he said, "I am an old Bird and hard to decieve. A good many people think they can do it, however, and now and then some one gets away with it."

I felt softened and repentent. Had he but patted me once more, I would have told all. But he was looking for a match for his cigar, and the opportunaty passed.

"Well," he said, "close up that active brain of yours for the night, Bab, and here are to 'don'ts' to sleep on. Don't break your neck in—in any way. You're a reckless young Lady. And don't elope with the first moony young idiot who wants to hold your hand. There will quite likly be others."

Others! How heartless! How cynical! Were even those I love best to worldly to understand a monogamous Nature?

When he had gone out, I rose to hide my Check Book in the crown of an old hat, away from Hannah. Then I went to the window and glansed out. There was no moon, but the stars were there as usual, over the roof of that emty domacile next door, whence all life had fled to the neighborhood of the Country Club.

But a strange thing caught my eye and transfixed it. There on the street, looking up at our house, now in the first throes of sleep, was the Stranger I had seen that afternoon when I had upset the milk wagon against the Park fense.

III

I shall now remove the Familey to the country, which is easier on paper than in the flesh, owing to having to take china, silver, bedding and edables. Also porch furnature and so on.

Sis acted very queer while we were preparing. She sat in her room and knited, and was not at home to Callers, although there were not many owing to summer and every one away. When she would let me in, which was not often, as she said I made her head ache, I tried to turn her thoughts to marriage or to nursing at the War, which was for her own good, since she is of the kind who would never be happy leading a simple life, but should be married.

But alas for all my hopes. She said, on the day before we left, while packing her jewel box:

"You might just as well give up trying to get rid of me, Barbara. Because I do not intend to marry any one."

"Very well, Leila," I said, in a cold tone. "Of course it matters not to me, because I can be kept in school untill I am thirty, and never come out or have a good time, and no one will care. But when you are an old woman and have not employed your natural function of having children to suport you in Age, don't say I did not warn you."

"Oh, you'll come out all right," she said, in a brutal manner. "You'll come out like a sky rocket. You'd be as impossable to supress as a boil."

Carter Brooks came around that afternoon and we played marbels in the drawing room with moth balls, as the rug was up. It was while sitting on the floor eating some candy he had brought that I told him that there was no use hanging around, as Leila was not going to marry. He took it bravely, and said that he saw nothing to do but to wait for some of the younger crowd to grow up, as the older ones had all refused him.

"By the way," he said. "I thought I saw you running a car the other day. You were chasing a fox terier when I saw you, but I beleive the dog escaped."

I looked at him and I saw that, although smiling, he was one who could be trusted, even to the Grave.

"Carter," I said. "It was I, although when you saw me I know not, as dogs are always getting in the way."

I then told him about the pony cart, and the Allowence, and saving car fare. Also that I felt that I should have some pleasure, even if *sub rosa*, as the expression is. But I told him also that I disliked decieving my dear parents, who had raised me from infancy and through meazles, whooping cough and shingles.

"Do you mean to say," he said in an astounded voice, "that you have *bought* that car?"

"I have. And paid for it."

Being surprized he put a moth ball into his mouth, instead of a gum drop.

"Well," he said, "you'll have to tell them. You can't hide it in a closet, you know, or under the bed."

"And let them take it away? Never."

My tone was firm, and he saw that I meant it, especialy when I explained that there would be nothing to do in the country, as mother and Sis would play golf all day, and I was not allowed at the Club, and that the Devil finds work for idle hands.

"But where in the name of good sense are you going to keep it?" he inquired, in a wild tone.

"I have been thinking about that," I said. "I may have to buy a portible Garage and have it set up somwhere."

"Look here," he said, "you give me a little time on this, will you? I'm not naturaly a quick thinker, and somhow my brain won't take it all in just yet. I suppose there's no use telling you not to worry, because you are not the worrying kind."

How little he knew of me, after years of calls and conversation!

Just before he left he said: "Bab, just a word of advise for you. Pick your Husband, when the time comes, with care. He ought to have the solidaty of an elephant and the mental agilaty of a flee. But no imagination, or he'll die a lunatic."

The next day he telephoned and said that he had found a place for the car in the country, a shed on the Adams' place, which was emty, as the Adams's were at Lakewood. So that was fixed.

Now my plan about the car was this: Not to go on indefanitely decieving my parents, but to learn to drive the car as an expert. Then, when they were about to say that I could not have one as I would kill myself in the first few hours, to say:

"You wrong me. I have bought a car, and driven it for— — days, and have killed no one, or injured any one beyond bruizes and one stitch."

I would then disapear down the drive, returning shortly in the Arab, which, having been used— — days, could not be returned.

All would have gone as aranged had it not been for the fatal question of Money.

Owing to having run over some broken milk bottles on the ocasion I have spoken of, I was obliged to buy a new tire at thirty-five dollars. I also had a bill of eleven dollars for gasoline, and a fine of ten dollars for speeding, which I paid at once for fear of a Notice being sent home.

This took fifty-six dollars more, and left me but $183.45 for the rest of the year, $15.28 a month to dress on and pay all expences. To add to my troubles mother suddenly became very fussy about my clothing and insisted that I purchace a new suit, hat and so on, which cost one hundred dollars and left me on the verge of penury.

Is it surprizing that, becoming desparate, I seized at any straw, however intangable?

I paid a man five dollars to take the Arab to the country and put it in the aforsaid shed, afterwards hiding the key under a stone outside. But, although needing relaxation and pleasure during those sad days, I did not at first take it out, as I felt that another tire would ruin me.

Besides, they had the Pony Cart brought every day, and I had to take it out, pretending enjoyment I could not feel, since acustomed to forty miles an hour and even more at times.

I at first invited Tom to drive with me in the Cart, thinking that merely to be together would be pleasure enough. But at last I was compeled to face the truth. Although protesting devotion until death, Tom did not care for the Cart, considering it juvenile for a college man, and also to small for his legs.

But at last he aranged a plan, which was to take the Cart as far as the shed, leave it there, and take out the car. This we did frequently, and I taught Tom how to drive it.

I am not one to cry over spilt milk. But I am one to confess when I have made a mistake. I do not beleive in laying the blame on Providence when it belongs to the Other Sex, either.

It was on going down to the shed one morning and finding a lamp gone and another tire hanging in tatters that I learned the Truth. He who should have guarded my interests with his very Life, including finances, had been taking the Arab out in the evenings when I was confined to the bosom of my Familey, and using up gasoline et cetera besides riding with whom I knew not.

Eighty-three dollars and 45 cents less thirty-five dollars for a tire and a bill for gasoline in the village of eight dollars left me, for the balance of the year, but $40.45 or $3.37 a month! And still a lamp missing.

It was terrable.

I sat on the running board and would have shed tears had I not been to angry.

It was while sitting thus, and deciding to return the Frat pin as costing to much in gasoline and patients, that I percieved Tom coming down the road. His hand was tied up in a bandige, and his whole apearance was of one who wishes to be forgiven.

Why, oh, why, must women of my Sex do all the forgiving?

He stood in the doorway so I could see the bandige and would be sorry for him. But I apeared not to notice him.

"Well?" he said.

I was silent.

"Now look here," he went on, "I'm darned lucky to be here and not dead, young lady. And if you are going to make a fuss, I'm going away and join the Ambulance in France."

"They'd better not let you drive a car if they care anything about it," I said, coldly.

"That's it! Go to it! Give me the Devil, of course. Why should you care that I have a broken arm, or almost?"

"Well," I said, in a cutting manner, "broken bones mend themselves and do not have to be taken to a Garage, where they charge by the hour and loaf most of the time. May I ask, if not to much trouble to inform me, whom you took out in my car last night? Because I'd like to send her your pin. I'd go on wearing it, but it's to expencive."

"Oh, very well," he said. He then brought out my key ring, although unable to take the keys off because of having but one hand. "If you're as touchy as all that, and don't care for the real story, I'm through. That's all."

I then began to feel remorceful. I am of a forgiving Nature naturaly and could not forget that but yesterday he had been tender and loving, and had let me drive almost half the time. I therfore said:

"If you can explain I will listen. But be breif. I am in no mood for words."

Well, the long and short of it was that I was wrong, and should not have jumped to conclusions. Because the Gray's house had been robbed the night before, taking all the silver and Mr. Gray's dress suit, as well as shirts and so on, and as their *chauffeur* had taken one of the maids out *incognito* and gone over a bank, returning at seven A.M. in a hired hack, there was no way to follow the theif. So Tom had taken my car and would have caught him, having found Mr. Gray's trowsers on a fense, although torn, but that he ran into a tree because of going very fast and skiding.

He would have gone through the wind-shield, but that it was down.

I was by that time mollafied and sorry I had been so angry, especialy as Tom said:

"Father ofered a hundred dollars reward for his capture, and as you have been adviseing me to save money, I went after the hundred."

At this thought, that my *fiancee* had endangered his hand and the rest of his person in order to acquire money for our ultamate marriage, my anger died.

I therfore submitted to an embrase, and washed the car, which was covered with mud, as Tom had but one hand and that holding a cigarette.

Now and then, Dear Reader, when not to much worried with finances, I look back and recall those halycon days when Love had its place in my life, filling it to the exclusion of even suficient food, and rendering me immune to the questions of my Familey, who wanted to know how I spent my time.

Oh, magic eyes of afection, which see the beloved object as containing all the virtues, including strong features and intellagence! Oh, dear dead Dreams, when I saw myself going down the church isle in white satin and Dutchess lace! O Tempora O Mores! Farewell.

What would have happened, I wonder, if father had not discharged Smith that night for carrying passengers to the Club from the railway station in our car, charging them fifty cents each and scraching the varnish with golf clubs?

I know not.

But it gave me the idea that ultimately ruined my dearest hopes. This was it. If Smith could get fifty cents each for carrying passengers, why not I? I was unknown to most, having been expatriated at School for several years. But also there were to stations, one which the summer people used, and one which was used by the so-called locals.

I was desparate. Money I must have, whether honestly or not, for mother had bought me some more things and sent me the bill.

"Because you will not do it yourself," she said. "And I cannot have it said that we neglect you, Barbara."

The bill was ninety dollars! Ye gods, were they determined to ruin me?

With me to think is to act. I am always like that. I always, alas, feel that the thing I have thought of is right, and there is no use arguing about it. This is well known in my Institution of Learning, where I am called impetuus and even rash.

That night, my Familey being sunk in sweet slumber and untroubled by finances, I made a large card which said: "For Hire." I had at first made it "For Higher," but saw that this was wrong and corected it. Although a natural speller, the best of us make mistakes.

I did not, the next day, confide in my betrothed, knowing that he would object to my earning Money in any way, unless perhaps in large amounts, such as the stock market, or, as at present, in Literature. But being one to do as I make up my mind to, I took the car to the station, and in three hours made one dollar and a fifteen cent tip from the Gray's butler, who did not know me as I wore large gogles.

I was now embarked on a Commercial Enterprize, and happier than for days. Although having one or to narrow escapes, such as father getting off the train at my station instead of the other, but luckily getting a cinder in his eye and unable to see until I drove away quickly. And one day Carter Brooks got off and found me changing a tire and very dusty and worried, because a new tube cost five dollars and so far I had made but six-fifteen.

I did not know he was there until he said:

"Step back and let me do that, Bab."

He was all dressed, but very firm. So I let him and he looked terrable when finished.

"Now," he said at last, "jump in and take me somewhere near the Club. And tell me how this happened."

"I am a bankrupt, Carter," I responded in a broken tone. "I have sold my birthright for a mess of porridge."

"Good heavens!" he said. "You don't mean you've spent the whole business?"

I then got my Check Book from the tool chest, and held it out to him. Also the unpaid bills. I had but $40.45 in the Bank and owed $90.00 for the things mother had bought.

"Everything has gone wrong," I admitted. "I love this car, but it is as much expence as a large familey and does not get better with age, as a familey does, which grows up and works or gets married. And Leila is getting to be a Man-hater and acts very strange most of the time."

Here I almost wept, and probably would have, had he not said:

"Here! Stop that, or I——" He stopped and then said: "How about the engagement, Bab? Is it a failure to?"

"We are still plited," I said. "Of course we do not agree about some things, but the time to fuss is now, I darsay, and not when to late, with perhaps a large familey and unable to seperate."

"What sort of things?"

"Well," I said, "he thinks that he ought to play around with other girls so no one will suspect, but he does not like it when I so much as sit in a hammick with a member of the Other Sex."

"Bab," he said in an ernest tone, "that, in twenty words, is the whole story of all the troubles between what you call the Sexes. The only diference between Tommy Gray and me is that I would not want to play around with any one else if—well, if engaged to anyone like you. And I feel a lot like looking him up and giving him a good thrashing."

He paid me fifty cents and a quarter tip, and offered, although poor, to lend me some Money. But I refused.

"I have made my bed," I said, "and I shall occupy it, Carter. I can have no companion in misfortune."

It was that night that another house near the Club was robed, and everything taken, including groceries and a case of champane. The Summer People got together the next day at the Club and offered a reward of two hundred dollars, and engaged a night watchman with a motor-cycle, which I considered silly, as one could hear him coming when to miles off, and any how he spent most of the time taking the maids for rides, and broke an arm for one of them.

Jane spent the night with me, and being unable to sleep, owing to dieting again and having an emty stomache, wakened me at 2 A.M. and we went to the pantrey together. When going back upstairs with some cake and canned pairs, we heard a door close below. We both shreiked, and the Familey got up, but found no one except Leila, who could not sleep and was out getting some air. They were very unpleasant, but as Jane observed, families have little or no gratitude.

I come now to the Stranger again.

On the next afternoon, while engaged in a few words with the station hackman, who said I was taking his trade although not needing the Money — which was a thing he could not possably know — while he had a familey and a horse to feed, I saw the Stranger of the milk wagon, et cetera, emerge from the one-thirty five.

He then looked at a piece of *mauve note paper*, and said:

"How much to take me up the Greenfield Road?"

"Where to?" I asked in a pre-emptory manner.

He then looked at a piece of *mauve note paper*, and said:

"To a big pine tree at the foot of Oak Hill. Do you know the Place?"

Did I know the Place? Had I not, as a child, rolled and even turned summersalts down that hill? Was it not on my very ancestrial acres? It was, indeed.

Although suspicous at once, because of no address but a pine tree, I said nothing, except merely:

"Fifty cents."

"Suppose we fix it like this," he suggested. "Fifty cents for the trip and another fifty for going away at once and not hanging around, and fifty more for forgetting me the moment you leave?"

I had until then worn my gogles, but removing them to wipe my face, he stared, and then said:

"And another fifty for not running into anything, including milk wagons."

I hesatated. To dollars was to dollars, but I have always been honest, and above reproach. But what if he was the Theif, and now about to survey my own home with a view to entering it clandestinely? Was I one to assist him under those circumstanses?

However, at that moment I remembered the Reward. With that amount I could pay everything and start life over again, and even purchace a few things I needed. For I was allready wearing my *Trouseau*, having been unable to get any plain every-day garments, and thus frequently obliged to change a tire in a *crepe de chine* petticoat, et cetera.

I yeilded to the temptation. How could I know that I was sewing my own destruction?

IV

Let us, dear reader, pass with brevaty over the next few days. Even to write them is a repugnent task, for having set my hand to the Plow, I am not one to do things half way and then stop.

Every day the Stranger came and gave me to dollars and I took him to the back road on our place and left him there. And every night, although weary unto death with washing the car, carrying people, changeing tires and picking nails out of the road which the hackman put there to make trouble, I but pretended to slumber, and instead sat up in the library and kept my terrable Vigil. For now I knew that he had dishonest designs on the sacred interior of my home, and was but biding his time.

The house having been closed for a long time, there were mice everywhere, so that I sat on a table with my feet up.

I got so that I fell asleep almost anywhere but particularly at meals, and mother called in a doctor. He said I needed exercize! Ye gods!

Now I think this: if I were going to rob a house, or comit any sort of Crime, I should do it and get it over, and not hang around for days making up my mind. Besides keeping every one tence with anxiety. It is like diving off a diving board for the first time. The longer you stand there, the more afraid you get, and the farther (further?) it seems to the water.

At last, feeling I could stand no more, I said this to the Stranger as he was paying me. He was so surprized that he dropped a quarter in the road, and did not pick it up. I went back for it later but some one else had found it.

"Oh!" he said. "And all this time I've been beleiving that you—well, no matter. So you think it's a mistake to delay to long?"

"I think when one has somthing Right or Wrong to do, and that's for your conscience to decide, it's easier to do it quickly."

"I see," he said, in a thoughtfull manner. "Well, perhaps you are right. Although I'm afraid you've been getting one fifty cents you didn't earn."

"I have never hung around," I retorted. "And no Archibald is ever a sneak."

"Archibald!" he said, getting very red. "Why, then you are— —"

"It doesn't matter who I am," I said, and got into the car and went away very fast, because I saw I had made a dreadfull Slip and probably spoiled everything. It was not untill I was putting the car up for the night that I saw I had gone off with his overcoat. I hung it on a nail and getting my revolver from under a board, I went home, feeling that I had lost two hundred dollars, and all because of Familey pride.

How true that "pride goeth before a fall"!

I have not yet explained about the revolver. I had bought it from the gardner, having promised him ten dollars for it, although not as yet paid for. And I had meant to learn to be an expert, so that I could capture the Crimenal in question without assistance, thus securing all the reward.

But owing to nervousness the first day I had, while practicing in the chicken yard, hit the Gardner in the pocket and would have injured him severely had he not had his garden scizzors in his pocket.

He was very angry, and said he had a bruize the exact shape of the scizzors on him, so I had had to give him the ten plus five dollars more, which was all I had and left me stranded.

I went to my domacile that evening in low spirits, which were not improved by a conversation I had with Tom that night after the Familey had gone out to a Club dance.

He said that he did not like women and girls who did things.

"I like femanine girls," he said. "A fellow wants to be the Oak and feel the Vine clinging to him."

"I am afectionate," I said, "but not clinging. I cannot change my Nature."

"Just what do you mean by afectionate?" he asked, in a stern voice. "Is it afectionate for you to sit over there and not even let me hold your hand? If that's afection, give me somthing else."

Alas, it was but to true. When away from me I thought of him tenderly, and of whether he was thinking of me. But when with me I was diferent. I could not account for this, and it troubled me. Because I felt this way. Romanse had come into my life, but suppose I was incapable of loving, although loved?

Why should I wish to be embrased, but become cold and fridgid when about to be?

"It's come to a Show-down, Bab," he said, ernestly. "Either you love me or you don't. I'm darned if I know which."

"Alas, I do not know," I said in a low and pitious voice. I then buried my face in my hands, and tried to decide. But when I looked up he was gone, and only the sad breese wailed around me.

I had expected that the Theif would take my hint and act that night, if not scared off by learning that I belonged to the object of his nefarius designs. But he did not come, and I was wakened on the library table at 8 A.M. by George coming in to open the windows.

I was by that time looking pale and thin, and my father said to me that morning, ere departing for the office:

"Haven't anything you'd like to get off your chest, have you, Bab?"

I sighed deeply.

"Father," I said, "do you think me cold? Or lacking in afection?"

"Certainly not."

"Or one who does not know her own mind?"

"Well," he observed, "those who have a great deal of mind do not always know it all. Just as you think you know it some new corner comes up that you didn't suspect and upsets everything."

"Am I femanine?" I then demanded, in an anxious manner.

"Femanine! If you were any more so we couldn't bare it."

I then inquired if he prefered the clinging Vine or the independant tipe, which follows its head and not its instincts. He said a man liked to be engaged to a clinging Vine, but that after marriage a Vine got to be a darned nusance and took everything while giving nothing, being the sort to prefer chicken croquets to steak and so on, and wearing a boudoir cap in bed in the mornings.

He then kissed me and said:

"Just a word of advise, Bab, from a parent who is, of course, extremely old but has not forgotten his Youth entirely. Don't try to make yourself over for each new Admirer who comes along. Be yourself. If you want to do any making over, try it on the boys. Most of them could stand it."

That morning, after changing another tire and breaking three finger nails, I remembered the overcoat and, putting aside my scruples, went through the pockets. Although containing no Burglar's tools, I *found a sketch of the lower floor of our house, with a cross outside one of the library windows*!

I was for a time greatly excited, but calmed myself, since there was work to do. I felt that, as I was to capture him unaided, I must make a Plan, which I did and which I shall tell of later on.

Alas, while thinking only of securing the Reward and of getting Sis married, so that I would be able to be engaged and enjoy it without worry as to Money, coming out and so on, my Ship of Love was in the hands of the wicked, and about to be utterly destroyed, or almost, the complete finish not coming untill later. But

> 'Tis better to have loved and lost
> Than never to have loved at all.

This is the tradgic story. Tom had gone to the station, feeling repentant probably, or perhaps wishing to drive the Arab, and finding me not yet there, had conversed with the hackman. And that person, for whom I have nothing but contempt and scorn, had observed to him that every day I met a young gentleman at the three-thirty train and took him for a ride!

Could Mendasity do more? Is it right that such a Creature, with his pockets full of nails and scandle, should vote, while intellagent women remain idle? I think not.

When, therefore, I waved my hand to my *fiancee*, thus showing a forgiving disposition, I was met but with a cold bow. I was heart-broken, but it is but to true that in our state of society the female must not make advances, but must remain still, although suffering. I therfore sat still and stared hautily at the water cap of my car, although seathing within, but without knowing the cause of our rupture.

The Stranger came. I shrink in retrospect from calling him the Theif, although correct in one sense. I saw Tom stareing at him banefully, but I took no notice, merely getting out and kicking the tires to see if air enough in them. I then got in and drove away.

The Stranger looked excited, and did not mention the weather as customery. But at last he said:

"Somehow I gather, Little Sister, that you know a lot of things you do not talk about."

"I do not care to be adressed as 'Little Sister,'" I said in an icy tone. "As for talking, I do not interfere with what is not my concern."

"Good," he observed. "And I take it that, when you find an overcoat or any such garment, you do not exhibit it to the Familey, but put it away in some secluded nook. Eh, what?"

"No one has seen it. It is in the Car now, under that rug."

He turned and looked at me intently.

"Do you know," he observed, "my admiration for you is posatively beyond words!"

"Then don't talk," I said, feeling still anguished by Tom's conduct and not caring much just then about the reward or any such mundane matters.

"But I *must* talk," he replied. "I have a little plan, which I darsay you have guest. As a matter of fact, I have reasons to think it will fall in with—er—plans of your own."

Ye gods! Was I thus being asked to compound a felony? Or did he not think I belonged to my own Familey, but to some other of the same name, and was therfore not suspicous.

"Here's what I want," he went on in a smooth manner. "And there's Twenty-five dollars in it for you. I want this little car of yours tonight."

Here I almost ran into a cow, but was luckaly saved, as a Jersey cow costs seventy-five dollars and even more, depending on how much milk given daily. When back on the road again, having but bent a mud guard against a fense, I was calmer.

"How do I know you will bring it back?" I asked, stareing at him fixedly.

"Oh, now see here," he said, straightening his necktie, "I may be a Theif, but I am not that kind of a Theif. I play for big stakes or nothing."

I then remembered that there was a large dinner that night and that mother would have her jewelery out from the safe deposit, and father's pearl studs et cetera. I turned pale, but he did not notice it, being busy counting out Twenty-five dollars in small bills.

I am one to think quickly, but with precicion. So I said:

"You can't drive, can you?"

"I do drive, dear Little—I beg your pardon. And I think, with a lesson now, I could get along. Now see here, Twenty-five dollars while you are asleep and therfore not gilty if I take your car from wherever you keep it. I'll leave it at the station and you'll find it there in the morning."

Is it surprizing that I agreed and that I took the filthy lucre? No. For I knew then that he would never get to the station, and the reward of two hundred, plus the Twenty-five, was already mine mentaly.

He learned to drive the Arab in but a short time, and I took him to the shed and showed him where I hid the key. He said he had never heard before of a girl owning a Motor and her parents not knowing, and while we were talking there Tom Gray went by in the station hack and droped somthing in the road.

When I went out to look *it was the key ring I had given him.*

I knew then that all was over and that I was doomed to a single life, growing more and more meloncholy until Death relieved my sufferings. For I am of a proud nature, to proud to go to him and explain. If he was one to judge me by apearances I was through. But I ached. Oh, how I ached!

The Theif did not go further that day, but returned to the station. And I? I was not idle, beleive me. During the remainder of the day, although a broken thing, I experamented to find exactly how much gas it took to take the car from the station to our house. As I could not go to the house I had to guess partly, but I have a good mind for estimations, and I found that two quarts would do it.

So he could come to the house or nearby, but he could not get away with his ill-gotten gains. I therfore returned to my home and ate a nursery supper, and Hannah came in and said:

"I'm about out of my mind, Miss Bab. There's trouble coming to this Familey, and it keeps on going to dinners and disregarding all hints."

"What sort of trouble?" I asked, in a flutering voice. For if she knew and told I would not recieve the reward, or not solely.

"I think you know," she rejoined, in a suspicous tone. "And that you should assist in such a thing, Miss Bab, is a great Surprize to me. I have considered you flitey, but nothing more."

She then slapped a cup custard down in front of me and went away, leaving me very nervous. Did she know of the Theif, or was she merely refering to the car, which she might have guest from grease on my clothes, which would get there in spite of being carful, especialy when changing a tire?

Well, I have now come to the horrable events of that night, at writing which my pen almost refuses. To have dreamed and hoped for a certain thing, and then by my own actions to frustrate it was to be my fate.

"Oh God! that one might read the book of fate!" Shakspeare.

As I felt that, when everything was over, the people would come in from the Club and the other country places to see the captured Crimenal, I put on one of the frocks which mother had ordered and charged to me on that Allowence which was by that time *non est*. (Latin for dissapated. I use dissapated in the sense of spent, and not debauchery.)

By that time it was nine o'clock, and Tom had not come, nor even telephoned. But I felt this way. If he was going to be jealous it was better to know it now, rather than when to late and perhaps a number of offspring.

I sat on the Terrace and waited, knowing full well that it was to soon, but nervous anyhow. I had before that locked all the library windows but the one with the X on the sketch, also putting a nail at the top so he could not open them and escape. And I had the key of the library door and my trusty weapon under a cushion, loaded—the weapon, of course, not the key.

I then sat down to my lonely Vigil.

At eleven P.M. I saw a sureptitious Figure coming across the lawn, and was for a moment alarmed, as he might be coming while the Familey and the jewels, and so on, were still at the Club.

But it was only Carter Brooks, who said he had invited himself to stay all night, and the Club was sickning, as all the old people were playing cards and the young ones were paired and he was an odd man.

He then sat down on the cushion with the revolver under it, and said:

"Gee whiz! Am I on the Cat? Because if so it is dead. It moves not."

"It might be a Revolver," I said, in a calm voice. "There was one lying around somwhere."

So he got up and observed: "I have conscientous scruples against sitting on a poor, unprotected gun, Bab." He then picked it up and it went off, but did no harm except to put a hole in his hat which was on the floor.

"Now see here, Bab," he observed, looking angry, because it was a new one—the hat. "I know you, and I strongly suspect you put that Gun there. And no blue eyes and white frock will make me think otherwise. And if so, why?"

"I am alone a good deal, Carter," I said, in a wistfull manner, "as my natural protecters are usualy enjoying the flesh pots of Egypt. So it is natural that I should wish to be at least fortified against trouble."

He then put the revolver in his pocket, and remarked that he was all the protecter I needed, and that the flesh pots only seemed desirable because I was not yet out. But that once out I would find them full of indigestion, headaches, and heartburn.

"This being grown-up is a sort of Promised Land," he said, "and it is always just over the edge of the World. You'll never be as nice again, Bab, as you are just now. And because you are still a little girl, although 'plited,' I am going to kiss the tip of your ear, which even the lady who ansers letters in the newspapers could not object to, and send you up to bed."

So he bent over and kissed the tip of my ear, which I considered not a sentamental spot and therfore not to be fussy about. And I had to pretend to go up to my chamber.

I was in a state of great trepadation as I entered my Residense, because how was I to capture my prey unless armed to the teeth? Little did Carter Brooks think that he carried in his pocket, not a Revolver or at least not merely, but my entire future.

However, I am not one to give up, and beyond a few tears of weakness, I did not give way. In a half hour or so I heard Carter Brooks asking George for a whisky and soda and a suit of father's pajamas, and I knew that, ere long, he would be

> In pleasing Dreams and slumbers light.
> Scott.

Would he or would he not bolt his door? On this hung, in the Biblical phraze, all the law and the profits.

He did not. Crouching in my Chamber I saw the light over his transom become blackness, and soon after, on opening his door and speaking his name softly, there was no response. I therfore went in and took my Revolver from his bureau, but there was somthing wrong with the spring and it went off. It broke nothing, and as for Hannah saying it nearly killed her, this is not true. It went into her mattress and wakened her, but nothing more.

Carter wakened up and yelled, but I went out into the hall and said:

"I have taken my Revolver, which belongs to me anyhow. And don't dare to come out, because you are not dressed."

I then went into my chamber and closed the door firmly, because the servants were coming down screaming and Hannah was yelling that she was shot. I explained through the door that nothing was wrong, and that I would give them a dollar each to go back to bed and not alarm my dear parents. Which they promised.

It was then midnight, and soon after my Familey returned and went to bed. I then went downstairs and put on a dark coat because of not wishing to be seen, and a cap of father's, wishing to apear as masculine as possable, and went outside, carrying my weapon, and being careful not to shoot it, as the spring seemed very loose. I felt lonely, but not terrafied, as I would have been had I not known the Theif personaly and felt that he was not of a violent tipe.

It was a dark night, and I sat down on the verandah outside the fatal window, which is a French one to the floor, and waited. But suddenly my heart almost stopped. Some one was moving about *inside*!

I had not thought of an acomplice, yet such there must be. For I could hear, on the hill, the noise of my automobile, which is not good on grades and has to climb in a low geer. How terrable, to, to think of us as betrayed by one of our own *menage*!

It was indeed a cricis.

However, by getting in through a pantrey window, which I had done since a child for cake and so on, I entered the hall and was able, without a sound, to close and lock the library door. In this way, owing to nails in the windows, I thus had the Gilty Member of our *menage* so that only the one window remained, and I now returned to the outside and covered it with a steady aim.

What was my horror to see a bag thrust out through this window and set down by the unknown within!

Dear reader, have you ever stood by and seen a home you loved looted, despoiled and deprived of even the egg spoons, silver after-dinner coffee cups, jewels and toilet articals? If not, you cannot comprehand my greif and stern resolve to recover them, at whatever cost.

I by now cared little for the Reward but everything for honor.

The second Theif was now aproaching. I sank behind a steamer chair and waited.

Need I say here that I meant to kill no one? Have I not, in every page, shown that I am one for peace and have no desire for bloodshed? I think I have. Yet, when the Theif apeared on the verandah and turned a pocket flash on the leather bag, which I percieved was one belonging to the Familey, I felt indeed like shooting him, although not in a fatal spot.

He then entered the room and spoke in a low tone.

The Reward was mine.

I but slipped to the window and closed it from the outside, at the same time putting in a nail as mentioned before, so that it could not be raised, and then, raising my revolver in the air, I fired the remaining four bullets, forgeting the roof of the verandah which now has four holes in it.

Can I go on? Have I the strength to finish? Can I tell how the Theif cursed and tried to raise the window, and how every one came downstairs in their night clothes and broke in the library door, while carrying pokers, and knives, et cetera. And how, when they had met with no violence but only sulkey silence, and turned on the lights, there was Leila dressed ready to elope, and the Theif had his arms around her, and she was weeping? Because he was poor, although of good famiey, and lived in another city, where he was a broker, my familey had objected to him. Had I but been taken into Leila's confidence, which he considered I had, or at least that I understood, how I would have helped, instead of thwarting! If any parents or older sisters read this, let them see how wrong it is to leave any member of the familey in the dark, especialy in *affaires de couer*.

Having seen from the verandah window that I had comitted an error, and unable to bear any more, I crawled in the pantrey window again and went up stairs to my Chamber. There I undressed and having hid my weapon, pretended to be asleep.

Some time later I heard my father open the door and look in.

"Bab!" he said, in a stealthy tone.

I then pretended to wake up, and he came in and turned on a light.

"I suppose you've been asleep all night," he said, looking at me with a searching glanse.

"Not lately," I said. "I—wasn't there a Noise or somthing?"

"There was," he said. "Quite a racket. You're a sound sleeper. Well, turn over and settle down. I don't want my little girl to lose her Beauty Sleep."

He then went over to the lamp and said:

"By the way, Bab, I don't mind you're sleeping in my golf cap, but put it back in the morning because I hate to have to hunt my things all over the place."

I had forgoten to take off his cap!

Ah, well, it was all over, although he said nothing more, and went out. But the next morning, after a terrable night, when I realized that Leila had been about to get married and I had ruined everything, I found a note from him under my door.

Dear Bab: After thinking things over, I think you and I would better say nothing about last night's mystery. But suppose you bring your car to meet me tonight at the station, and we will take a ride, avoiding milk wagons if possible. You might bring your check book, too, and the revolver, which we had better bury in some quiet spot.

Father.

P. S. I have mentioned to your mother that I am thinking of buying you a small car. *Verbum sap.*

* * * *

The next day my mother took me calling, because if the Servants were talking it was best to put up a bold front, and pretend that nothing had happened except a Burglar alarm and no Burglar. We went to Gray's and Tom's grandmother was there, *without her cruches.*

During the evening I dressed in a pink frock, with roses, and listened for a car, because I knew Tom was now allowed to drive again. I felt very kind and forgiving, because father had said I was to bring the car to our garage and he would buy gasoline and so on, although paying no old bills, because I would have to work out my own Salvation, but buying my revolver at what I paid for it.

But Tom did not come. This I could not beleive at first, because such conduct is very young and imature, and to much like fighting at dancing school because of not keeping step and so on.

At last, Dear Reader, I heard a machine coming, and I went to the entrance to our drive, standing in the shrubery to surprize him. I did not tremble as previously, because I had learned that he was but human, though I had once considered otherwise, but I was willing to forget.

> *How happy is the blameless Vestal's lot!*
> *The World forgeting, by the World forgot.*
> *Pope.*

However, the car did not turn into our drive, but went on. And in it were Tom, and that one who I had considered until that time my best and most intimate friend, Jane Raleigh.

Sans fiancee, *sans* friend, *sans* reward and *sans* Allowence, I turned and went back to my father, who was on the verandah and was now, with my mother and sister, all that I had left in the World.

And my father said: "Well, here I am, around as usual. Do you feel to grown-up to sit on my knee?"

I did not.

CHAPTER V
THE G. A. C.

APRIL 9th. As I am leaving this School to-morrow for the Easter Holadays, I revert to this Dairy, which has not been written in for some months, owing to being a Senior now and carrying a heavy schedule.

My trunk has now gone, and I have but just returned from Chapel, where Miss Everett made a Speach, as the Head has quinzy. She raised a large Emblem that we have purchaced at fifty cents each, and said in a thrilling voice that our beloved Country was now at war, and expected each and all to do his duty.

"I shall not," she said, "point out to any the Fields of their Usefulness. That they must determine for themselves. But I know that the Girls of this school will do what they find to do, and return to the school at the end of two weeks, school opening with evening Chapel as usual and no tardiness permitted, better off for the use they have made of this Precious Period."

We then sang the Star-Spangled Banner, all standing and facing the piano, but watching to see if Fraulein sang, which she did. Because there are those who consider that she is a German Spy.

I am now sitting in the Upper House, wondering what I can do. For I am like this and always have been. I am an American through and through, having been told that I look like a tipical American girl. And I do not beleive in allowing Patriotism to be a matter of words—words, emty words.

No. I am one who beleives in doing things, even though necesarily small. What if I can be but one of the little drops of Water or little grains of Sand? I am ready to rise like a lioness to my country's call and would, if permitted and not considered imodest by my Familey, put on the clothing of the Other Sex and go into the trenches.

What can I do?

It is strange to be going home in this manner, thinking of Duty and not of boys and young men. Usualy when about to return to my Familey I think of Clothes and *affairs de couer*, because at school there is nothing much of either except on Friday evenings. But now all is changed. All my friends of the Other Sex will have roused to the defense of their Country, and will be away.

And I to must do my part, or bit, as the English say.

But what? Oh what?

April 10th. I am writing this in the Train, which accounts for poor writing, etcetera. But I cannot wait for I now see a way to help my Country.

The way I thought of it was this:

I had been sitting in deep thought, and although returning to my Familey was feeling sad at the idea of my Country at war and I not helping. Because what could I do, alone and unarmed? What was my strength against that of the German Army? A trifle light as air!

It was at this point in my pain and feeling of being utterly useless, that a young man in the next seat asked if he might close the Window, owing to soot and having no other coller with him. I assented.

How little did I realize that although resembling any other Male of twenty years, he was realy Providence?

The way it happened was in this manner. Although not supposed to talk on trains, owing to once getting the wrong suit-case, etcetera, one cannot very well refuse to anser if one is merely asked about a Window. And also I pride myself on knowing Human Nature, being seldom decieved as to whether a gentleman or not. I gave him a steady glance, and saw that he was one.

I then merely said to him that I hoped he intended to enlist, because I felt that I could at least do this much for my Native Land.

"I have already done so," he said, and sat down beside me. He was very interesting and I think will make a good soldier, although not handsome. He said he had been to Plattsburg the summer before, drilling, and had not been the same since, feeling now very ernest and only smoking three times a day. And he was two inches smaller in the waste and three inches more in chest. He then said:

"If some of you girls with nothing to do would only try it you would have a new outlook on Life."

"Nothing to do!" I retorted, in an angry manner. "I am sick and tired of the way my Sex is always reproached as having nothing to do. If you consider French and music and Algebra and History and English composition nothing, as well as keeping house and having children and atending to social duties, *I do* not."

"Sorry," he said, stiffly. "Of course I had no idea—do you mean that you have a Familey of your own?"

"I was refering to my Sex in general," I replied, in a cold tone.

He then said that there were Camps for girls, like Plattsburg only more Femanine, and that they were bully. (This was his word. I do not use slang.)

"You see," he said, "they take a lot of over-indulged society girls and make them over into real People."

Ye gods! Over-indulged!

"Why don't you go to one?" he then asked.

"Evadently," I said, "I am not a real Person."

"Well, I wouldn't go as far as that. But there isn't much left of the way God made a girl, by the time she's been curled and dressed and governessed for years, is there? They can't even walk, but they talk about helping in the War. It makes me sick!"

I now saw that I had made a mistake, and began reading a Magazine, so he went back to his seat and we were as strangers again. As I was very angry I again opened my window, and he got a cinder in his eye and had to have the Porter get it out.

He got out soon after, and he had the impertinance to stop beside me and say:

"I hate to disapoint you, but I find I have a clean coller in my bag after all." He then smiled at me, although I gave him no encouragment whatever, and said: "You're sitting up much better, you know. And if you would take off those heals I'll venture to say you could *walk* with any one."

I detested him with feirceness at that time. But since then I have pondered over what he said. For it is my Nature to be fair and to consider things from every angel. I therfore said this to myself:

"If members of the Male Sex can reduce their wastes and increase their usefulness to their Native Land by camping, exercising and drilling, why not get up a camp of my own, since I knew that I would not be alowed to go away to train, owing to my Familey?"

I am always one to decide quickly. So I have now made a sketch of a Unaform and written out the names of ten girls who will be home when I am. I here write out the Purpose of our organisation:

To defend the Country and put ourselves into good Physical Condition.—Memo: Look up "physical" as it looks odd, as if mispelled.

Motto: To be voted on later.

Password: Plattsburg.

Dues: Ten dollars each in advance to buy Tent, etcetera.

Unaform: Kakhi, with orange-colored necktie. In times of danger the orange color to be changed to something which will not atract the guns of the Enemy.

Name: Girls' Aviation Corps. But to be known generally as the G. A. C. as because of Spies and so on we must be as secret as possable.

I have done everything thus in advance, because we will have but a short time, and besides I know that if everything is not settled Jane will want to run things, and probably insist on a set of By-Laws, etcetera, which will take to much time.

I have also decided to be Captain, as having organised the Camp and having a right to be.

10 P. M. I am now in my familiar Chamber, and Hannah says they intended to get new furnature but feel they should not, as War is here and everything very expencive.

But I must not complain. It is war time.

I shall now record the events from 5 P. M. to the present.

Father met me at the station as usual, and asked me if I cared to stop and buy some candy on the way home. Ye gods, was I in a mood for candy?

"I think not, father," I replied, in a dignafied way. "Our dear Country is now at war, and it is no time for self-indulgence."

"Good for you!" he said. "Evadently that school of yours is worth something after all. But we might have a bit of candy, anyhow, don't you think? Because we want to keep our Industries going and money in circulation."

I could not refuse under such circumstances, and purchaced five pounds.

Alas, war has already made changes in my Familey. George, the butler, has felt the call of Duty and has enlisted, and we now have a William who chips the best china, and looks like a German although he says not, and willing to put out the National Emblem every morning from a window in father's dressing room. Which if he is a Spy he would probably not do, or at least without being compeled to.

I said nothing about the G. A. C. during dinner, as I was waiting to see if father would give me ten dollars before I organised it. But I am a person of strong feelings, and I was sad and depressed, thinking of my dear Country at War and our beginning with soup and going on through as though nothing was happening. I therfore observed that I considered it unpatriotic, with the Enemy at our gates, to have Sauterne on the table and a Cocktail beforehand, as well as expencive tobacco and so on, even although economising in other ways, such as furnature.

"What's that?" my father said to me, in a sharp tone.

"Let her alone, father," Leila said. "She's just dramatising herself as usual. We're probably in for a dose of Patriotism."

I would perhaps have made a sharp anser, but a street piano outside began to play The Star-Spangled Banner. I then stood up, of course, and mother said: "Sit down, for heaven's sake, Barbara."

"Not until our National Anthem is finished, mother," I said in a tone of gentle reproof. "I may not vote or pay taxes, but this at least I can do."

Well, father got up to, and drank his coffee standing. But he gave William a dollar for the man outside, and said to tell him to keep away at meal times as even patriotism requires nourishment.

After dinner in the drawing room, mother said that she was going to let me give a Luncheon.

"There are about a dosen girls coming out when you do, Bab," she said. "And you might as well begin to get acquainted. We can have it at the Country Club, and have some boys, and tennis afterwards, if the courts are ready."

"Mother!" I cried, stupafied. "How can you think of Social pleasures when the enemy is at our gates?"

"Oh nonsense, Barbara," she replied in a cold tone. "We intend to do our part, of course. But what has that to do with a small Luncheon?"

"I do not feel like festivaty," I said. "And I shall be very busy this holaday, because although young there are some things I can do."

Now I have always loved my mother, although feeling sometimes that she had forgoten about having been a girl herself once, and also not being much given to Familey embrases because of her hair being marceled and so on. I therfore felt that she would probably be angry and send me to bed.

But she was not. She got up very sudenly and came around the table while William was breaking a plate in the pantrey, and put her hand on my shoulder.

"Dear little Bab!" she said. "You are right and I am wrong, and we will just turn in and do what we can, all of us. We will give the party money to the Red Cross."

I was greatly agatated, but managed to ask for the ten dollars for my share of the Tent, etcetera, although not saying exactly what for, and father passed it over to me. War certainly has changed my Familey, for even Leila came over a few moments ago with a hat that she had bought and did not like.

I must now stop and learn the Star-Spangled Banner by heart, having never known but the first verse, and that not entirely.

Later: How helpless I feel and how hopeless!

I was learning the second verse by singing it, when father came over in his *robe de nuit*, although really pagamas, and said that he enjoyed it very much, and of course I was right to learn it as aforsaid, but that if the Familey did not sleep it could not be very usefull to the Country the next day such as making shells and other explosives.

April 11th: I have had my breakfast and called up Jane Raleigh. She was greatly excited and said:

"I'm just crazy about it. What sort of a Unaform will we have?"

This is like Jane, who puts clothes before everything. But I told her what I had in mind, and she said it sounded perfectly thrilling.

"We each of us ought to learn some one thing," she said, "so we can do it right. It's an age of Specialties. Suppose you take up signaling, or sharp-shooting if you prefer it, and I can learn wireless telegraphy. And maybe Betty will take the flying course, because we ought to have an Aviator and she is afraid of nothing, besides having an uncle who is thinking of buying an Aeroplane."

"What else would you sugest?" I said freezingly. Because to hear her one would have considered the entire G. A. C. as her own idea.

"Well," she said, "I don't know, unless we have a Secret Service and guard your father's mill. Because every one thinks he is going to have trouble with Spies."

I made no reply to this, as William was dusting the Drawing Room, but said, "Come over. We can discuss that privatly." I then rang off.

I am terrably worried, because my father is my best friend, having always understood me. I cannot endure to think that he is in danger. Alas, how true are the words of Dryden:

"War, he sung, is Toil and Trouble,
Honour but an empty Bubble."

Noon: Jane came over as soon as she had had her breakfast, and it was a good thing I had everything written out, because she started in right away to run things. She wanted a Constitution and By-Laws as I had expected. But I was ready for her.

"We have a Constitution, Jane," I said, solemnly. "The Constitution of the United States, and if it is good enough for a whole Country I darsay it is good enough for us. As for By-laws, we can make them as we need them, which is the way laws ought to be made anyhow."

We then made a list, Jane calling up as I got the numbers in the telephone book. Everybody accepted, although Betty Anderson objected to the orange tie because she has red hair, and one of the Robinson twins could not get ten dollars because she was on probation at School and her Familey very cold with her. But she had loned a girl at school five dollars and was going to write for it at once, and thought she could sell a last year's sweater for three dollars to their laundress's daughter. We therfore admitted her.

All is going well, unless our Parents refuse, which is not likely, as we intend to purchace the Tent and Unaforms before consulting them. It is the way of Parents not to care to see money wasted.

Our motto we have decided on. It is but three letters, W. I. H., and is a secret.

Later: Sis has just informed me that Carter Brooks has not enlisted, but is playing around as usual! I feel dreadfully, as he is a friend of my Familey. Or rather *was*.

7 P. M.: The G. A. C. is a fact. It is also ready for duty. How wonderful it is to feel that one is about to be of some use to one's own, one's Native Land!

We held a meeting early this P. M. in our library, all doors being closed and Sentries posted. I had made some fudge also, although the cook, who is a new one, was not pleasant about the butter and so on.

We had intended to read the Constitution of the U. S. out loud, but as it is long we did not, but signed our names to it in my father's copy of the American Common Wealth. We then went out and bought the Tent and ten camp chairs, although not expecting to have much time to sit down.

The G. A. C. was then ready for duty.

Before disbanding for the day I made a short speach in the shop, which was almost emty. I said that it was our intention to show the members of the Other Sex that we were ready to spring to the Country's call, and also to assist in recruiting by visiting the different Milatary Stations and there encouraging those who looked faint-hearted and not willing to fight.

"Each day," I said, in conclusion, "one of us will be selected by the Captain, myself, to visit these places and as soon as a man has signed up, to pin a flower in his buttonhole. As we have but little money, the tent having cost more than expected, we can use carnations as not expencive."

The man who had sold us the tent thought this was a fine idea, and said he thought he would enlist the next day, if we would be around.

We then went went to a book shop and bought the Plattsburg Manual, and I read to the members of the Corps these rules, to be strictly observed:

1. Carry yourself at all times as though you were proud of Yourself, your Unaform, and your Country.

2. Wear your hat so that the brim is parallel to the ground.

3. Have all buttons fastened.

4. Never have sleeves rolled up.

5. Never wear sleeve holders.

6. Never leave shirt or coat unbuttoned at the throat.

7. Have leggins and trousers properly laced. (Only leggins).

8. Keep shoes shined.

9. Always be clean shaved. (Unecessary).

10. Keep head up and shoulders square.

11. Camp life has a tendency to make one careless as to personal cleanliness. Bear this in mind.

We then gave the Milatary Salute and disbanded, as it was time to go home and dress for dinner.

On returning to my domacile I discovered that, although the sun had set and the hour of twilight had arived, the Emblem of my Country still floated in the breese. This made me very angry, and ringing the door-bell I called William to the steps and pointing upward, I said:

"William, what does this mean?"

He pretended not to understand, although avoiding my eye.

"What does what mean, Miss Barbara?"

"The Emblem of my Country, and I trust of yours, for I understand you are naturalized, although if not you'd better be, floating in the breese *after sunset.*"

Did I or did I not see his face set into the lines of one who had little or no respect for the Flag?

"I'll take it down when I get time, miss," he said, in a tone of resignation. "But what with making the salid and laying the table for dinner and mixing cocktails, and the cook so ugly that if I as much as ask for the paprika she's likely to throw a stove lid, I haven't much time for Flags."

I regarded him sternly.

"Beware, William," I said. "Remember that, although probably not a Spy or at least not dangerous, as we in this country now have our eyes open and will stand no nonsense, you must at all times show proper respect to the National Emblem. Go upstairs and take it in."

"Very well, miss," he said. "But perhaps you will allow me to say this, miss. There are to many houses in this country where the Patriotic Feeling of the inhabatants are shown only by having a paid employee hang out and take in what you call The Emblem."

He then turned and went in, leaving me in a stupafied state on the door-step.

But I am not one to be angry on hearing the truth, although painfull. I therfore ran in after him and said:

"William, you are right and I am wrong. Go back to your Pantrey, and leave the Flag to me. From now on it will be my duty."

I therfore went upstairs to my father's dressing room, where he was shaveing for dinner, and opened the window. He was disagreable and observed:

"Here, shut that! It's as cold as blue blazes."

I turned and looked at him in a severe manner.

"I am sorry, father," I said. "But as between you and my Country I have no choice."

"What the dickens has the Country got to do with giving me influensa?" he exclaimed, glaring at me. "Shut that window."

I folded my arms, but remained calm.

"Father," I said, in a low and gentle tone, "need I remind you that it is at present almost seven P. M. and that the Stars and Stripes, although supposed to be lowered at sunset, are still hanging out this window?"

"Oh, that's it, is it?" he said in a releived tone. "You're nothing if you're not thorough, Bab! Well, as they have hung an hour and fifteen minutes to long as it is, I guess the Country won't go to the dogs if you shut that window until I get a shirt on. Go away and send William up in ten minutes."

"Father," I demanded, intencely, "do you consider yourself a Patriot?"

"Well," he said, "I'm not the shouting tipe, but I guess I'll be around if I'm needed. Unless I die of the chill I'm getting just now, owing to one shouting Patriot in the Familey."

"Is this your Country or William's?" I insisted, in an inflexable voice.

"Oh, come now," he said, "we can divide it, William and I. There's enough for both. I'm not selfish."

It is always thus in my Familey. They joke about the most serious things, and then get terrably serious about nothing at all, such as overshoes on wet days, or not passing in French grammer, or having a friend of the Other Sex, etcetera.

"There are to many houses in this country, father," I said, folding my arms, "where the Patriotism of the Inhabatants is shown by having a paid employee hang out and take in the Emblem between Cocktails and salid, so to speak."

"Oh damm!" said my father, in a feirce voice. "Here, get away and let me take it in. And as I'm in my undershirt I only hope the neighbors aren't looking out."

He then sneazed twice and drew in the Emblem, while I stood at the Salute. How far, how very far from the Plattsburg Manual, which decrees that our flag be lowered to the inspiring music of the Star-Spangled Banner, or to the bugel call, "To the Colors."

Such, indeed, is life.

Later: Carter Brooks dropped in this evening. I was very cold to him and said:

"Please pardon me if I do not talk much, as I am in low spirits."

"Low spirits on a holaday!" he exclaimed. "Well, we'll have to fix that. How about a motor Picnic?"

It is always like that in our house. They regard a Party or a Picnic as a cure for everything, even a heartache, or being worried about Spies, etcetera.

"No, thank you," I said. "I am worried about those of my friends who have enlisted." I then gave him a scornful glance and left the room. He said

"Bab!" in a strange voice and I heard him coming after me. So I ran as fast as I could to my Chamber and locked the door.

In Camp Girls Aviation Corps, April 12th.

We are now in Camp, although not in Uniform, owing to the delivery waggon not coming yet with our clothes. I am writing on a pad on my knee, while my Orderley, Betty Anderson, holds the ink bottle.

What a morning we have had!

Would one not think that, in these terrable times, it would be a simple matter to obtain a spot wherein to prepare for the defence of the Country? Should not the Young be encouraged to spring to the call, "To arms, to arms, ye braves!" instead of being reproved for buying a Tent with no place as yet to put it, and the Adams's governess being sent along with Elaine because we need a Chaperone?

Ye gods! A Chaperone to a Milatary Camp!

She is now sitting on one of the camp stools and embroidering a centerpeice. She brought her own lunch and Elaine's, refusing to allow her to eat the regular Milatary rations of bacon and boiled potatoes, etcetera, and not ofering a thing to us, although having brought chicken sandwitches, cake and fruit.

I shall now put down the events of the day, as although the Manual says nothing of keeping a record, I am sure it is always done. Have I not read, again and again, of the Captain's log, which is not wood, as it sounds, but is a Journal or Dairy?

This morning the man at the tent store called up and asked where to send the tent. I then called a meeting in my Chamber, only to meet with bitter disapointment, as one Parent after another had refused to allow their grounds to be used. I felt sad—helpless, as our house has no grounds, except for hanging out washing, etcetera.

I was very angry and tired to, having had to get up at sunrise to put out the Emblem, and father having wakened and been very nasty. So I got up and said:

"It is clear that our Families are Patriots in name only, and not in deed. Since they have abandoned us, The G. A. C. must abandon them and do as it thinks best. Between Familey and Country, I am for the Country."

Here they all cheered, and Hannah came in and said mother had a headache and to keep quiet.

I could but look around, with an eloquent gesture.

"You see, Members of the Corps," I said in a tence voice, "that things at present are intolerable. We must strike out for ourselves. Those who are willing please signafy by saying Aye."

They all said it and I then sugested that we take my car and as many as possable of the officers and go out to find a suitable spot. I then got my car and crowded into it the First and Second Lieutenants, the Sergeant and the Quartermaster, which was Jane. She had asked to be Veterinarian, being fond of dogs, but as we had no animals, I had made her Quartermaster, giving her charge of the Quarters, or Tent, etcetera. The others followed in the Adams's limousine, taking also cooking utensils and food, although Mademoiselle was very disagreeable about the frying pan and refused to hold it.

We went first to the tent store. The man in the shop then instructed me as to how to put up the Tent, and was very kind, ofering to send some one to do it. But I refused.

"One must learn to do things oneself if one is to be usefull," I said. "It is our intention to call on no member of the Male Sex, but to show that we can get along without them."

"Quite right," he said. "I'm sure you can get along without us, miss, much better than we could get along without you."

Mademoiselle considered this a flirtatious speach and walked out of the shop. But I consider that it was a General Remark and not personal, and anyhow he was thirty at least, and had a married apearance.

As there was not room for the Tent and camp chairs in my car, the delivery waggon followed us, making quite a procession.

We tried several farm houses, but one and all had no Patriotism whatever and refused to let us use their terratory. It was heartrending, for where we not there to help to protect that very terratory from the enemy? But no, they cared not at all, and said they did not want papers all over the place, and so on. One woman observed that she did not object to us, but that we would probably have a lot of boys hanging around and setting fire to things with cigarettes, and anyhow if we were going to shoot it would keep the hens from laying.

Ye gods! Is this our National Spirit?

I simply stood up in the car and said:

"Madame, we intend to have no Members of the Other Sex. And if you put eggs above the Stars and Stripes you are nothing but a Traitor and we will keep an eye on you."

We then went on, and at last found a place where no one was living, and decided to claim it in the name of the government. We then put up the tent, although not as tight as it should have been, owing to the Adams's chauffeur not letting us have his wrench to drive the pins in with, and were ready for the day's work.

We have now had luncheon and the Quartermaster, Jane, is burning the papers and so on.

After I have finished this Log we will take up the signaling. We have decided in this way: Lining up in a row, and counting one to ten, and even numbers will study flag signals, and the odds will take up telagraphy, which is very clearly shown in the Manual.

After that we will have exercises to make us strong and elastic, and then target practise.

We have as yet no guns, but father has one he uses for duck shooting in the fall, and Betty's uncle was in Africa last year and has three, which she thinks she can secure without being noticed. We have passed this Resolution: To have nothing to do with those of the other Sex who are not prepared to do their Duty.

Evening, April 12th. I returned to my domacile in time to take in Old Glory, and also to dress for dinner, being muddy and needing a bath, as we had tried bathing in the creek at the camp while Mademoiselle was asleep in the tent, but found that there was an oil well near and the water was full of oil, which stuck to us and was very disagreeable to smell.

Carter Brooks came to dinner, and I played the National Anthem on the phonograph as we went in to the Dining Room. Mother did not like it, as the soup was getting cold, but we all stood until it was finished. I then saluted, and we sat down.

Carter Brooks sat beside me, and he gave me a long and piercing glance.

"What's the matter with you, Bab?" he said. "You were rather rude to me last night and now you've been looking through me and not at me ever since I came, and I'll bet you're feverish."

"Not at all," I said, in a cold tone. "I may be excited, because of war and my Country's Peril. But for goodness sake don't act like the Familey, which always considers that I am sick when I am merely intence."

"Intence about what?" he asked.

But can one say when one's friends are a disapointment to one? No, or at least not at the table.

The others were not listening, as father was fussing about my waking him at daylight to put out the Emblem.

"Just slide your hand this way, under the table cloth," Carter Brooks said in a low tone. "It may be only intencity, but it looks most awfully like chicken pocks or somthing."

So I did, considering that it was only Politeness, and he took it and said:

"Don't jerk! It is nice and warm and soft, but not feverish. What's that lump?"

"It's a blister," I said. And as the others were now complaining about the soup, I told him of the Corps, etcetera, thinking that perhaps it would rouse him to some patriotic feelings. But no, it did not.

"Now look here," he said, turning and frowning at me, "Aviation Corps means flying. Just remember this,—if I hear of your trying any of that nonsense I'll make it my business to see that you're locked up, young lady."

"I shall do exactly as I like, Carter," I said in a friggid manner. "I shall fly if I so desire, and you have nothing to say about it."

However, seeing that he was going to tell my father, I added:

"We shall probably not fly, as we have no machine. There are Cavalry Regiments that have no horses, aren't there? But we are but at the beginning of our Milatary existence, and no one can tell what the next day may bring forth."

"Not with you, anyhow," he said in an angry tone, and was very cold to me the rest of the dinner hour.

They talked about the war, but what a disapointment was mine! I had returned from my Institution of Learning full of ferver, and it was a bitter moment when I heard my father observe that he felt he could be of more use to his Native Land by making shells than by marching and carrying a gun, as he had once had milk-leg and was never the same since.

"Of course," said my father, "Bab thinks I am a slacker. But a shell is more valuable against the Germans than a milk leg, anytime."

I at that moment looked up and saw William looking at my father in a strange manner. To those who were not on the alert it might have apeared that he was trying not to smile, my father having a way of indulging in "quips and cranks and wanton wiles" at the table which mother does not like, as our Butlers are apt to listen to him and not fill the glasses and so on.

But if my Familey slept mentaly I did not. *At once* I suspected William. Being still not out, and therfore not listened to with much atention, I kept my piece and said nothing. And I saw this. *William was not what he seemed.*

As soon as dinner was over I went into my father's den, where he brings home drawings and estamates, and taking his Leather Dispach case, I locked it in my closet, tying the key around my neck with a blue ribben. I then decended to the lower floor, and found Carter Brooks in the hall.

"I want to talk to you," he said. "Have you young Turks—I mean young Patriots any guns at this camp of yours?"

"Not yet."

"But you expect to, of course?"

I looked at him in a steady manner.

"When you have put on the Unaform of your Country," I said, "or at least of Plattsburg, I shall tell you my Milatary secrets, and not before."

"Plattsburg!" he exclaimed. "What do you know of Plattsburg?"

I then told him, and he listened, but in a very disagreeable way. And at last he said:

"The plain truth, Bab, is that some good-looking chap has filled you up with a lot of dope which is meant for men, not romantic girls. I'll bet to cents that if a fellow with a broken noze or a squint had told you, you'd have forgotten it the next minute."

I was exasparated. Because I am tired of being told that the defence of our Dear Country is a masculine matter.

"Carter," I said, "I do not beleive in the double standard, and never did."

"The what?"

"The double standard," I said with dignaty. "It was all well and good when war meant wearing a kitchin stove and wielding a lance. It is no longer so. And I will show you."

I did not mean to be boastfull, such not being my nature. But I did not feel that one who had not yet enlisted, remarking that there was time enough when the Enemy came over, etcetera, had any right to criticise me.

12 Midnight. How can I set down what I have discovered? And having recorded it, how be sure that Hannah will not snoop around and find this record, and so ruin everything?

It is midnight. Leila is still out, bent on frivolaty. The rest of the Familey sleeps quietly, except father, who has taken cold and is breathing through his mouth, and I sit here alone, with my secret.

William is a Spy. I have the proofs. How my hand trembles as I set down the terrable words.

I discovered it thus.

Feeling somewhat emty at bed time and never sleeping well when hollow inside, I went down to the pantry at eleven P. M. to see if any of the dinner puding had been left, although not hopeful, owing to the servants mostly finishing the desert.

William was in the pantrey.

He was writing somthing, and he tried to hide it when I entered.

Being in my *robe de nuit* I closed the door and said through it:

"Please go away, William. Because I want to come in, unless all the puding is gone."

I could hear him moving around, as though concealing somthing.

"There is no puding, miss," he said. "And no fruit except for breakfast. Your mother is very particuler that no one take the breakfast fruit."

"William," I said sternly, "go out by the kitchen door. Because I am hungry, and I am coming in for *somthing*."

He was opening and closing the pantrey drawers, and although young, and not a housekeeper, I knew that he was not looking in them for edables.

"If you'll go up to your room, Miss Bab," he said, "I'll mix you an Eggnogg, without alkohol, of course, and bring it up. An Eggnogg is a good thing to stay the stomache with at night. I frequently resort to one myself."

I saw that he would not let me in, so I agreed to the Eggnogg, but without nutmeg, and went away. My knees tremble to think that into our peacefull home had come "Grim-vizaged War," but I felt keen and capable of dealing with anything, even a Spy.

William brought up the Eggnogg, with a dash of sherry in it, and I could hear him going up the stairs to his chamber. I drank the Eggnogg, feeling that I would need all my strength for what was to come, and then went down to the pantry. It was in perfect order, except that one of the tea towles had had a pen wiped on it.

I then went through the drawers one by one, although not hopeful, because he probably had the incrimanating document in the heal of his shoe, which Spies usually have made hollow for the purpose, or sowed in the lining of his coat.

At least, so I feared. But it was not so. Under one of the best table cloths I found it.

Yes. *I found it.*

I copy it here in my journal, although knowing nothing of what it means. Is it a scheme to blow up my father's mill, where he is making shells for the defence of his Native Land? I do not know. With shaking hands I put it down as follows:

48 D. K.

48 D.F.

36 S. F.

34 F. F.

36 T. S.

36 S. S.

36 C. S.

24 I. H. K.

36 F. K.

But in one way its meaning is clear. Treachery is abroad and Treason has but just stocked up the stairs to its Chamber.

April 13th. It is now noon and snowing, although supposed to be spring. I am writing this Log in the tent, where we have built a fire. Mademoiselle is sitting in the Adams's limousine, wrapped in rugs. She is very sulky.

There are but nine of us, as I telephoned the Quartermaster early this morning and summoned her to come over and discuss important business.

Her Unaform had come and so had mine. What a thrill I felt as she entered Headquarters (my chamber) in kakhi and saluted. She was about to sit down, but I reminded her that war knows no intimacies, and that I was her Captain. She therfore stood, and I handed her William's code. She read it and said:

"What is it?"

"That is what the G. A. C. is to find out," I said. "It is a cipher."

"It looks like it," said Jane in a flutering tone. "Oh, Bab, what are we to do?"

I then explained how I had discovered it and so on.

"Our first duty," I went on, "is to watch William. He must be followed and his every movement recorded. I need not tell you that our mill is making shells, and that the fate of the Country may hang on you to-day."

"On me?" said Jane, looking terrafied.

"On you. I have selected you for this first day. To-morrow it will be another. I have not yet decided which. You must remain secreted here, but watching. If he goes out, follow him."

I was again obliged to remind her of my rank and so on, as she sat down and began to object at once.

"The Familey," I said, "will be out all day at First Aid classes. You will be safe from discovery."

Here I am sorry to say Jane disapointed me, for she observed, bitterly:

"No luncheon, I suppose!"

"Not at all," I said. "It is a part of the Plattsburg idea that a good soldier must have nourishment, as his strength is all he has, the Officers providing the brains."

I then rang for Hannah, and ofered her to dollars to bring Jane a tray at noon and to sneak it from the kitchin, not the pantrey.

"From the kitchin?" she said. "Miss Bab, it's as much as my life is worth to go to the kitchin. The cook and that new Butler are fighting something awfull."

Jane and I exchanged glances.

"Hannah," I said, in a low tone, "I can only say this. If you but do your part you may avert a great calamaty."

"My God, Miss Bab!" she cried. "That cook's a German. I said so from the beginning."

"Not the cook, Hannah."

We were all silent. It was a terrable moment.

I shortly afterwards left the house, leaving Jane to study flag signals, or wig-waging as vulgarly called, and *to watch*.

Camp, 4 P. M. Father has just been here.

We were trying to load one of Betty's uncle's guns when my Orderley reported a car coming at a furious gate. On going to the opening of the tent I saw that it was our car with father and Jane inside. They did not stop in the road, but turned and came into the field, bumping awfully.

Father leaped out and exclaimed:

"Well!"

He then folded his arms and looked around.

"Upon my word, Bab!" he said. "You might at least take your Familey into your confidence. If Jane had not happened to be at the house I'd never have found you. But never mind about that now. Have you or have you not seen my leather Dispach Case?"

Alas, my face betrayed me, being one that flushes easily and then turns pale.

"I thought so," he said, in an angry voice. "Do you know that you have kept a Board of Directors sitting for three hours, and that—Bab, you are hopeless! Where is it?"

How great was my humiliation, although done with the Highest Motives, to have my Corps standing around and listening. Also watching while I drew out the ribben and the key.

"I hid it in my closet, father," I said.

"Great thunder!" he said. "And we have called in the Secret Service!"

He then turned on his heal and stocked away, only stopping to stare at Mademoiselle in the car, and then driving as fast as possable back to the mill.

As he had forgotten Jane, she was obliged to stay. It was by now raining, and the Corps wanted to go home. But I made a speach, saying that if we weakened now what would we do in times of Real Danger?

"What are a few drops of rain?" I inquired, "to the falling of bullets and perhaps shells? We will now have the class in bandageing."

The Corps drew lots as to who would be bandaged, there being no volunteers, as it was cold and necesary to remove Unaform etcetera. Elaine got number seven. The others then practiced on her, having a book to go by.

I here add to this log Jane's report on William. He had cleaned silver until 1 P. M., when he had gone back to the kitchin and moved off the soup kettle to boil some dish towles. The cook had then set his dish towles out in the yard and upset the pan, pretending that a dog had done so. Hannah had told Jane about it.

At 1:45 William had gone out, remarking that he was going to the drug store to get some poizon for the cook. Jane had followed him and *he had really mailed a letter.*

April 14th. I have taken a heavy cold and am, alas, *hors de combat.* The Familey has issued orders that I am to stay in bed this A. M. and if stopped sneazing by 2 P. M. am to be allowed up but not to go to Camp.

Elaine is in bed to, and her mother called up and asked my Parents if they would not send me back to school, as I had upset everything and they could not even get Elaine to the Dentist's, as she kept talking about teeth being unimportant when the safety of the Nation was hanging in the Balance.

As I lie here and reflect, it seems to me that everywhere around me I see nothing but Sloth and Indiference. One would beleive that nothing worse could happen than a Cook giving notice. Will nothing rouze us to our Peril? Are we to sit here, talking about housecleaning and sowing women and how wide are skirts, when the minions of the German Army may at any time turn us into slaves? Never!

Later: Carter Brooks has sent me a book on First Aid. Ye gods, what chance have I at a wounded Soldier when every person of the Femanine Sex in this Country is learning First Aid, and even hoping for small accidents so they can practice on them. No, there are some who can use their hands (i. e. at bandageing and cutting small boils, etcetera. Leila has just cut one for Henry, the chauffeur, although not yellow on top and therfore not ready) and there are others who do not care for Nursing, as they turn sick at the sight of blood, and must therfore use their brains. I am of this class.

William brought up my tray this morning. I gave him a peircing glance and said:

"Is the Emblem out?"

He avoided my eye.

"Not yet, miss," he said. "Your father left sharp orders as to being disturbed before 8 A. M."

"As it is now 9:30," I observed coldly, "there has been time enough lost. I am *hors de combat*, or I would have atended to it long ago."

He had drawn a stand beside the bed, and I now sat up and looked at my Tray. The orange was cut through the wrong way!

Had I needed proof, dear log or journal, I had it there. For any *Butler* knows how to cut a breakfast orange.

"William," I said, as he was going out, "how long have you been a Butler?"

Perhaps this was a foolish remark as being calculated to put him on his guard. But "out of the fullness of the Heart the Mouth speaketh." It was said. I could not withdraw my words.

He turned suddenly and looked at me.

"Me, miss?" he said in a far to inocent tone. "Why, I don't know exactly." He then smiled and said: "There are some who think I am not much of a Butler now."

"Just a word of advise, William," I said in a signifacant tone. "A real Butler cuts an orange the other way. I am telling you, because although having grape fruit mostly, some morning some one may order an orange, and one should be very careful *these days*."

Shall I ever forget his face as he went out? No, never. He knew that I knew, and was one to stand no nonsense. But I had put him on his guard. It was to be a battle of Intellagence, his brains against mine.

Although regretful at first of having warned him, I feel now that it is as well. I am one who likes to fight in the open, not as a serpent coiled in the grass and pretending, like the one in the Bible, to be a friend.

3 P. M. No new developments. Although forbidden to go out nothing was said about the roof. I have therfore been up on it exchanging Signals with Lucy Gray next door by means of flags. As their roof slants and it is still raining, she sliped once and slid to the gutter. She then sat there and screamed like a silly, although they got her back with a clothesline which the Policeman asked for.

But Mrs. Gray was very unpleasant from one of their windows and said I was a Murderer at heart.

Has the Average Parent no soul?

Noon, April 14 (In Camp).

This is a fine day, being warm and bright and all here but Elaine and Mademoiselle—the latter not greatly missed, as although French and an Ally she thinks we should be knitting etcetera, and ordered the car to be driven away when ever we tried to load the gun.

A quorum being present, it was moved and seconded that we express wherever possable our disaproval in war time of

1. Cigarettes

2. Drinking

3. Low-necked dresses

4. Parties

5. Fancy deserts

6. Golf and other sports—except when necesary for health.

7. Candy.

We also pleged ourselves to try and make our Families rise early, and to insist on Members of our Families hoisting and taking down the Stars and Stripes, instead of having it done by those who may not respect it, or only aparently so.

Passed unanamously.

The class in Telegraphy reported that it could do little or nothing, as it is easy to rap out a dot but not possable to rap a dash. We therfore gave it up for The Study of the Rifle and Its Care.

Luncheon today: Canned salmon, canned beans and vanila wafers.

2 A. M., April 15th. I have seen a Spy at his nefarius work!

I am still trembling. At one moment I think that I must go again to Father and demand consideration, as more mature than he seems to think, and absolutely certain I was not walking in my sleep. But the next moment I think not, but that if I can discover William's plot myself, my Familey will no longer ignore me and talk about my studying Vocal next winter instead of coming out.

To return to William, dear Log or Journal. I had been asleep for some time, but wakened up to find myself standing in the dining room with a napkin in each hand. I was standing in the Flag Signal position for A, which is the only one I remember as yet without the Manual.

I then knew that I had been walking in my sleep, having done so several times at School, and before Examinations being usualy tied by my Room-mate with a string from my ankle to the door knob, so as in case of getting out of bed to wake up.

I was rather scared, as I do not like the dark, feeling when in it that Something is behind me and about to cluch at me.

I therfore stood still and felt like screaming, when suddenly the door of the Butler's pantry squeaked. Could I then have shreiked I would have, but I had no breath for the purpose.

Somebody came into the room and felt for the table, passing close by me and stepping by accident on the table bell, which is under the rug. It rang and scared me more than ever. We then both stood still, and I hoped if he or it heard my Heart thump he or it would think it was the hall clock.

After a time the footsteps moved on around the table and out into the hall. I was still standing in position A, being as it were frosen thus.

However, seeing that it was something human and not otherwise, as its shoes creaked, I now became angry at the thought that Treason was under the roof of my home. I therfore followed the Traitor out into the hall and looked in through the door at him. He had a flash light, and was opening the drawers of my father's desk. It was William.

I then concealed myself behind my father's overcoat in the hack hall, and considered what to do. Should I scream and be probably killed, thus dying a noble Death? Or should I remain still? I decided on the latter.

And now, dear Log or Journal, I must record what followed, which I shall do as acurately as I can, in case of having later on to call in the Secret Service and read this to them.

There is a safe built in my resadence under the stairs, in which the silver service, plates, etcetera, are stored, as to big for the Safe Deposit, besides being a nusance to send for every time there is a dinner.

This safe only my father can unlock, or rather, this I fondly believed until tonight. But how diferent are the facts! For William walked to it, after listening at the foot of the stairs, and opened it as if he had done so before quite often. He then took from it my father's Dispach Case, locked the safe again, and went back through the dining room.

It is a terrable thing to see a crime thus comitted and to know not what to do. Had William repaired again to his chamber, or would he return for the plates, etcetera?

At last I crept upstairs to my father's room, which was locked. I could not waken him by gently taping, and I feared that if I made a noise I would warn the lurking Criminal in his den. I therfore went to my bathroom and filled my bath sponge with water, and threw it threw the transom in the direction of my father's bed.

As it happened it struck on his face, and I heard him getting up and talking dreadfully to himself. Also turning on the lights. I put my mouth to the keyhole and said:

"Father!"

Had he but been quiet, all would have been well. But he opened the door and began roaring at me in a loud tone, calling me an imp of Mischeif and other things, and yelling for a towle.

I then went in and closed the door and said:

"That's right. Bellow and spoil it all."

"Spoil what?" he said, glareing at me. "There's nothing left to spoil, is there? Look at that bed! Look at me!"

"Father," I said, "while you are raging about over such a thing as a wet Sponge, which I was driven to in desparation, the house is or rather has been robbed."

He then sat down on the bed and said:

"You are growing up, Bab, although it is early for the burglar obsession. Go on, though. Who is robbing us and why? Because if he finds any Money I'll divide with him."

Such a speach discouraged me, for I can bear anything except to be laughed at. I therfore said:

"William has just taken your Dispach Case out of the safe. I saw him."

"William!"

"William," I repeated in a tence voice.

He was then alarmed and put on his slippers and dressing gown.

"You stay here," he observed. "Personally I think you've had a bad dream, because William can't possably know the combination of that safe. It's as much as I can do to remember it myself."

"It's a Spy's business to know everything, father."

He gave me a peircing glance.

"He's a Spy, is he?" he then said. "Well, I might have known that all this war preparation of yours would lead to Spies. It has turned more substantile intellects than yours."

He then swiched on the hall lights from the top of the stairs and desended. I could but wait at the top, fearing at each moment a shot would ring out, as a Spy's business is such as not to stop at Murder.

My father unlocked the safe and looked in it. Then he closed it again and disapeared into the back of the house. How agonising were the moments that ensued! He did not return, and at last, feeling that he had met a terrable Death, I went down.

I went through the fatal dining room to the pantrey and there found him not only alive, but putting on a plate some cold roast beef and two apples.

"I thought we'd have a bite to eat," he said. "I need a little nourishment before getting back into that puddle to sleep."

"Father!" I said. "How can you talk of food when knowing — —"

"Get some salt and pepper," he said, "and see if there is any mustard mixed. You've had a dream, Bab. That's all. The Case is in the safe, and

William is in his bed, and in about two minutes a cold repast is going to be in me."

Ye gods!

He is now asleep, and I am writing this at 2 A. M.

I, and I alone, know that there is a Criminal in this house, serving our meals and quareling with the cook as if a regular Butler, but really a Spy. And although I cry aloud in my anguish, those who hear me but maintain that I am having a nightmare.

I am a Voice crying in the Wilderness.

April 15th: 9 A. M. William is going about as usual, but looks as though he had not had enough sleep.

Father has told mother about last night, and I am not to have coffee in the evenings. This is not surprizing, as they have always considered me from a physical and not a mental standpoint.

My very Soul is in revolt.

6 P. M. This being Sunday, camp did not convene until 3 P. M. and then but for a short time. We flag-signaled mostly and are now to the letter E. Also got the gun loaded at last and fired it several times, I giving the orders as in the book, page 262, in a loud voice:

(1) "Hold the rifle on the mark." (2) "Aim properly." (3) "Squeeze the Triger properly." (4) "Call the shot."

We had but just started, and Mademoiselle had taken the car and gone back to the Adams's resadence to bring out Mr. Adams, as she considers gun-shooting as dangerous, when a farmer with to dogs came over a fense and objected, saying that it was Sunday and that his cows were getting excited anyhow and would probably not give any milk.

"These are War times," I said, in a dignafied manner. "And if you are doing nothing for the country yourself you should at least allow others to do so."

He was a not unreasonable tipe and this seemed to effect him. For he sat down on one of our stools and said:

"Well, I don't know about that, miss. You see — —"

"Captain," I put in. Because he might as well know that we meant business.

"Captain, of course!" he said. "You'll have to excuze me. This thing of Women in War is new to me. But now don't you think that you'll be doing the country a service not to interfere with the food supply and so on?" He then looked at me and remarked: "If I was you, miss or Captain, I would not come any to clost to my place. My wife was pretty well bruized up that time you upset our milk waggon."

It was indeed he! But he was not unpleasant about it, although remarking that if he had a daughter and a machine, although he had niether, and expected niether, the one would never be allowed to have the other until carefully taught on an emty road.

He then said:

"You girls have been wig-wagging, I see."

"We are studying flag signals."

"Humph!" he observed. "I used to know something about that myself, in the Spanish war. Now let's see what I remember. Watch this. And somebody keep an eye on that hill and report if a blue calico dress is charging from the enemies' Trenches."

It was very strange to see one who apeared to be but an ordinary Farmer, or Milkman, pick up our flags and wave them faster than we could read them. It was indeed thrilling, although discouraging, because if that was the regular rate of Speed we felt that we could never acheive it. I remarked this, and he then said:

"Work hard at it, and I reckon I can slip over now and then and give you a lesson. Any girl that can drive an automobile hell-bent" (these are his words, not mine) "can do most anything she sets her mind on. You leave that gun alone, and work at the signaling, and I guess I can make out to come every afternoon. I start out about 2 A. M. and by noon I'm mostly back."

We all thanked him, and saluted as he left. He saluted to, and said:

"Name's Schmidt, but don't worry about that. Got some German blood way back, but who hasn't?"

He then departed with his to dogs, and we held a meeting, and voted to give up everything but signaling.

Passed unanamously.

8 P. M. I am now at home. Dinner is over, being early on Sundays because of Servants' days out and so on.

Leila had a Doctor to dinner. She met him at the Red Cross, and he would, I think, be a good husband. He sat beside me, and I talked mostly

about her, as I wished him to know that, although having her faults as all have, she would be a good wife.

"She can sow very well," I told him, "and she would probably like to keep House, but of course has no chance here, as mother thinks no one can manige but herself."

"Indeed!" he said, looking at me. "But of course she will probably have a house of her own before long."

"Very likely," I said. "Although she has had a number of chances and always refuses."

"Probably the right Person has not happened along," he observed.

"Perhaps," I said, in a signifacant tone. "Or perhaps he does not know he is the right Person."

William, of whom more anon, was passing the ice cream just then. I refused it, saying:

"Not in war time."

"Barbara," mother said, stiffly. "Don't be a silly. Eat your desert."

As I do not like seens I then took a little, but no cake.

During dinner Leila made an observation which has somewhat changed my opinion of Carter Brooks. She said his mother did not want him to enlist which was why he had not. She has no other sons and probably never will have, being a widow.

I have now come to William.

Lucy Gray had been on Secret Service that day, but did the observing from the windows of their house, as my Familey was at home and liable to poke into my room at any moment.

William had made it up with the cook, Lucy said, and had showed her a game of Solitaire in the morning by the kitchin window. He had then fallen asleep in the pantrey, the window being up. In the afternoon, luncheon being over and the Familey out in the car for a ride, he had gone out into the yard behind the house and pretended to look to see if the crocuses were all gone. But soon he went into the Garage and was there a half hour.

Now it is one of the rules of this Familey that no house servants go to the Garage, owing to taking up the Chauffeur's time when he should be oiling up, etcetera. Also owing to one Butler stealing the Chauffeur's fur coat and never being seen again.

But alas, what am I to do? For although I reported this being in the Garage to mother, she but said:

"Don't worry me about him, Bab. He is hopelessly inefficient. But there are no Men Servants to be had and we'll have to get along."

1 A. M. I have been on watch all evening, but everything is quiet.

I must now go to bed, as the Manual says, page 166:

"Retire early and get a good night's rest."

April 16th. In camp.

Luncheon of sardines, pickels, and eclairs as no one likes to cook, owing to smoke in the eyes, etcetera.

Camp convened at 12 noon, as we spent the morning helping to get members of the Other Sex to enlist. We pinned a pink Carnation on each Enlister, and had to send for more several times. We had quite a Crowd there and it was very polite except one, who said he would enlist twice for one kiss. The Officer however took him by the ear and said the Army did not wish such as he. He then through (threw?) him out.

This morning I warned the new Chauffeur, feeling that if he had by chance any Milatary Secrets in the Garage he should know about William.

"William!" he said, looking up from where he was in the Repair Pit at the time. "*William!*"

"I am sorry, Henry," I said, in a quiet voice. "But I fear that William is not what he apears to be."

"I think you must be mistaken, miss." He then hamered for some time. When he was through he climbed out and said: "There's to much Spy talk going on, to my thinking, miss. And anyhow, what would a Spy be after in this house?"

"Well," I observed, in an indignant manner, for I am sensative and hate to have my word doubted, "as my father is in a business which is now War Secrets and nothing else, I can understand, if you can't."

He then turned on the engine and made a terrable noise, to see if hitting on all cylinders. When he shut it off I told him about William spending a half hour in the Garage the day before. Although calm before he now became white with anger and said:

"Just let me catch him sneaking around here, and I'll—what's he after me for anyhow? I haven't got any Milatary Secrets."

I then sugested that we work together, as I felt sure William was after my father's blue prints and so on, which were in the Dispach Case in the safe at night. He said he was not a Spy-catcher, but if I caught William at any nonsense I might let him know, and if he put a padlock on the outside of his door and mother saw it and raised a fuss, I could stand up for him.

I agreed to do so.

10 P. M. Doctor Connor called this evening, to bring Sis a pattern for a Surgicle Dressing. They spent to hours in the Library looking at it. Mother is rather upset, as she thinks a Doctor makes a poor husband, having to be out at night and never able to go to Dinners owing to baby cases and so on.

She said this to father, but I heard her and observed:

"Mother, is a doctor then to have no Familey life, and only to bring into the world other people's children?"

She would usualy have replied to me, but she merely sighed, as she is not like herself, being worried about father.

She beleives that my Father's Life is in danger, as although usualy making steel, which does not explode and is therfore a safe business, he is now making shells, and every time it has thundered this week she has observed:

"The mill!"

She refuses to be placated, although knowing that only those known to the foremen can enter, as well as having a medal with a number on it, and at night a Password which is new every night.

I know this, because we have this evening made up a list of Passwords for the next week, using a magazine to get them out of, and taking advertisements, such as Cocoa, Razers, Suspenders and so on. Not these actualy but others like them.

We then learned them off by heart and burned the paper, as one cannot be to carefull with a Spy in the house, even if not credited as such by my Parents.

Have forgotten the Emblem. Must take it in.

April 17th. In camp.

Henry brought me out in the big car, as mine has a broken spring owing to going across the field with it.

He says he has decided to help me, and that I need not watch the safe, etcetera, at night. I therfore gave him a key to the side door, and now feel much better. He also said not to have any of the Corps detailed to watch

William in the daytime, as he can do so, because the Familey is now spending all day at the Red Cross.

He thinks the Password idea fine, as otherwise almost anybody could steal a medal and get into the mill.

William seems to know that I know something, and this morning, while opening the door for me, he said:

"I beg pardon, Miss Bab, but I see Henry is driving you today."

"It is not hard to see," I replied, in a hauty manner. It is not the Butler's business who is driving me, and anyhow I had no intention of any unecessary conversation with a Spy.

"Your own car being out of order, miss?"

"It is," I retorted. "As you will probably be going to the Garage, although against orders, while Henry is out, you can see it yourself."

I then went out and sat in front in order to converce with Henry, as the back is lonely. I looked up at the door and William was standing there, with a very queer look on his face.

3 P. M. Mr. Schmidt is late and the Corps is practising, having now got to K.

Luncheon was a great surprize, as at 12:45 a car apeared on the sky line and was reported by our Sentry as aproaching rapidly.

When it came near it was seen to be driven by Carter Brooks, and to contain several baskets, etcetera. He then dismounted and saluted and said:

"The Commiseriat has sent me forward with the day's rations, sir."

"Very good," I returned, in an official manner. "Corps will line up and count. Odd numbers to unpack and evens to set the table."

This of course was figurative, as we have no table, but eat upon the ground.

He then carried over the baskets and a freezer of ice cream. He had brought a fruit salid, cold chicken, potatoe Chips, cake and ice-cream. It was a delightful Repast, and not soon to be forgoten by the Corps.

Mademoiselle got out of the Adams's car and came over, although she had her own lunch as usual. She then had the Chauffeur carry over a seat cushion, and to see her one would beleive she was always pleasant. I have no use for those who are only pleasant in the presence of Food or Strangers.

Carter Brooks sat beside me, and observed:

"You see, Bab, although a Slacker myself, I cannot bear that such brave spirits as those of the Girls' Aviation Corps should go hungry."

I then gave him a talking-to, saying that he had been a great disapointment, as I thought one should rise to the Country's Call and not wait until actualy needed, even when an only son.

He made no defence, but said in a serious tone:

"You see, it's like this. I am not sure of myself, Bab. I don't want to enlist because others of the Male Sex, as you would say, are enlisting and I'm ashamed not to. And I don't want to enlist just to wear a Unaform and get away from business. I don't take it as lightly as all that."

"Have you no Patriotism?" I demanded. "Can you repeat unmoved the celabrated lines:

"Lives there a man with Soul so dead,
He (or who) never to himself hath said:
This is my own, my Native Land."

I then choked up, although being Captain I felt that tears were a femanine weakness and a bad Example.

Mademoiselle had at that moment felt an ant somewhere and was not looking. Therfore she did not perceive when he reached over and put his hand on my foot, which happened to be nearest to him. He then pated my foot, and said:

"What a nice kid you are!"

It is strange, now that he and the baskets, etcetera, have gone away, that I continue to think about his pating my foot. Because I have known him for years, and he is nothing to me but a good friend and not sentamental in any way.

I feel this way. Suppose he enlists and goes away to die for his Country, as a result of my Speach. Can I endure to think of it? No. I did not feel this way about Tom Gray, who has gone to Florida to learn to fly, although at one time thinking the Sun rose and set on him. It is very queer.

The Sentry reports Mr. Schmidt and the dogs coming over the fense.

Evening. Doctor Connor is here again. He is taking Sis to a meeting where he is to make a Speach. I ofered to go along, but they did not apear to hear me, and perhaps it is as well, for I must watch William, as Henry is taking them in the car. I am therfore writing on the stairs, as I can then hear him washing Silver in the pantrey.

Mother has been very sweet to me this evening. I cannot record how I feel about the change. I used to feel that she loved me when she had time to do so, but that she had not much time, being busy with Bridge, Dinners, taking Leila out and Housekeeping, and so on. But now she has more time. Tonight she said:

"Bab, suppose we have a little talk. I have been thinking all day what I would do if you were a boy, and took it into that Patriotic head of yours to enlist. I couldn't bear it, that's all."

I was moved to tears by this afection on the part of my dear Parent, but I remembered being Captain of the Corps, and so did not weep. She then said that she would buy us an Emblem for the Camp, and have a luncheon packed each day. She also ofered me a wrist watch.

I cannot but think what changes War can make, bringing people together because of worry and danger, and causing gifts, such as flags and watches, and ofering to come out and see us in a day or so.

It is now 9 P. M. and the mention of the flag has reminded me that our own Emblem still fluters beneath the Starry Sky.

Later: William is now in the Garage. I am watching from the window of the sowing room.

The terrable thought comes—has he a wireless concealed there, by which he sends out clandestine messages, perhaps to Germany?

This I know. He cannot get into Henry's room, as the padlock is now on.

Later: He has returned, foiled!

April 18th. Nothing new. Working hard at signaling. Mr. Schmidt says I am doing well and if he was an Officer he would give me a job.

April 19th. Nothing new. But Doctor Connor had told Leila that my father looks sick or at least not well. When I went to him, being frightened, as he is my only Male Parent and very dear to me, he only laughed and said:

"Nonsense! We're rushed at the Mill, that's all. You see, Bab, War is more than Unaforms and saluting. It is a nasty Business. And of course, between your forgetting The Emblem until midnight, when I am in my first sleep, and putting it out at Dawn, I am not getting all the rest I really need."

He then took my hand and said:

"Bab, you haven't by any chance been in my Dispach Case for anything, have you?"

"Why? Is something missing?" I said in a startled tone.

"No. But sometimes I think—however, never mind about that. I think I'll take the Case upstairs and lock my door hereafter, and if the Emblem is an hour or to late, we will have to stand for it. Eight o'clock is early enough for any Flag, especialy if it has been out late the night before."

"Father," I said, in a tence voice. "I have before this warned you, but you would not listen, considering me imature and not knowing a Spy when I see one."

I then told him what I knew about William, but he only said:

"Well, the only thing that matters is the Password, and that cannot be stolen. As for William, I have had his record looked up by the Police, and it is fine. Now go to bed, and send in the Spy. I want a Scotch and Soda."

April 20th. Henry and I have searched the Garage, but there is no Wireless, unless in a Chimney. Henry says this is often done, by Spies, who raise a Mast out of the chimney by night.

To night I shall watch the Chimney, as there is an ark light near it, so that it is as bright as Day.

The cook has given notice, as she and William cannot get along, and as he can only make to salids and those not cared for by the other servants.

April 27th. After eight days I am at last alowed this Log or Journal, being supported with pillows while writing as Doctor Connor says it will not hurt me.

He has just gone, and I am sure kissed Leila in the hall while Hannah and the nurse were getting pen, ink, etcetera. Perhaps after all Romanse has at last come to my beloved sister, who will now get married. If so, I can come out in November, which is the best time, as December is busy with Xmas and so on.

How shall I tell the tradgic story of that night? How can I put, by means of a pen, my Experiences on paper? There are some things which may not be written, but only felt, and that mostly afterwards, as during the time one is to excited to feel.

On April 21st, Saturday, I had a bad cold and was not allowed to go to camp. I therfore slept most of the day, being one to sleep easily in daytime, except for Hannah coming in to feel if I was feverish.

My father did not come home to dinner, and later on telephoned that he was not to be looked for until he arived, owing to somthing very important at the Mill and a night shift going on for the first time.

We ate Dinner without him, and mother was very nervous and kept saying that with foremen and so on she did not see why father should have to kill himself.

Ye gods! Had we but realised the Signifacance of that remark! But we did not, but went to living in a Fool's Paradice, and complaining because William had put to much vinigar in the French Dressing.

William locked up the house and we retired to our Chambers. But as I had slept most of the day I could not compose myself to Slumber, but sat up in my *robe de nuit* and reflected about Carter Brooks, and that perhaps it would be better for him not to enlist as there is plenty to be done here at home, where one is safe from bullets, machine guns and so on. Because, although not Sentamental about him or silly in any way, I felt that he should not wish to go into danger if his mother objected. And after all one must consider mothers and other Parents.

I put a dressing gown over my *robe de nuit*, and having then remembered about the Wireless, I put out my light and sat in the window seat. But there was no Mast to be seen, and nothing but the ark light swinging.

I then saw some one come in the drive and go back to the Garage, but as Henry has a friend who has been out of work and sleeps with him, although not told to the Familey, as probably objecting,—although why I could not see, since he used half of Henry's bed and therfore cost nothing—I considered that it was he.

It was not, however, as I shall now record in this Log or Journal.

I had perhaps gone to sleep in my place of watching, when I heard a rapping at my Chamber door. "Only this and nothing more." Poe—The Raven.

I at once opened the door, and it was the cook. She said that Henry had returned from the mill with a pain in his ear, and had telephoned to her by the house 'phone to bring over a hot water bottle, as father was driving himself home when ready.

She then said that if I would go over with her to the Garage and drop some laudinum into his ear, she being to nervous, and also taking my hot water bottle, she would be grateful.

Although not fond of her, owing to her giving notice and also being very fussy about cake taken from the pantrey, I am one to go always where needed. I also felt that a member of the Corps should not shirk Duty, even a Chauffeur's ear. I therfore got my hot water bottle and some slippers, etcetera, and we went to the Garage.

I went up the stairs to Henry's room, but what was my surprize to find him not there, but only his friend. I then said:

"Where is Henry?"

The cook was behind me, and she said:

"He is coming. He has to walk around because it aches so."

Then Henry's friend said, in a queer voice:

"Now, Miss Bab, there is nothing to be afraid of, unless you make a noise. If you do there will be trouble and that at once. We three are going to have a little talk."

Ye gods! I tremble even to remember his words, for he said:

"What we want is simple enough. We want to-night's Password at the Mill. *Don't scream.*"

I dropped the hot water bottle, because there is no use pretending one is not scared at such a time. One is. But of course I would not tell them the Password, and the cook said:

"Be careful, Miss Bab. We are not playing. We are in terrable ernest."

She did not sound like a cook at all, and she looked diferent, being very white and with to red spots on her cheeks.

"So am I," I responded, although with shaking teeth. "And just wait until the Police hear of this and see what happens. You will all be arested. If I scream — —"

"If you scream," said Henry's friend in an awful voice, "you will never scream again."

There was now a loud report from below, which the neighbors afterwards said they heard, but considered gas in a muffler, which happens often and sounds like a shot. There was then a sort of low growl and somebody fell with a thump. Then the cook said to Henry's friend:

"Jump out of the window. They've got him!"

But he did not jump, but listened, and we then heard Henry saying:

"Come down here, quick."

Henry's friend then went downstairs very rapidly, and I ran to the window thinking to jump out. But it was closed and locked, and anyhow the cook caught me and said, in a hissing manner:

"None of that, you little fool."

I had never been so spoken to, especially by a cook, and it made me very angry. I then threw the bottle of laudinum at her, and broke a front tooth, also cutting her lip, although I did not know this until later, as I then fainted.

When I came to I was on the floor and William, whom I had considered a Spy, was on the bed with his hands and feet tied. Henry was standing by the door, with a revolver, and he said:

"I'm sorry, Miss Bab, because you are all right and have helped me a lot, especially with that on the bed. If it hadn't been for you our Goose would have been cooked."

He then picked me up and put me in a chair, and looked at his watch.

"Now," he said, "we'll have that Password, because time is going and there are things to be done, quite a few of them."

I could see William then, and I saw his eyes were partly shut, and that he had been shot, because of blood, etcetera. I was about to faint again, as the sight of blood makes me sick at the stomache, but Henry held a bottle of amonia under my nose and said in a brutal way:

"Here, none of that."

I then said that I would not tell the Password, although killed for it, and he said if I kept up that attitude I would be, because they were desperate and would stop at nothing.

"There is no use being stubborn," he said, "because we are going to get that Password, and the right one to, because if the wrong one you, to, will be finished off in short order."

As I was now desperate myself I decided to shriek, happen what may. But I had merely opened my mouth to when he sprang at me and put his hand over my mouth. He then said he would be obliged to gag me, and that when I made up my mind to tell the Password, if I would nod my Head he would then remove the gag. As I grew pale at these words he threw up a window, because air prevents fainting.

He then tied a towel around my mouth and lips, putting part of it between my teeth, and tied it in a hard knot behind. He also tied my hands behind me, although I kicked as hard as possable, and can do so very well, owing to skating and so on.

How awfull were my sensations as I thus sat facing Death, and remembering that I had often been excused from Chapel when not necesary, and had been confirmed while pretending to know the Creed while not doing so. Also not always going to Sunday School as I should, and being inclined to skip my Prayers when very tired.

We sat there for a long time, which seemed Eternities, Henry making dreadful threats, and holding a revolver. But I would not tell the Password, and at last he went out, locking the door behind him, to consult with the other Spies.

I then heard a whisper, and saw that William was not dead. He said:

"Here, quick. I'll unloose your hands and you can drop out the window."

He did so, but just in time, as Henry returned, looking fierce and saying that I had but fifteen minutes more. I was again in my chair, and he did not percieve that my hands were now untied.

I must stop here, as my hands tremble to much to hold my trusty pen.

April 28th. Leila has just been in. She kissed me in a fraternal manner, and I then saw that she wore an engagement ring. Well, such is Life. We only get realy acquainted with our Families when they die, or get married.

Doctor Connor came in a moment later and kissed me to, calling me his brave little Sister.

How pleasant it is to lie thus, having wine jelatine and squab and so on, and wearing a wrist watch with twenty-seven diamonds, and mother using the vibrator on my back to make me sleepy, etcetera. Also, to know that when one's father returns he will say:

"Well, how is the Patriot today?" and not smile while saying it.

I have recorded in this journal up to where I had got my hands loose, and Henry was going to shoot me in fifteen minutes.

We have thus come to Mr. Schmidt.

Suddenly Henry swore in an angry manner. This was because my father had brought the machine home and was but then coming along the drive. Had he come alone it would have been the end of him and the Mill, for Henry and his friend would have caught him, and my father is like me—he would die before giving the Password and blowing up all the men and so on in the Mill. But he brought the manager with him, as he lives out of town and there is no train after midnight.

My father said:

"Henry!"

So Henry replied:

"Coming, sir," and went out, but again locked the door.

Before he went out he said:

"Now mind, any noise up here and we will finish you and your father also. *Don't you overturn a chair by mistake, young lady.*"

He then went down, and I could hear my dear Parent's voice which I felt I would probably never hear again, discussing new tires and Henry's earache, which was not a real one, as I now knew.

I looked at William, but he had his eyes shut and I saw he was now realy unconscious. I then however heard a waggon in our alley, and I went to the window. What was my joy to see that it was Mr. Schmidt's milk waggon which had stopped under the ark light, with he himself on the seat. He was getting some milk bottles out, and I suppose he heard the talking in our Garage, for he stopped and then looked up. Then he dropped a milk bottle, but he stood still and stared.

With what anguished eyes, dear Log or Journal, did I look down at him, unable to speak or utter a sound. I then tried to untie the Towle but could not, owing to feeling weak and sick and the knots being hard.

I at one moment thought of jumping out, but it was to far for our Garage was once a Stable and is high. But I knew that if the Criminals who surounded my Father and the manager heard such a sound, they would then attack my Father and kill him.

I was but a moment thinking all this, as my mind is one to work fast when in Danger. Mr. Schmidt was still staring, and the horse was moving on to the next house, as Mr. Schmidt says it knows all his Customers and could go out alone if necesary.

It was then that I remembered that, although I could not speak, I could signal him, although having no flags. I therfore signaled, saying:

"Quiet. Spies. Bring police."

It was as well that he did not wait for the last to letters, as I could not remember C, being excited and worried at the time. But I saw him get into his waggon and drive away very fast, which no one in the Garage noticed, as milk waggons were not objects of suspicion.

How strange it was to sit down again as if I had not moved, as per orders, and hear my Father whistling as he went to the house. I began to feel very sick at my Stomache, although glad he was safe, and wondered what they would do without me. Because I had now seen that, although insisting that I was still a child, I was as dear to them as Leila, though in a diferent way.

I had not cried as yet, but at the thought of Henry's friend and the others coming up to kill me before Mr. Schmidt could get help, I shed a few tears.

They all came back as soon as my Father had slamed the house door, and if they had been feirce before they were awfull then, the cook with a handkerchief to her mouth, and Henry's friend getting out a watch and giving me five minutes. He had counted three minutes and was holding his Revolver to just behind my ear, when I heard the milk waggon coming back, with the horse galloping.

It stopped in the alley, and the cook said, in a dreadfull voice:

"What's that?"

She dashed to the Window, and looked out, and then turned to the other Spies and said:

"The Police!"

I do not know what happened next, as I fainted again, having been under a strain for some time.

I must now stop, as mother has brought the Vibrater.

April 29th. All the people in my father's Mill have gone together and brought me a riding horse. I have just been to the window of my Chamber to look at it. I have always wanted a horse, but I cannot see that I deserve this one, having but done what any member of the G. A. C. should do.

As I now have a horse, perhaps the Corps should become Cavalry. Memo: Take this up with Jane.

Later: Carter Brooks has just gone, and I have a terrable headache owing to weeping, which always makes my head ache.

He has gone to the War.

I cannot write more.

10 P. M. I can now think better, although still weeping at intervals. I must write down all that has happened, as I do not feel like telling Jane, or indeed anybody.

Always before I have had no Secrets from Jane, even in matters of the Other Sex. But I feel very strange about this and like thinking about it rather than putting it into speach.

Also I feel very kind toward everybody, and wish that I had been a better girl in many ways. I have tried to be good, and have never smoked cigarettes or been decietful except when forced to be by the Familey not understanding. But I know I am far from being what Carter Brooks thinks me to be.

I have called Hannah and given her my old watch, with money to for a new chrystal. Also stood by at Salute while my father brought in the Emblem. For William can no longer do it, as he was not really a Butler at all but a Secret Service Inspector, and also being still in the Hospital, although improving.

He had not told the Familey, as he was afraid they would not then treat him as a real Butler. As for the code in the pantrey, it was really not such, but the silver list, beginning with 48 D. K. or dinner knives, etcetera. When taking my Father's Dispach Case from the safe, it was to keep the real Spies from getting it. He did it every night, and took the important papers out until morning, when he put them back.

To-night my father brought in the Emblem and folded it. He then said:

"Well, I admit that Fathers are not real Substatutes for young men in Unaform, but in times of Grief they may be mighty handy to tie to." He then put his arms around me and said: "You see, Bab, the real part of War, for a woman—and you are that now, Bab, in spite of your years—the real thing she has to do is not the fighting part, although you are about as good a soldier as any I know. The thing she has to do is to send some one she cares about, and then sit back and wait."

As he saw that I was agatated, he then kissed me and sugested that we learn something more than the first verse of the National Hymn, as he was tired of making his lips move and thus pretending to sing when not actualy doing so.

I shall now record about Carter Brooks coming today. I was in a chair with pilows and so on, when Leila came in and kissed me, and then said:

"Bab, are you able to see a caller?"

I said yes, if not the Police, as I had seen a great many and was tired of telling about Henry and Henry's friend, etcetera.

"Not the Police," she said.

She then went out in the hall and said:

"Come up. It's all right."

I then saw a Soldier in the door, and could not beleive that it was Carter Brooks, until he saluted and said:

"Captain, I have come to report. Owing to the end of the Easter Holadays the Girls' Aviation Corps——"

I could no longer be silent. I cried:

"Oh, Carter!"

So he came into the room and turned round, saying:

"Some soldier, eh?"

Leila had gone out, and all at once I knew that my Patriotism was not what I had thought it, for I could not bear to see him going to War, especialy as his mother would be lonly without him.

Although I have never considered myself weak, I now felt that I was going to cry. I therfore said in a low voice to give me a Handkercheif, and he gave me one of his.

"Why, look here," he said, in an astounded manner, "you aren't crying about *me*, are you?"

I said from behind his Handkercheif that I was not, except being sorry for his mother and also for him on account of Leila.

"Leila!" he said. "What about Leila?"

"She is lost to you forever," I replied in a choking tone. "She is betrothed to another."

He became very angry at that, and observed:

"Look here, Bab. One minute I think you are the cleverest Girl in the World, and the next—you little stuped, do you still insist on thinking that I am in love with Leila?"

At that time I began to feel very queer, being week and at the same time excited and getting red, the more so as he pulled the Handkercheif from my eyes and commanded me: "Bab, look at me. Do I *look* as though I care for Leila?"

I, however, could not look at him just then. Because I felt that I could not endure to see the Unaform.

"Don't you know why I hang around this House?" he said, in a very savige manner. "Because if you don't everybody else does."

Dear Log or Journal, I could but think of one thing, which was that I was not yet out, but still what is called a Sub-Deb, and so he was probably only joking, or perhaps merely playing with me.

I said so, in a low tone, but he only gave a Groan and said:

"I know you are not out and all the rest of it. Don't I lie awake at night knowing it? And that's the reason I——" Here he stopped and said: "Damm it" in a feirce voice. "Very well," he went on. "I came to say Good-bye, and to ask you if you will write to me now and then. Because I'm going to War half because the Country needs me and the other half because I'm not going to disapoint a certain young Person who has a way of expecting people to be better than they are."

He then very suddenly stood up and said:

"I guess I'd better go. And don't you dare to cry, because if you do there will be Trouble."

But I could not help it, as he was going to War for my Native Land, and might never come back. I therfore asked for his Handkercheif again, but he did not listen. He only said:

"You are crying, and I warned you."

He then stooped over and put his hand under my Chin and said:

"Good-bye, sweetheart."

And kissed me.

He went out at once, slaming the door, and passed Leila in the lower Hall without speaking to her.

April 30th. I now intend to close this Log or Journal, and write no more in it. I am not going back to school, but am to get strong and well again, and to help mother at the Red Cross. I wish to do this, as it makes me feel usefull and keeps me from worrying.

After all, I could not realy care for any one who would not rise to the Country's Call.

May 3rd. I have just had a letter from Carter. It is mostly about blisters on his feet and so on, and is not exactly a love letter. But he ends with this, which I shall quote, and so end this Dairy:

"After all, Bab, perhaps we all needed this. I know I did.

"I want to ask you something. Do you remember the time you wrote me that you were *blited* and I sugested that we be blited together. How about changing that a bit, and being *plited*. Because if I am not cheered by something of the sort, my Patriotism is going to ooze out of the blisters on my heels."

I have thought about this all day, and I have no right to ruin his Career. I beleive that the Army should be encouraged as much as possable. I have therfore sent him a small drawing, copied from the Manual, like this

Which means "Afirmative."